PATRICIA SMILEY'S NOVELS

"Lively."

—*Entertainment Weekly*

"Snappy prose, a compelling heroine, and a healthy dose of suspense . . . a series that promises staying power."

—*Booklist*

"Breezy . . . a good read that's worth your while."

—*Midwest Book Review*

"Want a mystery that is a hoot? Try this book . . . Smiley's characters are vivid, funny, feisty, and no-nonsense, but the mystery is real."

—*Rendezvous*

"Smart, sassy."

—*Kirkus Reviews*

"Well-plotted, tension-filled . . . [with] plenty of humor. A fast, fun mystery . . . Just take a ride with Tucker in her Boxster, all the way to the shocking conclusion."

—*Lincoln Journal Star*

"Amusing . . . Fans of Sue Grafton will love this smart, feisty new addition to the genre."

—*Library Journal*

more . . .

FALSE PROFITS

"Smiley's feisty heroine boosts the bottom line."
—*Entertainment Weekly*

"Smiley's prose is like butter . . . with a keen eye for the telling detail . . . The plot hums along like Tucker in her snazzy Porsche Boxster."
—*Washington Post Book World*

"Hilarious."
—ELIZABETH GEORGE

"Fast, funny, and sure to find many fans. Smiley and Sinclair are off to a wonderful start."
—ROBERT CRAIS

"Clever and engaging . . . Fans of Evanovich's Stephanie Plum will appreciate the gutsy Tucker."
—*Booklist* (starred review)

"Smiley delivers a lively, often amusing, well-plotted novel . . . rife with tension and suspense."
—*South Florida Sun-Sentinel*

Also by Patricia Smiley

False Profits

PATRICIA SMILEY

COVER YOUR ASSETS

WARNER BOOKS

NEW YORK   BOSTON

Copyright © 2005 by Patricia Smiley
All rights reserved. Except as permitted under the U.S. Copyright Act of 1976, no part of this publication may be reproduced, distributed, or transmitted in any form or by any means, or stored in a database or retrieval system, without the prior written permission of the publisher.

Warner Books and the "W" logo are trademarks of Time Warner Inc. or an affiliated company. Used under license by Hachette Book Group USA, which is not affiliated with Time Warner Inc.

Cover design by Diane Luger
Cover photo by Herman Estevez

Warner Books
Hachette Book Group USA
237 Park Avenue
New York, NY 10169
Visit our Web site at www.HachetteBookGroupUSA.com

Printed in the United States of America

Originally published in hardcover by Mysterious Press
First Paperback Printing: July 2007

10 9 8 7 6 5 4 3 2 1

For William Solberg, my hero . . .

Acknowledgments

I WISH TO THANK the following people for their help and support in the writing of this book: Elizabeth George, Patricia Fogarty, Barbara Fryer, Steve Long, Elaine Medosch, Reg Park, Tim Polmanteer, and T. M. Raymond. I also thank Michael Barich and Martin Waine, PhD, for helping me better understand the anatomy of utility poles. If I got anything wrong, it was certainly no fault of theirs. Many thanks to my agent, Scott Miller of Trident Media Group, and my editor, Kristen Weber, for shepherding me through the process with insight, enthusiasm, and aplomb.

COVER
YOUR
ASSETS

- 1 -

i f life allows us only one great passion, Evan Brice was mine. I met him in a poetry class my junior year at UCLA. He was slumped in the seat in front of me, wearing an oversize black tuxedo jacket that hung on his bony shoulders like a bad prom rental. Definitely not my type: delicate hands, pasty skin, and a crumpled posture that made him seem frail.

At the time, I was working thirty hours a week scraping sticky-bun goop off the floor of a local bakery in order to earn money for tuition. I didn't have time for men, and I wouldn't have given Evan a second look if, at the moment I took the seat behind him, a ray of light from a nearby window hadn't set ablaze the red highlights in his shoulder-length brown hair. My first question had been, why didn't *my* hair look that shiny? Then I noticed that his was a rat's nest, and that led to my second question: why the good-hair, bad-hair dichotomy?

I constructed then debunked several theories about it during a boring discussion of *John Brown's Body*, including the possibility that he'd actually paid big bucks to some Beverly Hills celebrity stylist to create that do. Toward the end of class I surprised myself by reaching out to untangle a few of the snarls with my fingers. He turned slowly to blink at me with penetrating blue eyes. Then a quirky smile warmed his face. He leaned back compliantly, letting his hair cascade over the back of the chair as if he were at some beauty-salon shampoo bowl.

Later I'd learned that Evan wanted to be a poet. It wasn't hard to imagine him living in a Greenwich Village loft, scrounging through ashtrays for half-smoked ciga-rettes and writing tortured poems about his tormented past, except that he didn't have a tormented past, at least not back then. Evan was an Eagle Scout from an upscale neighborhood in West Los Angeles, the adored only child of parents who were a 1950s cliché. His background was an embarrassment to him, and he tried in increasingly dangerous ways to atone for his good fortune.

As it turned out, Evan was no Sylvia Plath. He wrote appallingly bad poetry that never seemed to improve even with the amazingly good drugs he took in search of his muse. The drugs made him anxious and unpredictable, which I interpreted as high-spirited and spontaneous, be-cause back then I was convinced that anyone who could love me deserved concessions.

And Evan did love me. In fact, he loved everything about me, including my name, Tucker Sinclair. He told me it delighted his tongue like a vintage Bordeaux. I'd never tasted vintage Bordeaux, but I was content to take his word for it. He also loved the idea that my father died before I was born, making me half an orphan, and that I'd been raised by a working-actor mom who wasn't always working and whose professional name was Pookie Kravitz. Most of all, he loved the fact that I'd never lived in a house. To Evan, my life up until then had been an ideal blend of pathos and poverty. Simply stated, it had the perfect cachet for the girlfriend of a struggling poet.

I loved Evan because he carried spiders out of the house alive, cradled in a tissue. Despite all that neo-bohemian crap, I sensed his gentleness and inner turmoil. I thought him incapable of hurting anyone except perhaps himself, but I was wrong. In the winter of our senior year, shortly after he'd asked me to marry him, Evan dumped me in a way that proved he was more than capable of inflicting pain.

For months his betrayal rubbed like a burr against every cell, but even the worst breakups are survivable. I'd gone on to complete my BA and then my MBA. I'd eventually married, divorced, and earned a degree of success as a business consultant with a reputation for inventiveness. Sporadically I'd hear about Evan through mutual friends. Hear that in the same ten years he'd gone on to become famous, not as a poet, but as a Hollywood agent hawking the dubious talents of supermodels who wanted to be superstars. Sometimes I'd read articles in entertainment magazines about some mega deal he'd done with the head of Paramount or Sony or Disney, or see pictures of him posing at the Cannes Film Festival or walking the red carpet at the premier of the latest blockbuster movie.

Occasionally I'd also hear darker rumors about parties, and punch bowls brimming with cocaine, but that was no longer my concern. My memories of Evan Brice still triggered a lot of what-ifs, even though I'd long since given up my one great passion theory. I never expected to see him again, but I had. Unfortunately, our brief reunion hadn't prepared me for the appearance of a Los Angeles Police Department homicide detective on the doorstep of my Zuma Beach cottage one sunny March morning two weeks later, telling me that Evan Brice had been found stabbed to death in a seedy Venice Beach apartment.

• • •

I WAS WORKING at home that morning, just as I had every morning for the past four months, ever since leaving my position as senior manager on the fast track to partner at Aames & Associates, a big downtown L.A. management consulting firm. I had loved my job and thought I'd be with the firm forever, until one of my clients was murdered and I suddenly found myself in very deep doo-doo. The firm's senior partners hadn't exactly supported me through the ordeal. My mother claims it was because they weren't operating at the highest level of their vibrations. She and I didn't always agree, but this time her assessment was right on.

By the time I got myself out of a potentially lethal jam, I'd found that climbing the career ladder at Aames & Associates had lost its allure. I resigned and started my own management consulting firm. I call it Sinclair and Associates, even though at the moment the Associates part is just wishful thinking.

I may have quit my job, but I hadn't severed all ties with the firm. I still had friends working there, including fellow consultant Venus Corday and my former administrative assistant, Eugene Barstok. Venus and I get together when the mood strikes us, but Eugene calls me at least two or three times a week. He considers it his personal responsibility to keep me posted on the behind-the-scenes politicking and backstabbing at Aames & Associates. It's gossip, but I love to hear him spin the details.

I was laboring over a project for Marvin Geyer, the owner of a small family-owned business that sold women's apparel by mail order. Sales were dropping faster than G-strings at a strip club, and he wanted to know why. The answer became apparent the moment I opened the catalog. It was full of merchandise that should have died a natural death back in the 1970s. Occasionally fashions get recycled, but I suspected that muumuus were down for the count.

I urged Mr. Geyer to consider updating the line, but he demurred. As a compromise, he agreed to test the market via a focus group, which I was organizing for him. I'd already mailed the invitations and was now in the process of selecting items from the catalog to parade in front of the group. I hoped that when Geyer heard the collective gagging of twenty impartial fashion mavens, it would sway him to my point of view.

As usual, I dressed for the day in old Levi's frayed at the knees, my favorite green flannel shirt, and a pair of wool slippers I wear for warmth against the damp morning fog even though they make my feet look like Old English sheepdogs. I may have run my fingers through my hair before starting the day, but I doubt I'd bothered with makeup. I do remember I was alone when the LAPD detective arrived. My mother, her boyfriend, and her West Highland white terrier, Muldoon, had already left for the day.

The detective didn't call in advance. He simply materialized at my door, clutching a slim black briefcase. He was a black man in his late thirties with a military bearing and bowed legs that disrupted the well-tended creases in his trousers. When he asked if he could talk to me about Evan, I could tell by the look on his face that whatever he had to tell me wasn't going to be good news. I checked his identification and ushered Detective Moses Green to a folding chair in the little alcove just off my living room that I use as a home office. I sat behind my desk, using it as a barrier between me and any bad news.

The room was awash in sunlight from the naked window. The brightness served to accentuate the craggy furrows Green had worried into his dark forehead. It also highlighted his large brown eyes, which were several shades darker than mine. Framing those eyes were ultralong lashes that reminded me of a llama's.

I'd already imagined the worst, so when Green told me Evan had been found murdered in the kitchen of that Venice apartment, I didn't cry. I didn't know what to feel. Shock? Anger? Mostly I felt numb. I stared at the large ruby stone on the detective's class ring and imagined Evan's blood seeping slowly from his body in everwidening crimson circles.

Green must have watched this scene play out many times before, but it hadn't dulled his humanity. He didn't exactly apply cold compresses or call 911, but he was respectful enough to leave space for my grief. Still, I wasn't naive enough to think that an LAPD homicide detective had come to hold my hand while I grieved for an old boyfriend. I suspected he was sitting on my folding chair for one reason: He knew I'd recently been in touch with Evan, and wanted to hear what, if anything, I could tell him about his death.

When he finally spoke again, his tone was polite. "Mrs. Brice said the three of you were friends in college, that you and her husband dated for a while."

I tensed, wondering what else Cissy Brice had told

him. Not the whole story, I was sure. I didn't want to get into that at the moment, so I just nodded. Then I changed the subject.

"Who killed him?"

"We don't know yet. He was stabbed multiple times with a knife from the kitchen. Somebody was obviously pretty angry with Mr. Brice, but they may not have come specifically to kill him. There was no forced entry, no ransacking, so it probably wasn't a burglary. We're interviewing neighbors to see if he had any visitors prior to his death. In the meantime, the coroner's investigator is sorting through fingerprints and blood samples. That's going to take a while. I hear the victim liked to party. A lot of people went in and out of that place, and it doesn't look like it's been cleaned in a while."

"Are you saying the apartment belonged to Evan?"

He nodded. "A rental. He used an alias on the contract, which raised a few red flags with us. There's a lot of gang-related drug activity in the neighborhood. Since the victim was a user, we're looking into a possible connection."

"You think he was dealing drugs from the place?"

"At this point, anything is possible."

Green balanced the briefcase on his knees and opened the lid. He pulled out a piece of paper in a see-through bag. "We found this at the crime scene. I'm hoping you can tell me what it means."

From my vantage point, the words on the page formed the shape of my grandma Felder's old sugar bowl, the one she got free from the Shell station for filling her Buick with gas. Even from a distance and even after all those years, I could tell that the handwriting was Evan's. My breath felt labored as I silently read the words:

To Tucker With Love and Regret

Dark warm room warning, warning
No, no, no, maybe, yes, oh baby
Springs groan, passion's screams
Make love not war she pleads
Sword slides into scabbard
A perfect fit it seems
Till morning comes
And questions
Far too late
For us
Red rose. Dead rose.
True love. Cruel myth.

I felt strangely embarrassed, wishing for Evan's sake and maybe for my own that the poem at least had been better. My gaze traveled from the paper to Green's face. I sensed him analyzing my every facial twitch and gesture. It made me anxious. I assumed he wanted it that way. Cops have an instinct for making even the innocent feel guilty.

"I'm not exactly Robert Frost, ma'am," he said, "but it sounds like Mr. Brice still had a thing for you."

"There was nothing between Evan and me but history," I said, knowing that the truth was much more complicated than that. "Last time I saw him, he told me he was in a drug recovery program. He felt sorry about our breakup back in college. He wanted to make amends for hurting me all those years ago. Maybe that's why he wrote the poem."

Green looked away briefly. Something about the broken eye contact made me wonder if he understood that kind of regret as well.

"Tell me about that last time," he said.

I explained that I'd gone with my mother to an agents' panel at the Screen Actors Guild. Evan had been one of the speakers. At the end of the evening he asked me out for coffee. I hesitated at first, but saying no to him had never been easy for me.

"How many times did you two get together?" he asked.

"Just that once. After that, we e-mailed each other and talked on the phone a few times."

"Mr. Brice must have had a lot of apologizing to do."

I searched Green's face for the snide look that matched the comment, but found only a neutral stare softened by the sweep of his dense eyelashes.

I gave him the benefit of the doubt and kept the defensiveness out of my tone. "We talked about other things, too, like work and all the fragile egos he had to manage. I let him unload. That's what friends do."

"Did he mention anybody he was having a problem with?"

"Not by name."

Green nodded. Then he shifted in his chair to look outside. Something near the shoreline had caught his attention, but I couldn't tell what.

"He ever talk about troubles in his marriage?"

I'd been peering over his shoulder to see what he was looking at, but the feigned casualness of his question wrenched me back into the room and put me on guard. I was obligated to tell Green what I knew, of course, but I felt shitty about that because it was only Evan's side of the story, and neither he nor Cissy had a perfect score with the truth.

"He told me there were problems," I said.

Green furrowed his brow in irritation when I waited for his "What kind of problems?" prompt. Nevertheless, he listened attentively as I related what seemed to me like the bad relationship cliché: Evan and Cissy had grown apart, had disagreed on everything from money management to child rearing. Evan worried that their constant bickering would damage the psyche of their seven-year-old daughter, Dara.

"When was the last time you heard from Mr. Brice?" Green asked.

"Sunday night. He called around midnight, but I let the machine pick up."

"Did you call him back?"

Guilty heat prickled my chest, making me feel trapped beneath my flannel shirt. I didn't want to admit that Sunday had been a bad day for me and I hadn't been in the mood to play any man's psychotherapist.

"No."

Green nodded solemnly. "Don't blame yourself, ma'am. Even if you *had* called him back, it wouldn't have mattered. A couple hours later, he'd have still been dead."

It's strange how guilt compounds when someone tries to take it from you. Until that moment I hadn't known the time of Evan's death. Now I felt sick wondering if that call to me had been his last.

"Did Mr. Brice indicate in his message that he and his wife had a blowup that morning? That she accused him of having an affair?"

I wondered where Green had gotten his information and whether Cissy's accusations were true. I hoped not. Evan hadn't given me any reason to suspect he was cheating on his wife, but I had to admit I was probably the last person he'd confide in about that.

"No," I said. "He sounded tired, and his nose was stuffy like he had a cold. He rambled for a while. Then he asked me to call him back."

Green picked up the poem and studied it. "Mrs. Brice seemed pretty upset when she read this."

His statement startled me, and then slowly the puzzle pieces snapped into place. The poem. The blowup. The affair.

"Are you suggesting Cissy Brice thought Evan was having an affair with *me*?"

Green raised his eyebrows slightly and let my words linger heavily in the air. Finally he said, "I didn't say that, ma'am, but is that what *you* think?"

My face felt warm with self-doubt and embarrassment. "I don't know . . . no, of course not."

"Have you ever known Mrs. Brice to be violent?"

Cissy had been a captivating young woman back in high school and college, a real charmer. She'd also been my best friend until she charmed Evan Brice out of my bed and into hers. At the time, her betrayal had felt like an act of violence, but it didn't make her a murderer now.

"No," I said finally. "At least not the kind of violence you're talking about."

"You're evading the question, Ms. Sinclair."

There was an edge to his tone. It occurred to me that Green's initial Mr. Sympathy routine might have been a ploy to offer the jilted ex-girlfriend a shot at revenge while helping him make a case against the obvious suspect in every murder: the spouse. If so, there was history between Cissy and me that Green hadn't figured into his strategy, history that would keep me from ever playing the revenge card.

"What's her motive?" I said.

He leaned back in the chair. "People kill for a lot of reasons: jealousy, revenge, financial gain. Take your pick. Apparently the victim was blowing money right and left on all sorts of things, including women and drugs. Maybe Mrs. Brice decided to preserve her assets while there were still some to preserve."

"So she turned Evan into Swiss cheese? I mean, how many times did you say he was stabbed?"

"I didn't say." He paused as if considering the wisdom of telling me. "Seventeen."

"Seventeen? How could she physically do that?"

"You mean, because she's a woman? Maybe you're too young to remember the Manson family, Ms. Sinclair. Susan Atkins stabbed Sharon Tate to death, then used the victim's blood to write 'PIG' on the door near her body."

"Fine. You made your point. As far as I know, Cissy was never physically violent. Aside from that, I haven't seen her in years. I don't feel comfortable speculating about what she may or may not be like now. I'm sorry."

Green's lips pressed together in a hard line. "I can accept that." He stared at me for a few moments and then added, "For now."

The narrowing of his eyes gave me the impression that he no longer trusted me, but I didn't care. I didn't like the idea that my reunion with Evan may have interfered with his already fragile marriage. I certainly didn't want to feel responsible for helping the police use our one meeting and a few phone calls to complicate a murder investigation. Green would soon find out that anyone who knew Evan could come up with a list of suspects that were at least as viable as Cissy, like a disgruntled client or a jealous lover, and certainly no one could rule out a possible connection to Evan's love affair with drugs.

Green asked several more perfunctory questions, which I answered to the best of my ability. I'd erased Evan's last telephone message, but I gave him the gist of it as accurately as I could. I also printed out the few, benign e-mails we'd exchanged. The detective told me he'd have to contact my mother to verify my whereabouts around the time Evan was murdered. He said it was routine, and I believed him. I wasn't his target. I was sure of that. I told him he could check with Pookie later that evening.

After I watched Moses Green's car turn from my road onto Pacific Coast Highway, I walked through the French doors to the deck to clear my head. The jet stream had now masked the sun and was bringing in some uninvited moisture, which blurred the horizon with haze. Near the shoreline, a half-dozen surfers peeled off wetsuits as waves pummeled the sand. A few feet down the beach, a springer spaniel waded through the surf, trying to fetch a Frisbee. His best intentions were thwarted again and again by the crashing waves.

The scene reminded me of the elusiveness of second chances. I couldn't shake the feeling that Evan might still be alive if I'd returned his call that night. I'd failed him, hadn't been there when he needed me most. There'd be no second chance to change that. I couldn't believe this was happening to me again.

Cold air began creeping through my flannel shirt, so I went inside and tried to purge my mind of all thoughts of Evan's death and tackle the mundane things that had to be done so life could move forward. I tidied the magazines on the coffee table. I went to my desk and halfheartedly tinkered with a list of questions I was writing for the focus group. Despite my best intentions, I couldn't keep my thoughts from drifting back to Evan's last message on my answering machine. He'd asked for nothing but my time—time I hadn't been willing to give him. His voice had been raspy. I'd thought he had a cold, but now I wondered if he'd been crying, overwhelmed by troubles he could no longer contain.

An unbearable heaviness settled in my chest. I couldn't concentrate. When I finally realized why, I pulled my address book from the desk drawer and carefully flipped through the pages until I spotted the entry. I listened to the dial tone for a long time, gathering my courage before dialing Cissy Brice's number.

- 2 -

the Brices' telephone rang at least eight times before a man answered. He explained in an even, emotionless tone that Cissy was unavailable. When I told him that the police had just left my house, he asked me to hold. Several minutes later he came back on the line. He explained that Cissy had appointments scheduled for most of the day, but that I was welcome to pay my respects in person if I came over by ten o'clock. That didn't give me much time. According to my watch it was nearly nine, and I was far from ready to meet the day.

I went to the bathroom mirror and slapped on a little makeup. I put on my tomato red pantsuit, pausing briefly to consider whether black might have been a more appropriate color to wear on a condolence call. Then I reminded myself that red had been Evan's favorite color. That was all the validation I needed.

As I was leaving the house, I glanced toward the kitchen counter and saw the light on my answering machine blinking, signaling a new message. I hadn't heard the telephone ring, so the call had probably come in while I was in the bathroom. I pushed the Play button and heard the voice of Eugene Barstok.

For the past few days my former administrative assistant had been calling me every morning at exactly nine o'clock. Technically, he was on vacation from Aames & Associates. He'd planned to take a road trip to visit friends in Palm Springs, but he had been forced to cancel because his cat, Liza, had come down with a respiratory infection and couldn't travel. Eugene would never leave her behind. I guess after a couple of days of being cooped up in his apartment, he began to feel isolated; hence, the daily phone calls to me. Eugene was sensitive. I hoped he wouldn't feel slighted, but I didn't have time to call him back at the moment.

I put the top down on the Boxster, hoping the cold March wind would brace me for what was to come, but the temperature was mild, and the air rushing by my face was neither hot nor cold. Forty-five minutes later I was nearing the Brices' address.

Benedict Canyon is one of a series of ravines that slash through the Santa Monica Mountains, linking Los Angeles to the San Fernando Valley. Canyon living has a mystique all its own. It's where the hills begin to close in on you, nudging the eclectic array of houses within a hairsbreadth of the street, where finding a place to park is a joke, and driving slow along the narrow, twisting road is a risk few are willing to take. Somehow it seemed a fitting place for Evan to have lived.

Just past the crest of the hill, I turned onto a side street and was surprised to find it lined with news vans. Tall trees and a rock wall camouflaged the Brices' house, but I was able to see the address on a plaque next to an ornate metal gate.

Across the street, a man with a camera perched on his shoulder was trampling a bed of impatiens that bordered a neighbor's yard. He was trying to get a good shot of a tall, blonde woman speaking into a microphone: Darcy Daniels. I'd seen her on TV a couple of times after she'd marshaled a win on the reality show *Staying Alive* into a permanent gig as a reporter on the tabloid TV show *Celebrity Heat*. It was comforting to know that looking good in a thong bikini could still get you places in this world.

I inched my car toward the gate and gave my name to a rent-a-cop with thighs the size of Doric columns. As he conferred by cell phone with the powers-that-be inside the house, I heard a tapping sound on the side of my car. Startled, I turned and saw Darcy Daniels. Her cameraman stood next to her, pointing his lens directly at me. Up close, Darcy looked older than she did on TV. Staying alive had obviously taken its toll.

"Excuse me," she said, aiming her microphone for my mouth. "Are you a friend of the family?" Without waiting for a response, she lobbed a verbal grenade. "My sources tell me that Evan Brice's murder was a drug deal gone bad. Care to comment?"

I felt a white-hot anger to think that she was turning Evan's death into some kind of cheesy entertainment. I ignored her question, driving away just as the gate jerked open in short, hiccuping spurts.

I made my way to the top of a private knoll, amazed by the remoteness of the surrounding area. Undulating hills covered by dull, green trees and brittle grass, tense with the threat of fire, stood as a backdrop to a wide expanse of lawn that rose up gently to greet the surrounding hills before dropping off into a ravine as if it had suddenly lost its will to go on. It was odd to realize that a mile or so beyond this urban wilderness were eight million people, many of them packed in so close together, they could hear their neighbor's john flush. At least they were alive to appreciate the irony.

The Brices' place was a surprisingly modest ranch house. I wondered if they liked the intimacy of a small place, or if the architectural plans for an expansive Tuscan villa were gathering dust in a closet somewhere because all of Evan's discretionary income had disappeared up his nose.

A little girl's pink bike lay on the flagstone driveway. Near it was a forest green Jaguar with a personalized license plate that read SEXY CC. A lone Adirondack chair, similar to those on the beach in front of my house, stood on the lawn at the edge of the canyon. I felt a crushing sadness as I imagined Evan sitting there writing poetry and trying to make sense of his life. I took a deep breath and walked toward the house.

A man somewhere in his thirties answered the door. He was about my height, five-nine or so, with bleached blond hair and the small sharp features of a fox. A pink hankie that looked like the chute from Paratrooper Barbie blossomed from the breast pocket of his dove gray sports jacket. He introduced himself as Jerome Fielding, Evan's personal assistant, in the same dispassionate voice I recognized from our earlier telephone conversation. Maybe he didn't care about Evan's death, or perhaps he was just trying to hold it together for the sake of a house in mourning.

To my relief, no one else was around. The house was still except for the syncopated rhythm of our footsteps on the hardwood floors, and the echoing silence. A few seconds later, we emerged from a sliding glass door and stepped onto a patio that surrounded an angular swimming pool and a small cabana.

Cissy Brice stood in front of a round metal table, arranging a bouquet of red tulips in a heavy crystal vase. I was impressed that she hadn't changed much in the past ten years. She wasn't beautiful in the Hollywood sense of the word, but she had a flawless complexion, eyes the color of Texas bluebonnets, and enough capped teeth to help send her dentist's children to Harvard. Her hair was red now. She was wearing it pushed off her face with a headband that looked like a Brunhilde braid. It was probably the latest in Beverly Hills chic, but it made her look as though she were on her way to a yodeling contest.

She was wearing a black dress, which provided a fitting background for the platinum cross she wore around her neck. I'd never known Cissy to be religious, but I could see how losing your mate to violent death could move you in that direction. The cross was encrusted with large diamonds. It looked as if it had cost more than the weekly wages of a hundred illegal immigrants sharing jerry-rigged living quarters in some Pacoima garage.

Clinging to Cissy's leg was a fragile-looking girl of six or seven whom I presumed was Dara. The child was sucking her thumb and fingering a faded rag that looked as if it might have been a pink baby blanket a thousand wash cycles ago. She had dark smudges under her eyes, and burnished brown hair, which reminded me so much of Evan's that I was taken aback. When Dara saw me, she buried her head among the folds of Cissy's black dress.

Cissy didn't look up. She caressed her daughter's hair with one hand and, with the other, tried to make the tulip stems crisscross symmetrically in the vase. Unfortunately, she hadn't clipped off the bottom leaves, which made the stalks hopelessly tangled. She tried to pull one out but managed only to eject the entire bouquet in one snarled mess. I guess no one had told her that in floral arranging, as in everything else, planning is the key to success.

It wasn't until Jerome cleared his throat that Cissy finally lifted her gaze. A brief frown appeared on her forehead, as if she resented his intrusion. A moment later she spotted me. Our eyes locked as both of us calculated our next move before the spell was broken.

A wan smile brushed across her lips. "I see you made it past the vultures."

"Just barely."

"Ever since Evan was murdered, they follow me everywhere. It feels like I'm living in prison."

"I'm sorry."

Cissy disentangled the child from her leg and walked toward me. When she was within touching distance, she took my hand and squeezed it gently. "Thanks for coming, Tuckie." She stepped back and surveyed me like a proud mom checking out her daughter's first prom dress. "You're as beautiful as ever."

I tried to remember the last time a man had told me that, but I couldn't recall a single incidence. I felt uncomfortable holding her hand, so I let mine drop away.

"You must be devastated," I said.

She put a finger to her lips to shush me. In a voice louder than necessary she said, "Tucker, I want you to meet my daughter, Dara. Honey, come meet Mommy's friend from a long time ago."

Without the support of her mother's leg, Dara looked as if she'd been set adrift in a hostile sea. She didn't look up, just shook her head and let her chin loll on the blanket around her neck as if she'd given up all hope of rescue.

"Sorry," Cissy said. "Dara's not feeling well today. Are

you, honey? Maybe if you say 'pretty please,' Jerome will get you some banana cream pie."

A disapproving frown appeared on Jerome's face, but nonetheless, he picked up his cue. He took Dara's hand, the one that wasn't picking at the remnants of the blanket's satin binding, and guided her toward the sliding glass door as Cissy watched her child's every hesitant footstep until the house swallowed her completely.

Cissy stared at the door until moisture filled her eyes and spilled down her cheeks. "Now she's just like us, Tuckie. She'll grow up without a daddy and be cheated out of all those memories. Did you know my uncle walked me down the aisle when Evan and I got married? In some ways, it was the saddest day of my life." Her voice had a hollow detachment to it, as if she were talking in her sleep.

My body felt as if some vital organ had suddenly stopped functioning. I understood her pain. Both Cissy and I had lost our fathers at an early age. Mine died before I was born, so I'd grown up without expectations. Frank Jerrard had been around long enough to teach his daughter that a man's adoration was her birthright. In many ways, life had been easier for me.

"My world is falling apart," she said in a voice that was barely above a whisper, "and I don't know what to do about it."

It felt lame, but I said it anyway. "Is there anything I can do to help?"

She roughly brushed away the tears. "No, but thanks for asking."

I kept quiet until she regained her composure. "Cissy, the police told me—"

She interrupted. "Told you what? That I killed my husband?"

I hesitated. "Not exactly . . ."

"Well, whatever they told you, it isn't true. I've never even been to Evan's apartment. Besides, I was with Mom that night. I told them, but they won't believe me. They're trying to scare me into saying I did it. One of the cops said if I was implicated in any way, they could put Dara into protective custody. My daughter means everything to me, Tucker. *Everything.* You of all people should know I would *never* take her daddy away from her."

There was fierceness in her tone, and the ring of truth to her words. I looked at the mascara smeared by her tears, at the fingers nervously twisting the chain of her necklace, and knew I believed her. When I told her so, relief softened her expression. She picked up the tulips one by one and began tearing off the lower leaves and fitting them into the vase.

"The police told me you saw the poem," I said. "I want to make sure you don't think it meant Evan and I were together again."

Cissy let out a sigh of frustration. "I know you're a better person than that, Tuckie. Look, Evan and I had a fight on Sunday. So what? We didn't have a perfect marriage. He cheated on me, but I wasn't afraid he'd leave me for another woman. He didn't have sex with people he loved; he had sex with people who loved drugs, and he wasn't exactly discriminating. I was afraid he'd get something horrible like AIDS. If you'd ever loved an addict, you'd understand what it was like for me."

To her credit, she caught herself and quickly added, "I know you loved Evan once, Tucker, but that was before cocaine hijacked his life." She paused before placing the final tulip in the vase, stroking it gently just as she had earlier stroked Dara's hair. "Look," she went on.

"None of that stuff matters anymore. I'm sorry for what I did to you back then. I don't know what was wrong with me, but I'd like to think I've changed. I hope you can forgive me."

Apologies are like blind dates. You occasionally accept one, but they seldom live up to the hype.

"Let the dead past bury its dead," I said.

She frowned. "That sounds familiar."

"It's Henry Wadsworth Longfellow. 'A Psalm of Life.'" I could have added that it was one of Evan's favorite poems, but I didn't. Maybe she already knew.

When I finally got up to leave, Cissy offered to walk with me to the car. We moved together in silence until we reached the driveway.

"Tucker?" Her voice was soft and tentative. "I don't know what your schedule is like, but I know Mom would love to see you."

I felt a stab of guilt. "I'll try to give her a call sometime soon."

Cissy nodded, but I could see the disappointment in her face.

I'd just slid into the front seat of my car and was searching in my purse for the key when she said, "You know . . . maybe there is something you can do to help."

She was trying to keep her expression neutral, but I caught a faint glimmer of uncertainty and perhaps a little fear as well.

"Sure, name it."

"That apartment in Venice where Evan was killed—it was his. He wanted a place where he could get away from the office and work without being bothered. He liked the neighborhood, because it was sort of funky and anonymous."

"The police say he used a fake name on the rental agreement."

"They're making it sound like it was something sinister. It wasn't. Everybody in the entertainment business makes up phony names. Do you think Madonna calls up the Peninsula Hotel and says, 'Hey, guys. It's the Material Girl. Book me in for a couple of nights'? No. Somebody would leak the news to the paparazzi. She'd never have any peace and quiet. Evan didn't use his real name to rent the place because he didn't want the locals bugging him about his work, that's all."

I didn't want to add to her burden by telling her the police suspected Evan of using an alias as a cover for his drug dealing, so I just shrugged.

"He was hardly ever at the apartment," she went on, "so he hired the little girl across the hall to open and close the curtains, pick up the junk mail—you know, make it look lived in. Anyway, somebody has to close up the place. The furniture is rental, so that's easy. Everything else needs to be packed up and donated to charity." She paused as her eyes welled with tears. "Mom said she'd do it, so I gave her all of the paperwork—the rental contracts, stuff like that. But I think it's going to be too hard on her. I know it's asking a lot, but maybe you could help. The papers are still at her place. You could pick them up. It would give you an excuse to see her again."

I hesitated, wondering how to say no tactfully. Frankly, the idea of going to the scene of Evan's murder didn't exactly appeal to me. Facing Claire Jerrard again after all these years didn't sound so great, either. After Frank died and Cissy began dating Evan, Claire and I drifted apart— my choice, not hers. Maybe I hadn't handled the situation very well, but it was too late to change that now.

I knew I'd waited too long to respond when I saw Cissy's cheeks flush with embarrassment. "Never mind, Tuckie. It was a bad idea." Then the fierceness crept back into her voice. "But I want you to know, in spite of what you may think, Mom never stopped loving you."

I leaned back against the headrest and let out the breath I'd been holding. There were a thousand reasons why I shouldn't do what Cissy had just asked me to do. In the end, my thoughts kept coming back to one thing: second chances.

I turned slowly to face her. "I'll need Evan's address."

a fter I left Cissy's house, it occurred to me that the logical person to handle the apartment closure was Evan's personal assistant, Jerome Fielding. I wondered why Cissy hadn't asked him. That seemed odd. On the other hand, I'd sensed some tension between the two of them. Perhaps Jerome's loyalties didn't extend beyond Evan, and Cissy resented him for that. I knew it was a bad idea for me to get involved with Cissy Brice again. I should have gone back inside and told her I'd changed my mind about helping, except that I'd given my word. I couldn't take it back without feeling like a jerk.

According to Cissy, the police had taken the original rental agreements for both the apartment and the furniture as evidence. They'd given her copies, which she'd handed over to her mom. Claire Jerrard's job had been to notify the management company of the family's intent to vacate the apartment, make arrangements to clean the place, and remove the rental furniture. I was responsible for doing that now. I decided to pick up the documents at Claire's place on my way home just to get it over with.

Members of the media were still congregated around the Brices' front entrance as I retraced my path down the driveway. As soon as the gate opened, I stepped on the gas and didn't look back until Darcy Daniels became a mere speck in my rearview mirror.

No one had to give me directions to the Jerrard family home. The map coordinates were indelibly stamped on my memory. Only a few high-rises interrupted my view of the western skyline as I turned left at Fox Studios onto Motor Avenue, heading toward Cheviot Hills, the West L.A. neighborhood that had displaced acres of orange groves and bean fields back in the 1930s and '40s. When I crossed Monte Mar, the congestion of Pico Boulevard was replaced by winding roads and hillside lots crowned by pricey real estate. Only one or two For Sale signs were visible, and almost no examples of the latest L.A. remodeling craze: tearing down a perfectly good house in order to squeeze a McMansion onto a fifty-foot lot. I turned off the ignition at curbside and looked around for any signs of the upper middle class searching for greater meaning in their lives, but all I saw was a Latino gardener herding garden debris with an outlawed leaf blower.

Claire's house was a well-maintained two-story English traditional with dormer windows. I felt melancholy gazing at the neatly trimmed hedge that surrounded the property. Even though Frank Jerrard had been gone for years, in my mind's eye I could still see him out in the yard in his chinos and plaid shirt, laboring with hand clippers to make the hedge boxy but not so flat that the white flowers wouldn't bloom. His life had seemed so effortless compared to mine. In high school I used to fantasize about how things might have been if I'd grown up in this house instead of an apartment in Palms where my mother struggled to make ends meet.

A black Mercedes S-class sedan was parked in the driveway. The vanity plate read, "1GR8MOM." The car was obviously a gift from Cissy—Evan, too, I assumed. Claire deserved it. After Frank died, she had gone through a rough time financially and almost lost the house. The crisis had warped Cissy into viewing money as a protective cloak. In fact, for a long time it was the only thing she cared about—until I introduced her to Evan.

I knocked on the door, and when it finally opened, I realized I'd been holding my breath. Claire was standing at the threshold wearing a lavender warm-up suit, the type meant for driving your SUV to the grocery store, not for serious exercise. She was thinner than I'd ever seen her, and her hair was now completely white and cut short. Aside from that, she hadn't changed much in the past ten years. We hugged long enough for me to smell her flowery hair shampoo and feel her ribs beneath the jacket.

"Tucker, it's been too long."

Her voice was deep and husky from years of smoking. She once told me that she had learned the proper way to hold a cigarette from her college sorority sisters back when smoking had been considered first sophisticated, then rebellious, and finally merely a way to keep your weight at 120 pounds. I hoped she'd quit by now. Cancer is a heavy price to pay for a size six.

Standing in the foyer, I could clearly see into the living room. The couch was covered with the same brown and blue floral print I remembered from high school. On top of the seldom-played piano were the silver-framed family photographs, some done in vintage tints by an artist's hand before the computer mouse ruled the world. From a nearby window, a beam of light fell across a picture of Frank Jerrard. Tiny dust particles floated around his face, making him look as if he were encased in some kitschy snow globe.

Claire led me to what had always been the true center of life in the Jerrard household: the kitchen. We gravitated naturally to our traditional places across from each other at the breakfast bar. Sitting there felt just like the old days, when I'd come over to visit and she'd listen to my problems without seeming to pry.

Without asking, Claire poured freshly brewed coffee. As she placed a cup on the counter in front of me, I noticed a tissue tucked into the elastic wristband of her jacket. It made her seem vulnerable and old, which caused a heaviness to settle in my chest. She followed my eyes to the tissue and smiled as if she knew what I was thinking. She took my hands in hers and looked at me for a long moment.

"So," she said, "tell me about your life."

"There's not much to tell. I got married, divorced. Now I'm struggling to keep my head above water. You know, typical American-dream stuff."

There was a tinge of sadness in her smile, as though she regretted missing out on the events in my life. I didn't want to dwell on the past, so I moved on to Pookie and Bruce and my current campaign to convince Marvin Geyer that muumuus were costumes, not haute couture. As always, she listened without interrupting, offering only an occasional sympathetic nod. When it was her turn, she told me about her garden club and her prize-winning camellias.

I waited for a lull in the conversation. "I guess Cissy told you I volunteered to close Evan's apartment."

She flashed a wry smile. "Yes, she just called, but knowing my daughter, it was probably something short of volunteering. I hope it isn't too much of a burden for you.

It's just . . . I didn't realize the family was responsible for cleaning the crime scene. When I found out, I didn't have enough oomph to do anything . . ." Her voice trailed off into a sigh. "Well, that doesn't really matter, does it? You're here. That's all that counts. I only wish it had been pleasant news that brought you back."

"I'm sorry about Evan," I said. "It must be hard on you."

"Evan has always been a dilemma for me. What's hard about his death is knowing the police think my daughter killed him."

Claire's tone was tinged with resentment, but I chalked it up to worry and grief. I understood why her feelings toward Evan might be conflicted. For years her daughter had lived with his substance abuse and infidelity. Cissy's life couldn't have been easy. Now his death was putting her future in jeopardy. I thought about reassuring Claire that Moses Green was looking at other suspects, too, but in fact, I wasn't at all sure that he was. I was sure of one thing: If Cissy remained in the detective's crosshairs, it would destroy the only family Claire had left.

"I thought Evan was finally getting his life back on track."

"We thought so, too, but after he got out of rehab, he seemed anxious all the time, as though the weight of the world was on his shoulders."

I didn't want to tell her, but for a lot of people sobriety was sobering.

"Do you know what was bothering him?"

She hesitated. "No."

"Look, Claire, maybe it's time Cissy talked to a lawyer."

She held up her hands in a gesture of futility. "I agree, but she thinks it will just make her look guilty."

"How can that be? She was with you the night Evan

died. I don't understand why the cops are still focusing on her."

Claire seemed tense, fiddling with the tissue in her jacket sleeve. "Unhappy marriages raise eyebrows."

"Maybe, but I'm sure there are other suspects, like friends Evan partied with."

"Those people weren't his friends. They were users who either wanted clout in the entertainment business or access to drugs."

A loud noise interrupted our conversation. I glanced out the window and saw the gardener firing up something that looked like a weapon from *The Texas Chainsaw Massacre*. I was waiting for him to put on a leather mask and wield the tool like a samurai sword. Instead, he began hacking away at the hedge, moving with purpose. It was clear by the stony look on his face that beauty and possibility didn't bring him the same joy they had brought to Frank Jerrard.

Claire didn't seem to notice the noise. A moment later she pushed back the stool and walked to the coffeepot for a refill. In the old days she would also have been going for a smoke. There were no cigarettes this time. I was glad about that. Nevertheless, she took a long time before returning to her chair at the breakfast bar.

"You know, Tucker, I wasn't thrilled about having Evan as a son-in-law. I told Cissy that a man who cheats once will cheat again, but she wouldn't listen to me."

"They stayed together," I said. "That says something."

"Yes, but if she'd stayed away from him in the first place, none of this would be happening."

I wasn't sure why she was bringing this up now. Cissy and Evan had been married for at least nine years. If Claire wanted to salve my wounded ego after all this time, I wasn't interested.

"Look, Claire, that's ancient history. I've been dumped by dozens of guys since Evan."

She paused for a moment. "You're right. Ancient history. I'm sorry. I'll get those contracts."

She rose from her chair and began searching through a hand-painted wooden organizer sitting on the kitchen counter. Whatever she was looking for wasn't there, so she moved on to a drawer across the room that appeared to be filled with appliance manuals and paper doilies. After a short search, she pulled out several pieces of legal-length paper, which I assumed were the copies of the furniture contract and the apartment rental agreement. She laid them on the counter beside her, pausing for a moment as if to debate some issue in her head; then she pulled a trifold brochure from the drawer.

"There's something I want to show you," she said. "It's the program from a poetry reading. Evan wrote something shortly before he died. He wanted to try it out on an audience. I don't know why Cissy invited me. Moral support, maybe."

I could tell by the distance in her tone that she wasn't a big fan of Evan's poetry. "Pretty bad, huh?"

"Truthfully? Yes, but another of his poems was printed in the program. It's quite nice. I think it's about you."

She handed me the brochure. From the cover I saw that the event had been held two months before at a café in West Hollywood called Poet's Corner. I flipped through the pages until I found Evan's piece. I recognized it immediately. It was a love poem he'd composed for me shortly after we met, one of the few he'd written that hadn't been derivative. Now, after almost ten years, I was reading it again. The words were equal parts angst and longing, but they possessed a purity of emotion that caused a lump to form in my throat.

I'm not sure how long I stood there lost in the moment, but at some point I sensed Claire staring at me. I glanced up and saw on her face an unguarded, critical frown. I was taken aback. Obviously Moses Green wasn't the only person who questioned the nature of my recent reunion with Evan Brice.

"Claire, I hope you know this was written back in college."

Her frown softened but did not disappear. "Yes, that's what you said—ancient history."

I was frustrated and a little annoyed, but mostly hurt that she would think I was capable of that kind of payback. I waited for the silence to pass. Meanwhile, I returned my gaze to the program. Ten people, including Evan, were listed as readers at the event. As I scanned down the page, I was surprised to see another familiar name: James Brodie. I asked Claire if she knew him.

"Evan introduced me to several people that night," she said. "I don't remember any names. Why?"

"Just curious. He was a close friend of Evan's in college. It's got to be the same guy."

I didn't tell her, but Brodie had been a friend of mine as well, until he'd been swept up along with Evan in the vortex of rhyming couplets and cocaine. In my experience, old friends are often the ones we trust most with our secrets. James Brodie had been one of his closest old friends. I wondered if Evan had confided in him up to the end.

I could tell by the droop of Claire's shoulders that our conversation was wearing her down. As I stood to leave, I wondered if I'd ever stop drumming up ways to feel responsible for her pain—probably not. I owed Claire

Jerrard, if for no other reason than because she'd told me my yellow taffeta little-piece-of-heaven prom dress from J. C. Penney made me look like Julia Roberts in *Pretty Woman*, even though the image in the mirror looked more like Big Bird in *Sesame Street*, or for playing mother when my own was playing sidekick to the real star in some forgettable film so she could pay the rent on our one-bedroom apartment. But mostly because she'd assured me that Frank Jerrard's death was a tragedy that couldn't have been prevented, even though I knew how terribly wrong she was about that. Suddenly, old memories began carving out a hollow cavity in my chest that I felt compelled to fill with words.

"Don't worry," I said. "I'll close the apartment. I'll take care of everything. Hopefully I'll be finished by the end of the week."

"I can't thank you enough for what you're doing for Cissy."

I didn't have the heart to tell her I wasn't doing anything for Cissy. I was doing it for her or for Evan or maybe even for Dara. What the hell, maybe I was just doing it for myself.

"No problem," I said, "really."

Relief eased the crease between her eyebrows, which should have made me feel good instead of merely dutiful. As I said my good-byes and headed for the car, I wondered if James Brodie could tell me anything about Evan's death. For a moment, I considered trying to locate him. On the other hand, I knew that if I did, I'd eventually be smacking my palm against my forehead and thinking, *Stupid idea? Who knew?* Besides, I couldn't allow myself to get sidetracked. My number one priority was closing Evan's apartment. Let the police handle the rest.

- 4 -

i sat in my car in front of Claire's house, studying the rental contract. The police had the original, so maybe they thought there was something hidden between the lines that might lead them to Evan's killer. If so, I couldn't see it. Except for the fake name, the document looked pretty standard. The only thing that seemed odd was the rent. It was incredibly low for property so close to the beach.

Apparently, the coroner's office had finished collecting evidence at the apartment, but they still had the key. Since there was no on-site manager, Claire told me I'd have to get a spare from the girl Evan had hired to look after his place. Her name was Monique Ruiz. She was a student at a local community college who was trying to make ends meet and had seemed grateful for the extra cash.

Venice was roughly on my way home, so I decided to swing by the apartment and see if she was at home. I figured it wouldn't be all that difficult to arrange for the return of the rental furniture. I'd pack up everything else and call some charity to haul it away, just as Cissy had instructed. There was a battered-women's shelter in Santa Monica that was always looking for items to sell in their thrift shop. I'd call them.

Finding somebody to clean the apartment was another issue. That job required more than a Merry Maid with a bottle of Lysol and an old T-shirt. It had to be somebody who was knowledgeable in the handling of human tissue, body fluids, and blood. I'd once read an article in the *Los Angeles Times* about a company that made its living sanitizing death scenes, but I couldn't remember the name. A creepy image flashed through my head of men with industrial vacuums sucking up Evan's spilled life. I shook off the chill and headed toward Venice.

I followed Pacific Avenue, a narrow street lined with run-down houses, weathered one- and two-story apartment buildings, and a few small businesses, including a market and a tattoo parlor, all wearing the same look of weary determination. The area reminded me of the group of friends, mostly Evan's, I had hung out with back in college: gritty, unkempt, and perhaps a little dangerous.

On Seagate Pathway, a slender lane that dead-ended at the beach, I turned left behind an older-model Volvo, its red paint oxidized from weather and neglect. I inched along until I spotted Evan's address on a three-story brick building at the end of the street, where the pavement met the sand. Detective Green had implied that the apartment was seedy, but I'd lived in worse places.

There were no news vans with antennas and satellite dishes blocking my way here. No reporters, either. Even without a media presence, the street was jammed with cars parked in every inch of space except for one, and the Volvo in front of me got to it first. The driver looked to be somewhere in her fifties with shoulder-length, dishwater blond hair. After she had pulled into the spot, she held up both hands in a gesture that said, *Better luck next time.* Yeah, right. I ended up paying nine dollars to park in a private lot a couple of blocks away. I put up the Boxster's convertible top and headed toward the beach.

Evan had rented his apartment using the name Thomas Chatterton, which was an interesting choice. Chatterton was an impoverished English poet of the late 1700s, rumored to be a drug addict and a liar of such great magnitude that critics rejected him as a fake and a forger. He never saw his poetry in print. At age eighteen he poisoned himself in a small London garret rather than starve to death. His work had never resonated with me, but his life had the kind of pathos that appealed to Evan. I imagined him smiling each time he picked up his junk mail.

Despite Cissy's explanation that Evan wanted a quiet place to work, I didn't completely understand why he had felt it necessary to use an alias on the rental contract. She claimed he didn't want to be bothered with paparazzi or wannabe actors looking for an agent. The truth was, most people in L.A. were jaded by the celebrities in their midst. Besides, he wasn't a high-profile actor; he was an agent. It was hard to believe that legions of groupies followed him everywhere. Maybe he was on some kind of ego trip, but I suspected he used the nom de guerre for other reasons. Perhaps, as Detective Green had suggested, he wanted to be closer to his drug sources, or maybe he was creating his vision of a bohemian poet's Greenwich Village lifestyle in those few stolen hours by the beach. I also couldn't discount the possibility that his reason for renting the apartment was murkier than drugs or stolen hours. It just didn't seem likely to me.

I checked the mailboxes on the lobby wall and found a label for M. Ruiz on number 307. Since there was no elevator, I walked up three flights of stairs. When I reached the landing, I saw a row of doors on each side of a central hallway. As I neared Evan's unit, my heart began to pound, half expecting to see or—worse—to smell something that might challenge my good intentions. Thankfully, there was no police tape and no official-looking seal on the door to indicate that the apartment had ever been a crime scene.

Green had told me there were no signs of forced entry and no ransacking, so it wasn't a burglary. Assuming Evan hadn't inadvertently left the door unlocked, he must have let his killer in. All the speculation was taxing my brain, so I moved on to Monique Ruiz's door and knocked. No one answered. A moment later I knocked again, this time louder.

"No one's home."

It was an old voice, weak and gravelly. I turned to see an elderly woman standing in the entrance of the apartment a couple of doors down from Evan's place, clinging to a walker that had two green tennis balls skewered on its front legs. Her spine was bowed by osteoporosis, and her brow was etched with the omnipresent look of seriousness born of chronic pain.

"You from the police?" Her tone sounded brittle and wary.

I said no and introduced myself as a friend of the family. I told her I'd come to pick up Mr. Chatterton's apartment key.

At the mention of the name she shuddered, ruffling the white sausage curls that lay in symmetrical rows atop her head.

"I'm sorry for your loss," she said. "I hear his real name was something else. That was a surprise. We're all pretty scared about what happened, but Monique is very sensitive. I guess she couldn't take the commotion, so she went to stay with her aunt for a few days." She paused for a moment to look at me. "You could almost be his sister. Your hair's dark like his, but I see now your eyes are brown. And you're too tall. Mr. Chatterton was a small-boned man. I used to be five-four myself, but I keep shrinking."

She told me her name was Rose Miller and that she'd lived in the building for twelve years. She spoke in that open, almost naive manner that a lot of older people have. She'd been in the hospital the night Evan was murdered. When she came home the following day, she'd found a note from Monique Ruiz slipped under her door.

"She left her car parked in the lot out back," Rose said. "I guess she didn't want me to worry when I didn't see her around."

"If her car's out back, how did she get to her aunt's?"

"I'm not sure. She has a boyfriend. Maybe he drove."

"Did she say when she'd be back?"

A concerned look crossed her face. "No, but I hope it's soon, because she keeps an eye on me."

"You know where her aunt lives?"

She paused for a moment to think. "Let's see, her name is Estela—Sandoval, I think—but I don't remember where she lives. Up the coast somewhere. Monique's folks live in West Covina, though. Maybe you can check with them. Her father's name is William, but in Spanish."

I tried to recall some rusty high school Spanish. "Guillermo?"

"I think so. My memory's not so good anymore. Not like it used to be. Mr. Ruiz never liked the idea of Monique living here alone. He thinks she's safer at home with the family. I guess I'm selfish, but I hope he doesn't make her move away."

"Who keeps an eye on you when Monique's not here?"

"I have a daughter in Scottsdale, but I guess that

doesn't count. She's quite a golfer. Do you play?" I told her no, and she added, "Me, neither. I'm more of a walker—at least I used to be."

Not recently, I gathered. She looked too frail. It must have been an effort just to get up and down the stairs to pick up her mail. I wondered what it felt like to be old and alone and with a daughter too busy shagging golf pros to come visit her mother in the hospital. Considering my abysmal history with relationships, imagining that wasn't much of a stretch.

I hesitated to leave Rose Miller alone, but I didn't know what else to do. As a compromise, I wrote my telephone number on the back of a business card and asked if she would have Monique call me when she returned.

"You can reach me at that number anytime," I added, "in case you need anything while Monique's gone."

"My goodness, do I sound that bad? My daughter says I complain too much. I guess she's right. Don't worry, dear. I'll be fine."

"I'm sure you will, but keep the number just in case. It's my cell phone number, so I usually answer."

She studied the card. "Everybody's got a cell phone these days. Monique's parents pay for hers, I guess so they can keep tabs on her."

"Monique has a cell phone? Do you have the number?"

"It's only for emergencies; otherwise she has to pay extra." Her tone sounded like a dire warning.

"I won't talk long, I promise. Besides, this is sort of an emergency."

She frowned in thought, obviously worried about respecting Monique's bottom line. Finally she said, "Well, I guess it wouldn't hurt."

It took Rose a while to find Monique's number. By the time she did, her breathing had become labored. With all that white hair caressing her pale face, Rose reminded me of an aging cherub, which made me think of my grandma Felder singing hymns off-key at church. I suddenly had a bad case of the guilties, so before I left, I lied and told her I was on my way to the market. Did she need anything? After a little prodding, she produced a list of three or four staple items and a white envelope. Inside was a crisp twenty-dollar bill that looked as if it had just come back from the Fluff 'n Fold.

Since I'd paid nine bucks for the privilege of parking all day in a weed-infested square of sandy dirt, I decided to walk to the market on Pacific that I'd passed earlier. On the way, I dialed Monique Ruiz's cell phone number and got a recorded message. The voice sounded tense and hurried. "Hi, this is Monique. Please leave a message." There was a pause as I waited for some kind of beep. None came. A moment later, I heard her voice again. "Nonny, call me at the beauty shop, okay?"

There was no way to know when the recording had been made. The idea that Monique Ruiz had stopped off for a consolation perm before going to her aunt's place sounded a little far-fetched. Regardless, I left a message asking her to call me. Just to be thorough, I checked with information for a Guillermo Ruiz in West Covina. The number was unlisted.

When I trudged back up the stairs to deliver Rose's groceries, she greeted me at the door as though I were a member of the Prize Patrol.

"Oxnard," she said. "That's where the aunt lives. I remembered the minute you left. I don't know the phone number, though. Monique is usually good about telling me how to reach her, but I guess she forgot this time."

That was understandable. I tried to put myself in

Monique's shoes. She was young and had already been put on a short leash by her family. It made sense that she'd be freaked out by a homicide committed across the hall from her. It was interesting that she'd gone to her aunt's place and not home to her parents. Maybe she didn't want them to know about the crime, for fear they'd strip away her newfound independence.

On the other hand, maybe Rose was only speculating about the reason for Monique's trip. Perhaps the girl hadn't even known about Evan's death and had merely gone away on a planned vacation to enjoy a different stretch of beach for a few days.

I wondered who Nonny was and why Monique wanted her to know that she'd stopped at the beauty shop. At least scheduling an impromptu hair appointment fit better with my vacation theory. Only I was sure I'd detected tension in Monique's recorded voice message. That led to a grislier thought: Evan's killer forged the note from Monique and slipped it under Rose's door, and Monique Ruiz was lying somewhere in a shallow grave, beautifully coiffed and gummy with hair spray. Obviously, I was out of control.

After helping Rose put away her groceries, I headed downstairs. When I got to the lobby, I noticed the woman with the Volvo standing on the sidewalk across the street, dressed in a red kimono and a pair of blue flip-flops. She was glaring at a late-model Toyota, which was parked at an odd angle to the curb, with its rear end sticking out into the street. She looked as though she was jotting down the license plate number in a small notebook. When she noticed me watching her, she shook her head in dismay as if she'd just unlocked the secret of man's inhumanity to man: bad parking etiquette.

I went back to my car and watched a half-dozen people play beach volleyball while I called the information operator to get the telephone number for Estela Sandoval. In a rare display of telephone company compassion, he gave me her address as well.

I told myself that driving sixty miles one way to Oxnard to pick up Evan's apartment key was above and beyond my commitment to Cissy. On the other hand, I didn't know how long Monique Ruiz would be out of town, and I didn't want to let this project drag on for days. For the moment, my work on Marvin Geyer's focus group project was under control. I had no other jobs in the pipeline to work on. Besides, I was curious to find out what happened to Monique Ruiz, if her hair turned out okay, and if she was coming back to take care of Rose. Maybe I'd even ask her if she'd been home the night Evan died, and what, if anything, she'd seen or heard.

I prorated the nine-buck parking fee, declared it a wash, and headed north.

– 5 –

Oxnard is a seaside town best known for its impeccable strawberries and improbable name. It's about an hour north of Los Angeles and surrounded by some of the most fertile agricultural land in the world. Unfortunately, its unspoiled beaches and small-town atmosphere have been discovered, leaving its fate up for grabs as slow-growth advocates and developers wage war. I wondered how deep Estela Sandoval's roots extended into that rich Oxnard soil.

The address for Monique Ruiz's aunt led me to an apartment house in a neighborhood with modest single-family homes. The units were perched above a row of carports and bordered by a wraparound balcony that looked as if it were on the verge of collapsing from the weight of the crushed-rock facade. A dilapidated sign hanging on the front of the building read, "Studios, One and Two Bedrooms," and "No Vacancy."

There was a unifying theme to the place: rust. From the reddish-brown dome cover of an abandoned barbecue to the corroded window bars, everything was in an advanced stage of neglect. Weeds grew through the cracked cement in the driveway, where a black Chevy Silverado pickup was parked. The pickup, at least, looked new.

I tried the latch on a wire-mesh gate just left of the building, but it wouldn't budge. My tomato red pantsuit notwithstanding, I was about to look for footholds in the wire so I could climb the fence, when I noticed a security intercom system that was nearly obscured behind a piece of plywood.

I pushed the plywood aside and checked the names adjacent to the intercom buttons. Five of the six read "Sandoval." Since I didn't know which apartment belonged to Monique's aunt, I pushed all the buzzers. Nothing happened. I waited a minute or two and pushed them again.

"That thing don't work."

A pretty Latina, no more than seventeen years old, stood about four feet behind me. Her eyebrows had been shaved and redrawn into thin semicircles that gave her expression a permanent air of surprise. On her upper right arm was a tattoo of an arrow piercing a heart and the name "Oscar." There was a world-weary look on her face that had no right to be there for at least ten more years. A chubby baby was slung over her left hip. He wore a Tommy Hilfiger T-shirt and a droopy disposable diaper that smelled as though it was carrying a full load. The shirt made a fashion statement, but it seemed a little too skimpy for the chilly March air.

"Who you looking for?" she said.

"Estela Sandoval."

"What you want her for?"

The baby's deep, racking cough interrupted our conversation. The girl cooed and kissed his cheek, trying to comfort him.

"Actually I'm looking for Monique Ruiz."

Her eyes narrowed. "She's not here."

"You sure? She said she was coming to visit her aunt."

"Monique's got a lot of aunts."

The gate apparently wasn't locked, just ornery, because the girl pushed hard on it a couple times with her free hip, and it popped opened with an arthritic groan. The baby resumed his ragged coughing until a plug of stringy snot dropped from his nose onto his mom's shirt. I memorized every precious detail from the five-alarm diaper to the nose googies. It was enough to dash anyone's fantasies of motherhood.

I waited until she disappeared through the door of apartment 2. Then I followed her path through the side yard, up a flight of stairs, and along the rickety-looking balcony, determined to knock on each of the other five apartment doors until I found either Monique or her aunt.

A boy of around eight answered the door of number 6. Inside, a sleeping toddler was strapped in a car seat parked in front of a TV, which was blaring cartoons. I asked for Estela Sandoval. The boy pointed to a small bungalow next door.

The bungalow was surrounded by a chain-link fence and subdivided by a cement sidewalk that had managed to claw its way through the hard-packed dirt. A hand-painted sign on the front door read, "Estela's Salón de Belleza." Another sign read, "Abierto." At least that explained Monique's telephone message about being at a beauty shop. As I turned the knob and walked inside, I heard a door slam somewhere toward the back of the house.

Just inside to the right were several matching chairs and a small round table dolled up with a bouquet of faded plastic flowers. To the left, in what was originally meant as the living room, were two beauty operator stations, each with its own sink and styling chair.

There were two women in the place. One sat under a hair

dryer, reading *La Opinión*. The newspaper obscured her face, but the spider veins on her legs told me she was too old to be Monique Ruiz. The other was standing in the kitchen, eating what looked like a chile relleno. Estela Sandoval, I assumed. It was difficult to determine her age, but I guessed late forties. Lush brown hair tinged with auburn highlights crouched in springy curls around her shoulders. The sheen on her flawless skin looked more oily than dewy. At least two hundred pounds of dense flesh hugged her five-foot frame, leaving her arms and legs unnaturally splayed like the limbs of a gingerbread man.

When Estela saw me, she looked around the shop as if she'd just noticed the accumulation of grime and was embarrassed by it. She left the food and picked up a nearby broom and a clamshell dustbin and started hurriedly sweeping up hair that had drifted around one of the styling chairs.

"Sorry, I didn't see you come in. Do you want an appointment?" Her voice was slightly nasal, with an accent that had survived despite at least a generation of acculturation.

Even if I hadn't been wearing my tomato red pantsuit, I would have looked out of place in her shop. The expression of caution on her face told me she knew that, too. I decided against faking interest in a cut and blow-dry and got right to the point.

"I'm looking for your niece."

She flashed a warm smile laced with affection. "Which one? I got quite a few."

"Monique Ruiz."

The smile disappeared along with any interest in sweeping. She propped the cleaning tools against the counter near a funky blue backpack.

"Why do you want her? She in some kind of trouble?" Her voice sounded overly tense. I wondered what kind of a family brouhaha I'd stumbled into.

I told her I'd come from L.A. to pick up the key to Evan's apartment. She looked relieved and then puzzled. "You drove all this way for a key? Why? Your friend can't get into his place or what?"

I didn't want to get into it with her, so I told her my friend was moving. It wasn't exactly a lie, but even so, the aunt's eyes watched me cautiously, as if she was used to people holding out on her.

"Can you tell me where Monique is?" I said.

The timer on the hair dryer clicked off. Estela seemed relieved by the distraction. She raised the hood to check her client's hair.

"She's not here."

I felt frustrated. "Do you know where she is?"

"No." She paused for a moment to think. "But all you want is a key, right? Just a key."

I nodded.

The woman under the dryer stopped reading the news-paper and reached into a purse by her feet, pulling out a tin of Altoids. She popped a couple into her mouth as Estela guided her head back under the dryer, reset the timer, and motioned me toward the front door.

"Maybe I can get a hold of Monique about your friend's apartment key," she said. "Give me your number. I'll call you. Monique's a good girl. If she has something that belongs to your friend, she'll give it back."

"Why don't you call her now? I'll wait. As you said, I drove a long way."

"No, no, I can't. I'm busy now." She nodded toward the woman under the dryer. "I have a customer."

To highlight her predicament, she walked over and turned off the timer. For some reason Estela Sandoval was stalling. That irked me. There was little I could do about it at the moment, so I gave her both my home and cell phone numbers.

"By the way," I said, "who's Nonny?"

She looked startled. "Monique's sister. It's a nickname. Why?"

"Just curious."

I left the salon and parked the car down the street from Estela's Salón de Belleza. I rolled down the windows for air and watched and waited for anybody who looked as if she might be Monique Ruiz. Unfortunately, the only person who walked by was an old woman pushing a baby stroller that looked sturdy enough to survive a crash at Indy.

Apparently, the lady with the spider veins was the last customer of the day, because after she left the shop, Estela flipped the sign on the door to "Cerrado" and headed toward the apartment building next door.

"Nice car. How much you pay for it?"

The voice startled me. I whipped my head around to see Latina Madonna standing on the curb, peering through the open window of the Boxster. I'd been so intent on spying on Estela Sandoval's shop that I hadn't noticed her approaching the car. Her baby was fast asleep, draped over her shoulder like a fox stole.

It took a moment for my pulse to slow and my mind to process her question. It was incredibly cheeky, but she didn't seem to notice. I considered telling her the car was a gift from my ex-husband, the remnant of a failed marriage, but somehow I didn't think she'd care.

Finally I said, "Why do you ask?"

She shrugged. The movement produced a hoarse whimper from the baby. I calculated how much cough medicine a Boxster could buy. It made me feel guilty enough to wish I had my eleven-year-old Corolla back. She jiggled the kid for a moment or two until he quieted down.

"Having such a fancy car might make some people think you have a lot to lose."

With that, she kissed the baby's head and walked back toward the apartment building, leaving me wondering if I'd just been threatened.

-6-

i t was dark by the time I left Oxnard and headed home. On the drive I thought about Estela Sandoval and Latina Madonna. I suspected both were playing dumb about the whereabouts of Monique Ruiz. That funky blue backpack on Estela's counter didn't look as if it came from her closet. It didn't belong to the woman under the dryer either; she had a purse. It seemed more like something Monique Ruiz might have left behind in her rush to escape out a back door to avoid talking to me. I wondered where she was now and why everyone was lying to protect her.

For a moment I gave my imagination free rein. Monique Ruiz had a key to Evan's apartment. She'd also left town around the time of the murder. When I'd asked to see her niece, Estela Sandoval had immediately jumped to the conclusion that Monique was in some kind of trouble. So why weren't the police breathing down Monique's neck? And what about her boyfriend? What role, if any, might he have played in Evan's death?

On the other hand, it was possible that Estela Sandoval had only used the word "trouble" because life had taught her to expect the worst. Maybe Monique Ruiz was merely a sheltered young woman, protecting little old ladies from bad hair days. Hopefully she'd call me tonight, so I could judge for myself.

I was relieved when I finally arrived home. I had inherited the beach cottage from my grandmother Anne Sinclair. It was built in the 1940s, and for years she had used it primarily as a family getaway. Over time, her surviving children, Sylvia and Donovan, had lost interest in the place. Eventually, she turned it over to a management company that farmed it out to vacationers looking for a short-term taste of California oceanfront living.

I'd never actually met my grandmother. After my father died, the Sinclairs made it clear that our branch of the family tree was being pruned back. Read, lopped off. So I was caught off guard when I learned that Anne Sinclair had died and left the beach house to me.

While I was surprised, my uncle Donovan was blasé. He didn't even show up for the reading of the will, preferring instead to remain ensconced in his villa in Provence. On the other hand, my aunt Sylvia was horrified and has made taking the house away from me her raison d'être. Most of her dirty tricks have failed, but a few months back, she'd petitioned the court to reopen probate, claiming she'd found a new will that left the house to her. Our respective attorneys were still exchanging nasty letters, while my pile of legal bills neared critical mass.

It's not that my aunt needed the house or the money the sale of it would bring. She's loaded. She has no real emotional attachment to the place, either. She just doesn't want *me* to have it. I suppose I should be grateful that I'm finally experiencing one of those dysfunctional family psychodramas all my friends keep raving about.

Anyway, it should come as no surprise that I'd never

seen the cottage until the probate judge had, in effect, handed me the keys. The place looks like a little brown shoebox on the sand, but when I walked through the door that first time, it was love at first sight.

The house was suffering from renter's ennui, but with some cosmetic work and a few repairs, I managed to fix it up without compromising its rustic integrity. The existing furnishings included an iron bedstead and an old steamer trunk that belonged to my grandmother. I'd integrated both those pieces into the new decor. I also added a hooked rooster rug for the kitchen floor, and hand-painted seashell tiles above the stove. I had my living room furniture re-covered in a soothing celery-and-rose-colored fabric. For the deck I bought a set of white wicker furniture, which, even on the sunniest days, you can hardly tell is plastic.

My mother's lime green Beetle was parked in my driveway, which meant she and her boyfriend were back from looking at real estate. I spent a moment or two letting exhaustion sweep through my body and mourning the loss of independence that comes with having visitors who stay too long.

Pookie Kravitz is not my mother's real name, of course, but when she began her acting career in her twenties, she thought the name had more pizzazz than either Mary Jo Felder or Mary Jo Sinclair. She'd never been too thrilled with "Mom," either, so I've always called her Pookie.

Being an actor hasn't been an easy life, but until recently it seemed to suit her. Bruce was about to change all that. She'd met him four months back while searching for her power animal at a shaman boot camp in British Columbia. While she was away, I took care of Muldoon. After boot camp, she and Bruce traveled to a kahuna workshop in Maui. When they returned to L.A., they moved in with me—temporarily, just until they found a place of their own. The only problem was, I knew from past experience that "temporary" had a completely different meaning in my mother's lexicon.

Something had happened while they were traveling that made my mother decide to leave acting in order to help Bruce open a yoga studio so he could satisfy the "living a productive life" clause in a trust created by his generous but not stupid grandfather. I didn't mind that she was giving up her recurring role as a celery stalk in a thirty-second spot for a produce co-op called Lettuce Entertain You, but not to babysit some guy in his sixties who was so serene he seemed lobotomized.

I opened the back door and stepped into my kitchen, which is one of those small apartment-type arrangements that have an open counter with a view to the living room and, in my case, to the beach beyond. "Mustang Sally" was playing on the stereo. On the coffee table, burning incense coiled toward the ceiling, making the air heavy with the smell of lavender. Nearby, a bottle of champagne lolled against the side of an ice bucket.

Through the open French doors, I saw two silhouettes on the deck, swaying against a backdrop of dim light from a crescent moon. Pookie and Bruce were doing some kind of jerky bump-and-grind routine. My mother is a good dancer, but Bruce looked as though he'd just had a run-in with a power line.

Muldoon, my mother's Westie, was sprawled on my white fake-wicker lounge chair, looking bored, or maybe he was just embarrassed for them. He was snuggled up with a yellow cashmere sweater, a gift from my neighbor Mrs. Domanski, a woman who is a soft touch for big brown eyes and very dry martinis. Muldoon looked up at me as though he were caught in the Sturm und Drang of greeting etiquette: cashmere, Tucker; cashmere, Tucker. In the end he stayed put, but it didn't bother me. I'd lost out before to less impressive things than cashmere.

I scanned the room from Anne Sinclair's steamer trunk to the couch and easy chair, to the wire colander filled with seashells, and immediately sensed that something was wrong. Then I spotted it. A lacquered-blue room divider covered with crimson flowers was now blocking off my office alcove from the rest of the house. It hadn't been there this morning. Bruce!

He was into feng shui and had rearranged everything in my house at least once. He'd peppered the living room with *Ficus benjamina* trees because woody trunks meant something good. He'd also brought home two canaries, which I promptly made him return to the Fish and Chirps store from which they'd come. All because he was convinced that the stuff in my house inhibited the free flow of my chi. Personally, I think my chi would be a lot freer if it didn't have to flow around Bruce.

I tried to cut him some slack because he made my mother happy, but the room divider was just too much. I folded it up and leaned it against the wall. After that, I doused the incense and switched off the stereo. From out on the deck, Muldoon produced a rolling growl to let me know he'd noticed. It sounded like *gr-r-r-OOF*.

Pookie waved and glided in from the deck. She was wearing vintage 1970s flowered bell-bottoms and a matching orange tube top. It was risky garb for a woman half her age, but my mother takes care of her body the way a classical pianist takes care of her hands, and it shows. Her hair is short and blond, and her eyes are blue.

She's five-three and 105 pounds, even though she's not as fragile as those numbers suggest. She eats right, exercises religiously, and banishes wrinkles with Botox injections she discovered when FDA approval was just a glimmer in her dermatologist's eye.

My mother and I don't look anything alike. I favor my dad, at least according to the few people in my world who knew him. I'm a reedy five-nine, with shoulder-length brown hair and brown eyes that my grandpa Felder says are the color of Old Grand-Dad Kentucky bourbon.

Bruce greeted me with a "Yo" and slipped into a pair of leather clogs wide enough to accommodate his toes, which I swear could fan out and forklift Fay Wray to the top of the Empire State Building. He followed Pookie inside, inadvertently closing the door in Muldoon's face. The little Westie waited patiently with his nose pressed to the glass. When I let him in, he padded over to the coffee table to lick condensation from the ice bucket.

I nodded toward the champagne. "So what are you celebrating?"

Pookie fluttered her eyelashes and flashed me an ingenue look, the one that had gotten her cast in young-mom commercials well into her forties. "We're celebrating my eyes."

"Why? Did they do something special I don't know about?"

"Bruce says they looked inside his heart and found splintered aspects in his soul. Didn't you, honey?"

With a resonant burst of air that moved through at least two octaves, Bruce said, "H-h-a-h-h-h," and articulated himself into downward-facing dog on a blue yoga mat placed alongside the couch, where my dried flower arrangement used to be.

Muldoon doesn't care much for loud sounds and started to bark.

"I guess that's better than finding plaque in his arteries."

Pookie rolled her eyes and sank onto the couch, next to a stack of mail, probably Bruce's bills. He's what you call "not good with money," and lately she'd been handling his checkbook. Both Bruce and the trust attorneys liked it that way.

"So, did you buy that place you were looking at?" I asked.

Pookie sighed. "No. Mrs. Gwee said we'd have to tear down walls to redirect the chi. That would cost a fortune. The trust lawyers would never go for it."

"I have an idea. Hire six longshoremen with sledge-hammers, and your problem disappears."

"Very funny, Tucker. I'll have you know, Mrs. Gwee is *the* feng shui expert on the Westside. We're lucky she's working with us, aren't we, sweetie?"

"H-h-a-h-h-h."

I felt a headache coming on.

"Bruce, why don't you pour Tucker a glass of champagne? I think she needs an attitude adjustment."

I could tell that wasn't going to happen anytime soon, because Bruce had just rolled himself up with his head squeezed between his knees, like a croquet ball stuck in a wicket. He had a vacant smile on his face, as if he was thinking, "Champagne? What champagne? Do we have champagne?"

Muldoon was giving Bruce's body the once-over, trying to determine if any part of it was humpable. Suddenly, alcohol sounded like a good idea. I went to the kitchen to get my own glass. When I came back to the bucket and tipped the bottle, nothing came out. It was empty. I mumbled something like "shit" and collapsed onto the couch next to Pookie, rubbing my temples to chase away the pain.

Muldoon came over and rested his nose on my foot. He pretended to be asleep, but his ears were rotating as though he was trying to pick up any interesting sounds, like maybe a refrigerator door opening. Pookie put down the mail she was sorting.

"What's wrong with you tonight, Tucker? You're no fun at all."

It was an attempt at levity, but her tone held an undercurrent of concern. My mother doesn't like surprises, especially bad-news surprises. I almost felt guilty spoiling her celebration, but she'd learn the news about Evan's murder sooner or later, either on TV or in the newspaper. It was better if she heard it from me. When I laid out the story, her face grew pale.

"I told you Evan Brice would come to a bad end."

True, my mother had never liked Evan. She thought he was trouble, and had made it clear she'd never be happy until I had a total Evanectomy. However, considering the current circumstances, her attitude sucked.

"You know, Pookie, I was hoping you'd come up with something more creative than 'I told you so.'" The words came out angrier than I'd intended.

Pookie reacted as if I'd slapped her. "Oh, sweetie, I'm sorry. I really am. Are you okay?"

The sentiment was unfashionably late, but I nodded.

"What happened?" she said. "Who killed him?"

"Apparently, the police think it was Cissy."

"Cissy? No way. She'd have to give up her tickets to the Oscars and all those free designer gowns. If you ask me, I'd say it had something to do with drugs."

"I don't think so. From what I know, Evan was clean and sober."

"Don't be naive, Tucker. He spent a couple of weeks in a luxury hotel and called it rehab, but when he got out, I bet the first person he called was his dealer. I've seen it happen over and over—"

"Careful, Goldie," Bruce warned. "Bad karma."

It annoyed me when he called her that. It was as though he considered it a waste of time to learn my mother's name, because she was just another woman he didn't plan to stay with for very long. Pookie didn't look annoyed, though. She looked amused.

"This isn't gossip, honey. My friend Sheila did the makeup for one of Evan's clients on a biker flick that just wrapped. She said he came to the set a few times, acting crazy. She swore he was loaded, and believe me, Sheila knows loaded when she sees it."

"You weren't there, Goldie."

"Hey," I said. "Gossip is a legitimate form of communication in this house."

Pookie looked sheepish. "It's okay, Tucker. Bruce is right. I wasn't there."

My head was really throbbing now. My face was warm, and my attitude resentful. Bruce was turning my mother into a wimp.

"A friend of mine was murdered," I said to him. "I'd like to hear about anyone who has any idea how he got that way."

"What goes around comes around," he said.

"Can it, Bruce." I picked up Muldoon and stomped toward my bedroom. I got as far as the kitchen.

"Stella called."

I turned and saw Bruce sitting on the yoga mat with his eyes closed.

"Stella? You mean Estela Sandoval? When?"

"Earlier."

I waited for more, and when it didn't come, I said, "Well? What did she say?"

"She has the key."

"That's it? Damn it, Bruce, if you can't take a friggin message, don't answer my phone."

"Tucker, please—"

"Back off, Mother."

There was an uncomfortable lull in the conversation before Bruce spoke again. "You can pick it up tomorrow . . . after one . . . at Rose's place."

I walked into my bedroom with Muldoon still in my arms and closed the door. Sometime later I checked my cell phone voice mail and found a tearful message from Cissy Brice. By the time I called her back, she sounded calmer.

"I'm sorry I bothered you, Tuckie, but I was a mess. Mom wasn't home. I had to talk to somebody."

"What's going on? Is Dara okay?"

"Yes, but that detective called again, the Moses Green guy. He wanted me to go downtown to Parker Center to take a lie detector test. Can you believe it?"

"What did you tell him?"

"I told him no, of course. Then he said 'no' was a guilty person's answer. He sounded mean. It scared me. He can't make me do it, can he?"

"I don't know. I think it's routine for the police to ask members of the victim's family to take polygraphs, but you should consult a lawyer about these kinds of decisions, not your mom or me."

"Don't worry, Tuckie. It's over now. I don't think he'll bother me anymore."

Her naïveté was astonishing. Somewhere deep inside she had to know that this cat-and-mouse game with Moses Green wasn't over by a long shot. In fact, it was just beginning.

- 7 -

At seven o'clock the next morning, I woke up to the sound of whimpering. It was Muldoon reminding me once again that the house had no doggie door. Pookie and Bruce were still asleep—at least, their bedroom door was closed—so I let Muldoon out to chase gulls. When he came back inside, I wiped the wet sand off his paws. I showered and dressed in a pair of denim jeans and a red turtleneck.

The first order of business was to find somebody to clean the Venice apartment. I checked the Smart Yellow Pages under cleaning, crime, and industrial, but didn't find what I was looking for. As a last resort, I called Detective Green for help. He wasn't allowed to make specific recommendations and suggested I check the Internet. He didn't bring up Cissy's name, so I decided to leave well enough alone.

At his suggestion, I logged on and typed in "crime scene cleanup." I shouldn't have been surprised to find numerous companies listed, including several in the Los Angeles area. I called all of them until I found one that advertised service "24/7/365." The company's owner, Max Farnsworth, offered to come to the scene, assess the damage, and provide a written proposal, which would include the extent of work to be done, as well as an estimate of the cost. He told me his company also handled any necessary restoration—repainting, repairing, or replacing—and could also help file the applicable insurance claims. I told him I didn't need a written proposal. If he would send his technicians to Evan's apartment that afternoon, the job was his. We could negotiate the fine print when he got there. We agreed to meet at two p.m.

I was scheduled to pick up the apartment key from Rose at one o'clock. There were several hours of productive time before then, so I decided to work on the focus group. The invitations had gone out to randomly selected shoppers in the L.A. area who had a history of buying by mail order. Mr. Geyer had insisted that the artwork include one of his signature muumuus, so I was hoping the mailing list included at least a few Don Ho groupies.

The group was meeting in three weeks, but in truth, my interest was halfhearted. Maybe that was why my business wasn't growing as fast as it should be. On the other hand, maybe I didn't lack initiative; maybe I was just hungry. As usual, I'd forgotten to eat breakfast. I needed brain food, something hearty. Eggs Benedict? I'd never actually made that before, but I'd ordered it in restaurants. How hard could it be?

I scoured the bread drawer for English muffins. There weren't any, but I did come up with a slice of stale wheat bread. That would have to do. There wasn't even a remote possibility I'd find Canadian bacon in the refrigerator, but I did find an egg—the last one.

I pulled down Pookie's tattered, orangey-colored *Betty Crocker's Cookbook* from the shelf and checked the index for poaching instructions. The recipe was simple:

fill a skillet with water, turn the burner to high, slip the egg into the boiling water, and simmer until done. Even I could do that.

When Muldoon heard the egg break against the side of the skillet, he began pawing my leg. I ignored him, because by that time I'd found Betty's hollandaise sauce recipe and was shocked to read that it required two more egg yolks and a half cup of butter. Scratch that idea. I didn't have two more eggs. Besides, my arteries would thank me in the morning.

I was looking inside the refrigerator for a hollandaise substitute—cheddar cheese or something else yellow—when I heard the telephone ringing. I glanced at my watch. Nine o'clock. It had to be Eugene. I'd forgotten to return his call from yesterday. I braced myself for the consequences.

Eugene is what you might call "intense." He's a loyal friend and a great organizer of paper. He responds to structure, and he loves animals. People are another story. He especially dislikes large crowds of them. But that's not the extent of his problems. Other things upset him as well—like change. I also suspect he has a phobia that has something to do with raking leaves, but don't quote me on that one.

On the advice of his therapist, he's taken up knitting to combat his stress. After completing truckloads of slipper-socks and sweater-vests, it seems to be helping, but he's not completely cured. Recently he'd decided to increase his "medication" by volunteering to knit a dozen tasseled berets for patients at a local nursing home. Unfortunately, with having to nurse his cat, Liza, he'd fallen behind on his self-imposed schedule.

Eugene interrupted in the middle of my "hello."

"Something's wrong with my right wrist. I was just

finishing my ninth beret when it started hurting." He sounded out of breath, not a good sign.

"Wow," I said. "Nine. That's a lot of tasseled berets. Maybe you should stop."

"You don't understand, Tucker. People are counting on me. What if I have carpal tunnel syndrome? What if I can't knit anymore?"

I popped the slice of wheat bread into the toaster and checked the egg. It was starting to firm up in the simmering water. I felt empowered.

"Why not do something else for a while, until your wrist heals?"

"Like what?"

"I don't know . . . what about needlepoint? Or tatting? That's almost a lost art. You could bring it back. Start a new trend."

"That's not funny, Tucker."

"Okay, I'm sorry. Why not try something completely different, then? Learn to play mah-jongg."

"My mother played mah-jongg every Wednesday afternoon with a group of eighty-year-old widows who'd slit your throat for a five-dollar pot. I need relaxation, not hand-to-hand combat."

"Skydiving?"

"Tucker!"

"So call your therapist. Maybe she has some ideas."

"She's on maternity leave."

I glanced at the skillet. The egg looked done, but when I poked the yolk with a fork, it drooled into the water, forming a tiny appendage.

"Somebody must be taking her calls," I said.

"I suppose so, but I couldn't possibly discuss my issues with a stranger."

"It's an emergency, Eugene. Maybe you should make an exception this one time."

While I was listening to him expose the flaws in my hypothesis, the toast popped up. Muldoon looked at me as if to say, *Bread? That's not a good snack.* I set the toast on the counter and poked the yolk again. It was now as hard as a hockey puck.

I consulted the recipe again and saw that I was supposed to lift the egg out gently with a slotted spatula. Unfortunately, I couldn't find one in my utensil drawer. I did, however, find barbeque tongs. Those should work. I carefully grabbed the edge of the egg's white part and lifted it out of the pan. For a brief moment, it hung from the tongs like rubber barf. Then it fell to the floor. In less than five seconds, the egg was gone and Muldoon was licking his chops.

I patiently waited for Eugene to finish his white paper on the psychological ramifications of sharing secrets with a surrogate therapist. When he was finished, I said, "Listen, here's my best advice. Stop knitting berets. Put ice on your wrist, do some biofeedback, and try to relax."

"I can't relax." He sounded glum. "I have too many things on my mind. Maybe I should just go back to the office and immerse myself in mindless busywork."

I felt a twinge of guilt. Eugene had felt abandoned when I left Aames & Associates. To make matters worse, I'd asked Venus to leave with me. I hadn't offered Eugene a job, because I was trying to protect him. I thought his fragile psyche needed more security than my start-up business could offer. In the end, Venus had turned down my business proposal, which had mollified Eugene's hurt feelings to some extent.

Regrettably, after I left the firm, the human resources

director had transferred Eugene to the front desk to answer the telephone and greet visitors, a job he hated. He saw it as punishment for his loyalty to me. Maybe he was right, but I couldn't offer him a permanent job just yet. Not until business picked up. Still, I had to do something to make him feel better, so I laid out a few sketchy details about Mr. Geyer and the focus group project I was working on.

"Look," I said, "I could use some help getting organized. Why don't you stop by for a couple of hours tomorrow? I can't pay you much, but I promise there won't be any heavy wrist activity." He didn't respond right away, which concerned me. "Of course, it's only an idea. After all, you're on vacation. Maybe you'd rather—"

"I'll be there at nine."

As soon as I hung up the telephone, I was forced to admit that my first attempt at eggs Benedict looked alarmingly like dry, stick-in-the-throat toast—my normal breakfast. I smeared a little peanut butter on the bread and ate it over the sink.

When I was finished eating, Muldoon decided to take a nap on the living room couch. I went into my office and picked up my things-to-do list, glancing down the page at the two items noted there: (1) buy laundry detergent and (2) Eric's wedding. The last entry had a big question mark after it.

Eric Bergstrom is my ex-husband. He was getting remarried, and I'd been debating going to the wedding. I wasn't still in love with him, but we'd stayed friends after our divorce. I'd always thought of him as a person I could call on for help at any time and for any reason. A little red-haired girl named Becky Quinn had changed all that. I was having a hard time facing the fact that he wasn't mine anymore. I was having an even harder time accepting that he seemed happy about it. The problem was, if I didn't go to the wedding, everybody would think I was a sore loser. If I went alone, they'd just think I was a generic loser.

Bruce claimed that going to the wedding would bring closure. As much as I hated to admit it, he was probably right. Unfortunately, I couldn't attend the ceremony unless I found a killer date. The guy didn't have to know a fish knife from a putty knife; all he had to do was look good glad-handing in the reception line and try not to embarrass me in front of Eric's aunt I-told-you-she-was-wrong-for-you Lena. Unfortunately, there was no one in my life at the moment who matched that description, which left me only one choice for a date. I decided to delay working on the focus group and use my productive time to stop by and relay the invitation in person.

Pookie and Bruce still hadn't emerged from the bedroom, so before I left the house, I filled Muldoon's bowl with low-fat kibble, because Pookie thought the pup had packed on a little weight on my watch. As expected, Muldoon took one whiff of those dry, unappetizing pellets and backed away. I could almost tell what he was thinking by the look of dismay in his soulful brown eyes: *Yeech!*

I didn't feel comfortable micromanaging his diet, so at the last minute I spooned a glob of oily peanut butter into his dish. He was still trying to lick the stuff off the roof of his mouth as I grabbed my fleece vest from the bedroom closet and headed for the car.

• • •

MY FORMER EMPLOYER occupies an entire floor of one of those inscrutable smoky-glass high-rises in downtown

L.A. As in many other consulting firms, the corporate culture at Aames & Associates is on the conservative side. In fact, you'd be hard-pressed to find a female consultant wearing earrings in any metal but gold and in any size larger than a Tums tablet. As for male consultants, the partners once denied employment to a well-qualified candidate because he wore a pair of argyle socks to his interview. Someone should have clued the guy in that wearing anything short of plain and dark meant never having to say, "Honey, I got the job!" Luckily, my days of working for a company that measured a man's worth by his footwear were over.

When I arrived at the ground-floor cafeteria, which had been dubbed the *barf*eteria by those familiar with its cuisine, it was empty except for a woman typing on her laptop computer and a middle-aged man in a business suit, arguing with Mrs. Kim, the cafeteria's owner, over the price of an orange. I sat at one of the tables and called Venus on my cell phone. She informed me she was finishing up some paperwork but would be down in a few minutes.

During the years that Venus Corday and I had been coworkers at Aames & Associates, we'd developed a friendship that's hard to sum up on a Hallmark card. She's still a consultant there, working mostly with manufacturing companies. Even though she'd decided against leaving the firm to work with me, a shadowy rumor had begun circulating through the hallways of Aames & Associates that she *was* planning to defect. When the buzz reached the windowed offices of the senior partners, they panicked because they couldn't afford to lose her knowledge of the nuances of just-in-time inventory. They countered by offering her a substantial raise. The raise was hard-earned and long overdue. The source of the rumor is still unknown.

I was in the process of destroying my stomach lining with one of Mrs. Kim's house specialties—the dregs of this morning's coffee, aged into battery acid on the warmer—when Venus finally walked through the door. She's in her late thirties, with a genetic makeup that isn't easy to sort out. Her great-grandmother came from Barbados so she's got that whole English, Caribbean, African thing going. I suspect that the clan may have added a few more genes to the pool in San Francisco's Chinatown before they eventually settled in L.A.

Regardless of what had gone into Venus's genetic mix, the end product is a thing of beauty: unfathomable brown eyes, creamy-caramel skin, and long black hair, which today was twisted into a neat chignon. The designer suit she wore was a flowing mango-colored getup that hugged curves like a European sports car. In fact, sitting next to her sometimes makes me feel like the celery in a Bloody Mary. The suit partially explained why she's still a senior manager at Aames & Associates and not a partner. The other part is attitude. Venus doesn't suffer fools. That doesn't sit well with people who make promotion decisions.

Venus ambled over to join me at the table, lugging a bottle of water big enough to survive a trip through the Sahara for her *and* the Land Rover. Don't ask me why, but the H_2O just reeked of a new weight-loss scheme. Venus has tried and failed at every diet on the bookstore shelves, mainly because she's in love with eating, particularly chocolate.

"Let me guess," I said, pointing to the water. "You've just been accepted into firefighter school."

"Joke all you want, Tucker, but I am in the *zone*. My body is loose, and my mind is clear."

"And your Godivas are where?"

She laughed. "Don't mess with me, girl." She sat in the chair across from mine. "So what's so important that it couldn't wait for happy hour?"

I hesitated to tell her about Evan Brice's murder. I knew it would upset her, but she was my closest friend. She'd want to know. For the next few minutes I explained about the investigation and my efforts to help Cissy close the Venice apartment. By the time I was finished, she'd swallowed enough liquid to fill a dolphin tank at Sea World.

"I swear, Tucker, dead people cling to you like cat hair on a funeral suit. Somebody should invent an aerosol."

"Hey, this is L.A. People die here. I can't help it if I know some of them personally."

"You ever ask yourself why, after all these years, this Cissy girl is making *you* run her errands? Especially since she knows you and the dead husband had a thing for each other."

"That's right—*had*," I said, perhaps too defensively. "I told you, that was back in college. Besides, Cissy isn't making me do anything. I volunteered."

"Uh-huh, I bet. So what if the police are right and she killed Evan? Who's to say she didn't bring you into the equation to throw suspicion off her and onto you?"

"Oh, come on, Venus. How could she possibly do that?"

"I don't know, but something doesn't sound right to me. I say get out before things turn bad."

"I can't. I promised."

Venus shook her head in frustration. "You're making a mistake, but suit yourself." She glanced at her watch. "I can't believe you came all this way to discuss dead boyfriends. If there's something else, lay it on me quick. I gotta get back to work."

"I need you to be my date for Eric's wedding."

She studied my demeanor for a moment to make sure I was serious. "Is it casual or formal?"

"Formal. Black-tie, sit-down dinner."

"DJ?"

"Live orchestra."

"Small, intimate?"

"I doubt it. Knowing Eric, I'd guess he invited three hundred of his closest friends, and money is no object."

"Then I'd have to say not just no, but hell no. You know the rules. You gotta take a man to a shindig like that, and he has to be a stud, because you don't want anybody thinking you're not still a contender."

"By 'stud' I assume you mean some good-looking guy who's incapable of carrying on an intelligent conversation?"

She leaned back and crossed her arms over her ample chest. "Men weren't made for talking philosophical shit over tea at the Ritz, honey. That's why God made girlfriends. You follow me on this?"

"Okay, okay," I said. "Maybe I'll invite Eugene."

She rolled her eyes. "Eugene is a twenty-five-year-old bony-assed kid whose social life consists of an annual birthday party for his cat."

"Liza isn't just a cat; she's—"

"Look, Tucker, forget about Eugene. You know he can't take the pressure. If you take him to a party like that, he'll end up floating like a dead bug in the vodka punch."

I hated to admit it, but Venus was probably right. Forcing Eugene to deal with a noisy crowd of strangers could trigger another yarn bender. I didn't think I could deal with one more knitted poodle cover for my spare toilet paper rolls.

"There's nobody else I can ask," I said.

Venus looked incredulous. "Just when was the last time you had a date?"

That sounded like a math quiz, and I wasn't interested. "Forget about the wedding. I'm not going."

"Huh-uh, no way. You gotta go. What about asking Deegan?"

Joe Deegan was an LAPD homicide detective I'd met while he was investigating the death of my client. At the time, there had been some sizzle between us. We'd never acted on it, mostly because I wasn't looking for an extra pair of jeans in my laundry basket. Besides, he saw my independence as stubbornness, and I saw his old-fashioned politeness as macho bullshit. That didn't leave much room for a meaningful relationship.

"What *about* Deegan?" I said.

"Seen him lately?"

"No."

"Maybe it's about time you did."

"No," I said emphatically.

Venus took one last gulp of water and shrugged, "You say 'tomayto'; I say 'tomahto'." When she stood to leave, her stomach made a sound like a Maytag in the final rinse cycle. "Just don't rule it out, Tucker. Besides, haven't you had enough of those 'E' men? Eric, Evan—shit, even Eugene. I think it's time you moved on in the alphabet. Why not start with Joe?"

After she was gone, I swirled the dead coffee around in the foam cup for a while, watching the sludge stick to the sides and wondering if I should take her advice. Venus was right about a lot of things. Maybe she was right about Deegan, too. In theory, he'd make a good date for Eric's wedding. He was easy on the eyes, funny, and on occasion even charming. Plus, if I showed up with a six-foot-two hunky cop, Eric's lutefisk-eating aunt Lena might stop telling everybody what a low-rent catch I'd been.

It sounded good, but I had to look at the downside of asking Deegan as well. He was a homicide detective. I'd have to monitor his dinner conversation to make sure he didn't try to demonstrate blood-spatter patterns with the tomato bisque.

I kept telling myself it was only one night. As long as the champagne flowed, I figured we could make nice for a few hours. I just wasn't sure if Deegan would agree to my plan. What if he said no? What if he laughed when I asked him? That would be humiliating but survivable. After tossing the idea around in my head for a few more minutes, I decided that as much as it mortified me to invite him, I would, because sometimes you just have to take charge of your life.

It was almost noon. The café was beginning to fill up with the forty-five-minute lunch crowd confronted with Mrs. Kim's daily special, which today looked like canned sloppy Joe mix dumped unceremoniously over a crusty-looking hamburger bun.

My stomach was still lurching from the smell of it as I headed out the door. On the way to my car, I told myself that even if Deegan agreed to hold my hand during my ex-husband's nuptials, convincing anybody that Tucker Sinclair was in any way, shape, or form anything close to being a contender was like convincing the barfeteria crowd that Mrs. Kim's sloppy Joes were haute cuisine.

Whatever happened, seeing Deegan would give me an

opportunity to press him for information on the Evan Brice murder investigation. He had to know Moses Green. They were both homicide detectives at Pacific Station. They probably gossiped about cases at the doughnut machine.

I decided to stop by and ask him before I lost my nerve completely.

- 8 -

hirty-five minutes after leaving Venus, I pulled into the visitors' parking lot at the LAPD's Pacific Community Police Station, a two-story brick building surrounded by a low block wall. As I walked toward the lobby, a late-model blue Crown Victoria with multiple antennas that practically screamed, *I am a city-issued vehicle,* maneuvered up the driveway. When I turned to look, the woman behind the wheel braked hard. Moments later, Joe Deegan sprang from the passenger-side seat.

Deegan is six feet two, lean, and has a tiny dimple at the tip of his nose that matches a somewhat larger one on his chin. It must have been casual day at the station, because he wore tight Levi's 501s and a blue-gray T-shirt a shade darker than his eyes. A badge hung from his belt. A gun in a leather holster on his chest peeked out from underneath a brown leather jacket that looked as though it had come from some baby bovine on its way to veal scaloppine.

A smile crinkled the corners of his eyes. "Hey, Stretch, long time no see."

"I guess we've both been busy."

He acknowledged that line of bullshit with a nod. "Yeah, I guess that's it, all right."

"I was wondering if you had a few minutes," I said.

He raised his eyebrows in mock surprise. "What's the deal? You finally drop me off your shit list?"

"People don't have to agree on everything to stay friends."

"No, not everything, just some things."

The driver of the Crown Vic, a woman somewhere in her twenties, leaned over to get a better listen. She was young enough to be a rookie, but she was obviously a quick study, because a placid mask of cynicism already controlled her facial muscles. Her full lips were highlighted with gloss the color of light brown sugar. Her dark hair was twisted into a smooth, thick knot at the nape of her neck. Just looking at that well-mannered hair depressed me. Even on a good day mine had more cowlicks than the Double R Bar Ranch.

Whatever else this young woman was, she was drop-dead gorgeous. I wondered if she was Deegan's new partner or if perhaps she was already something more than that.

"Look," I said to him, "can we go someplace and talk—privately?"

Deegan shifted his weight as he thought about that. Finally, he said something to the woman in the car, and she drove off. When she was out of sight, he placed his hand lightly on the back of my arm and guided me to the back of the station past a sign that read, "Do Not Enter." He led me through a sea of black-and-white police cars to a grassy median in the middle of the parking lot, where a eucalyptus tree loomed over a picnic table shaded by a leaf-patterned umbrella. We sat on benches across from each other but far enough apart to avoid exchanging any body heat.

Even though it was still early, a security light above the table was on. The glare bounced garishly off the flat grayness of the asphalt parking lot and the overcast March sky. A breeze agitated a scrap of aluminum foil, pushing it over the grass. Without taking his eyes off me, Deegan bent down, picked up the foil, and crumpled it into a ball. Then he waited.

I was already having second thoughts about coming to see him. I stalled by asking about his sister, only because I'd met her briefly at a holiday party the previous December.

"Which sister?" he said. "I have three."

I felt sheepish telling him I couldn't remember her name.

"Yeah, I guess we didn't get that far." He looked at me for a moment, as if he was going to open a new line of conversation. Obviously, he changed his mind at the last moment. "If you're talking about Claudia, she's pregnant."

"Again? That was quick. I mean, it's none of my business, but didn't she just have one?"

His look of disapproval made me squirm. "So why'd you stop by?"

I paused, wondering if I should leave before I got myself into real trouble. "I need a favor."

He leaned forward and gave me his gotcha smile. "Ah, I get it. Now that your ex is out of the picture, you need somebody to change a lightbulb."

I stood up so fast, the umbrella wobbled. "You know something? You're a butthead."

He laughed. "Just tell me the truth, Stretch. If you had anybody else to ask this favor of, you wouldn't be here. Am I right?"

Of course he was right. That pissed me off even more than his lightbulb crack. So I lied.

"No, you are *not* right. You and I didn't always see eye to eye, but I thought we were friends. Obviously I was wrong."

He scrunched up his face as though he smelled something bad. "If I buy that line of bullshit, will you tell me why you're here?"

"After what you just said?"

He stood and hooked his thumbs inside the front pockets of his jeans—something Eric would never have done.

"What?" he said. "You want me to apologize or something?"

"For starters."

He rolled his eyes. "Okay, I'm sorry I implied you needed anything from anybody. How's that?"

"*That* doesn't sound like an apology."

The frown on his face told me I'd pushed too far. "You always have to drive, don't you, Stretch?"

I vaguely sensed my arms crossing tightly across my chest. "Okay, let's call a truce."

He paused for a moment. Finally he nodded, and we both sat down. Deegan began working the aluminum foil, rolling it around in his hands and squishing it with his thumbs. For a moment I sensed nothing except the crackle of that foil and the aroma of his body lotion. The scent was pear. The jar had come from a cosmetics counter at Nordstrom. That much I knew. What I didn't know was how it had gotten from the shopping mall into Deegan's bathroom. I guess there were a lot of things I didn't know about him.

I took a deep breath. "I came to ask if you'll go with me to my ex's wedding."

Deegan looked as if I'd just hit him in the face with a pie. "You mean like a date?"

"Definitely not like a date. All you have to do is listen to a little DUM-DUM-TA-DUM, throw some rice, and you're free to go. And don't worry, I'll pay for the tuxedo rental."

"Gee, Stretch, you make it sound so romantic."

"Cut the crap, Deegan. Look, if you do this for me, I'll owe you one, okay?"

He raised his eyebrows suggestively. "Can I get that in writing?"

I swallowed a hard lump of irritation. "That's not necessary, because unlike some people, *I* always keep my promises."

He opened his mouth as if to defend himself but apparently changed his mind.

"So when is the big event?"

I gave him the date. We spent several minutes discussing the details before he pulled an antique watch from an inside jacket pocket. It had a heavy silver chain and a hairy braided tail dangling from a loop near the stem. I imagined that the tail was a lock of hair commemorating his first lay, a girl named Ula, an exchange student from Finland with hairy armpits, who'd taken one look at Deegan and said, "I don't think I'm in Lapland anymore."

He checked the time. "I have to get back to work."

I thought about asking him to fill me in on Evan Brice's murder investigation, but I suspected it was a waste of time. Deegan was tight-lipped about his work. Besides, if he knew I was connected to another homicide, he might not take me to Eric's wedding. It was better to call Moses Green directly.

Deegan walked with me to the visitors' lot where I'd left my car. When I slid into the front seat, he leaned down so his eyes were in line with mine.

"By the way, Stretch, you don't have to worry about paying any rental fees. I have my own tux. I even know how to do the tie myself."

I was surprised, but didn't want to admit it. Just before I drove away, he handed me the bunched-up foil and asked if I'd take care of it for him. I said sure and threw it on the passenger's seat. I was almost at the beach when I glanced over at the foil and noticed that Deegan had sculpted it into the shape of a goofy little heart.

- 9 -

hen I turned onto Evan's street, I saw a Latino in his late teens, standing in front of a black Honda Civic parked in front of the building. He had a wide, sensuous mouth and hair no longer than a five o'clock shadow. He wore wraparound sunglasses, a heavy silver crucifix, and a black silky shirt. The shirt was unbuttoned and exposed pectorals that were chiseled either by hours of lifting weights or by minutes of inject-ing steroids. A tattoo of a busty woman undulated up his arm. Her breasts were strategically etched at the curve of his biceps.

From a second-floor balcony across the street, the woman I'd seen driving the Volvo leaned over the railing and shouted something at him, but I couldn't hear what she was saying. With one languid movement, the guy gave her the finger. Then he slid into the front seat of the car and drove off. I slipped into the vacated spot, thank-ing White Cloud, the spirit guide of parking places, for making me a victor by default in the L.A. curb wars.

Rose answered her door dressed in a loose-fitting cot-ton housedress zippered up the front. Her hair was newly coiffed. She had abandoned her walker for a sturdy four-legged cane. I stepped into her living room and was immediately engulfed in a wave of heat that must have been pushing ninety degrees. I waited until she turned her back before using my hand to fan myself with the same urgency Icarus must have felt trying to get across the Aegean. Unfortunately, Rose turned just in time to catch me at it.

"Oh, my, I'm sorry," she said. "One good thing about living alone. Nobody tells you to turn down the heat. Rudy—that's my husband—he was always hot. He's been gone twelve years now. Are you married?"

I told her no. She nodded as if I'd said something profound.

"Better to be single and alone than married and miserable," she said. "I tried to tell my daughter that. She didn't listen, of course. Twelve bridesmaids! My goodness. There was hardly enough room for the guests."

Rose found Evan's keys and handed them to me. There were two on the ring. I assumed one was to the door and the other to the mailbox.

"I guess Monique made it home okay."

"Yes. She's at work now. She came early to do my hair, but she couldn't wait around to comb it out. I can manage that part by myself. I just can't get my arms up high enough to set the curlers anymore."

"Monique has a second job?"

She paused for a moment to think. "Yes, she works over at that tire place on Marine. It doesn't pay much, but they give her a good deal on retreads. I never learned to drive myself. That was a big handicap after Rudy died."

I wondered if anybody actually used retreads anymore and, if they did, where they fell in the pecking order of employee perks. I told Rose that a crew was coming to clean Evan's apartment. She offered to let me stay with her while they worked. She also volunteered to let me use some moving boxes she had squirreled away in her storage unit, but warned me she hadn't looked at them for years. It was possible termites had gotten to them by now. Creatures lurking in dark spaces nibbling on cardboard gave me a bad case of the heebie-jeebies, but I needed boxes in order to pack up the charity donations. Anything was better than driving around in bumper-to-bumper traffic looking for a box store.

At around 1:50 p.m., I went down to the lobby to wait for the cleaning crew. While I was there, I picked up the letters in Evan's mailbox, rationalizing that if the police were monitoring the mail for clues, they'd have left me a note. I was only mildly surprised to find the box full. I remembered Cissy telling me that one of Monique's duties was picking up the junk mail. Apparently, she had abandoned the job.

As it turned out, not all the stuff was junk. Several envelopes looked like bills, including a notice from the gas company, and an envelope from a medical clinic in Santa Monica. Everything was addressed to Thomas Chatterton. Seeing that name again made me wonder if the police had missed the point. Maybe Evan Brice hadn't been murdered at all. Maybe Thomas Chatterton was the intended victim. I wondered if Moses Green would be interested in hearing my theory. The likelihood seemed remote. For now, I stuffed the mail into my vest pocket and made a mental note to remind Cissy to file a change-of-address notice with the post office.

Max Farnsworth and his technicians arrived shortly after two p.m. in a red van with biohazardous-waste warnings printed on both side panels. Farnsworth was a wiry, intense man in his fifties, with large, earnest eyes and oversize ears. He supervised the unloading of various pieces of equipment, including barrels, masks, and several white, hooded HAZMAT suits. It didn't take long. I guess if you clean up blood for a living, you want to make quick work of it. I gave Farnsworth the key to Evan's apartment and told him to knock on Rose's door when he was finished.

I decided to see if the mice had spared any of the packing boxes. Rose warned me there wasn't much light inside the building, so I borrowed a mini flashlight she kept by her bed, and headed outside.

The storage unit turned out to be a shed in the parking lot that was large enough to displace at least three cars. It didn't match the building's original architecture in either age or design. I assumed it was an afterthought, moved in to enable *Homo sapiens*'s obsession for collecting useless junk. Luckily, most of the boxes were serviceable. I carted a few upstairs and propped them against the wall near Evan's door. Rose was delighted to hear that they were still in good shape.

"I was trying to remember how long they've been down there," she said. "I moved here just after Rudy died—May eighteenth. For a long time I remembered that day every month: June eighteenth, one month since Rudy died. July eighteenth, two months without Rudy. Then one month I forgot to think about how long I'd been a widow, and that was it. You ever lose somebody you loved?"

"No one like Rudy."

"Well, you will some day, I'm sorry to say. You never get over it, but you do get beyond it. I guess that's the best I can say. What about your folks? They live around here?"

"Just my mother."

She acknowledged my guarded tone with a nod. "Well, she's probably not perfect, but enjoy her while you can. She won't be around forever, you know."

While I waited for the cleaning crew to finish, Rose and I watched a *Perry Mason* marathon. During commercials she regaled me with the personal history of each of its stars. Who knew that Della Street and Paul Drake were married in real life?

It was just before five o'clock. Perry was in the process of tricking yet another bad guy into confessing on the witness stand, when I heard a knock on the door. It was Max Farnsworth. I thanked Rose for entertaining me, grabbed my purse, and joined Max in the hallway, where he gave me a rundown of everything the crew had done. It was more information than I wanted to know.

Fortunately, the apartment was small and the crime scene was confined mostly to the kitchen. The biggest problem was that blood had saturated the kitchen's industrial carpet. The crew had removed it, so it would have to be replaced. Also, the kitchen needed repainting. I decided to delay those decisions. Perhaps the apartment owners preferred to do the work themselves. Farnsworth asked if I wanted a walk-through. I declined. I didn't know how I'd react to being in Evan's apartment, and didn't want witnesses. I signed his contract, listing Cissy's home address for billing purposes.

After Farnsworth left, I found myself facing Evan's door. The last thing I wanted to do was go inside, but the packing boxes were still propped up against the wall in the hallway. I should at least put them inside. I also needed to see how much work remained to be done.

Evan's key ring was looped over my index finger,

which provided an overwhelming sense of forward motion that propelled me toward his front door. It was the same unstoppable momentum that must have gotten the old woman's pig to jump over the sty. The hand began to hold the key; the key began to turn the lock; the lock began to open the door, so Tucker could get herself into deeper doo-doo in time for supper tonight.

Once the door was open, I lingered near the threshold for a moment, holding my breath for as long as I could. Slowly I allowed small doses of air to register in my olfactory processing center as industrial cleaners trapped in stagnant air. I set my purse down near the threshold and carried the boxes inside before pulling the door closed until I heard the latch bolt slide quietly into the slot.

The living room was narrow, with two small double-hung windows. It was now too dark outside to see much, but the building was on the beach. The view must be amazing. A telephone sat on the window ledge. I'd have to remind Cissy or Claire to have the service cut off.

Forming a tight cluster near the windows was the rental furniture: couch, coffee table, two canvas director's chairs, and a home entertainment center, which housed a TV and VCR. The only other piece was a long worktable, pushed against the wall just left of the front door. It was strewn with copies of *Variety* and *Hollywood Reporter*. The arrangement seemed out of balance. I wondered if the police had moved things around and forgotten where they belonged.

To my left, a small kitchen branched off the living room. As I moved toward it, I saw where the carpet had been hacked out, leaving pieces of jagged padding and hook fasteners against the plywood floor. I tensed, half expecting to feel Evan's presence hovering over the Old

Dutch Cleanser in some afterlife limbo, waiting to guide me to his killer. Instead, all I felt were cold prickles up and down my neck, and a growing concern that being here was maybe not such a good idea.

I backed away from the kitchen and, despite my uneasiness, headed through the living room to take a quick look at the rest of the place. There was a bathroom at the center of a long hallway, which was anchored at each end by a bedroom. The smaller of the two rooms was empty. Looming large in the main bedroom was a canopied wooden bedstead. It looked expensive. Draped from the frame was a gauzy fabric that appeared to be mosquito netting on loan from the set of *Call Me Bwana*. The linens had been pulled off and then haphazardly thrown back on. The earthy textures and patterns looked rich and sensual, as if a woman with attitude had put her foot down: I'll sleep with you in this dump, but not on a rental bed. I wondered who that woman had been—certainly not Cissy. She'd never been to the apartment.

Perched on top of a small bedside chest of drawers were a dozen red roses, fighting to keep their heads high in a dry vase. I thought about the poem found at the crime scene. What had it said? "Red rose, dead rose. True love, cruel myth." I didn't know what Evan had meant by those words. Roses had never been a part of our relationship. In fact, I didn't remember him ever sending me flowers of any kind. Perhaps the roses were a gift, but for whom or from whom? Self-doubt swept over me as I wondered whether the poem had been written for me or for somebody else.

My gaze left the roses and continued around the room. Aside from the flowers and a few ghostly hangers in the closet, the place either had been stripped clean by the police or was that way when they arrived. As I walked toward the bed, I spotted a splash of color on the nightstand next to the flower vase. It was a key ring made up of red and green beads stitched to a flimsy piece of leather. One of the threads had broken loose, and several beads were missing. Even so, it looked as if the design had once been some kind of flower. Another rose?

The workmanship was marginal, as if an amateur hobbyist or a child had crafted it. I thought of Evan's daughter, Dara, and wondered if she'd made it for Evan. If so, Cissy would want to keep it. In any event, it wasn't evidence, or it wouldn't be sitting out in plain sight. I slipped it into my pants pocket.

Out of curiosity, I opened the top drawer of the bedside chest and found a half-empty box of condoms and a pair of reading glasses, the type you buy from the drugstore. When I tried to close the drawer again, it jammed. I jiggled it a few times to free the blockage, but with no success. Frustrated, I yanked the drawer out and stared into the black cavity but saw nothing. I removed the next drawer down and felt around with my hand until I touched something that was wedged back there. It was a videotape. I didn't spend much time wondering what was on it and why it was hidden in Evan's bedside chest. Instead, I hurried to the living room and popped it into the VCR.

The soundtrack started before the picture. The music was jazzy but of poor sound quality. The image that came into view had a home movie feel to it: jerky camera work and grainy picture quality. A camera panned what looked like a doctor's office and stopped on a man's face. He appeared to be lying on an examining table. His eyes fluttered. His mouth contorted as if he were in the midst of gallbladder surgery without anesthetic. Then a satisfied smile spread to the outer corners of his eyes. The camera lens slowly pulled back to reveal the reason for the patient's good humor: he was stark naked and encouraging a hard-on that was already as big as a dachshund. Evan, I thought, you dog, you.

Just then the camera cut to the office door, where a blonde woman with pouty lips and a nurse's cap appeared. Her outfit, or lack thereof, confirmed that I hadn't just stumbled onto an old episode of *ER*. The action was gross. I should have turned it off immediately, but it was so icky I couldn't stop watching. Five minutes into the scene I decided the only way this flick could get any worse was if Nurse Pouty-lips and the donkey from *Shrek*—well, never mind.

I was about to turn off the VCR when a woman entered the room. She was wearing a lab coat with "Dr. Luster" embroidered on the left breast pocket. A woman doctor? Wow, I thought, a feminist porno flick. What will they think of next? She looked young—late teens, I guessed, maybe younger—but the lascivious look in her eyes made her seem older. Her complexion was flawless, as was her figure. I studied her bleached blond hair and brown eyes. It was an unusual combination. She looked vaguely familiar, but it took a moment before I realized who she was. When I did, a low but audible "Sheee-it" hissed through my lips. The good doctor was a much younger but still recognizable Lola Scott.

Anyone who had ever glanced, however furtively, at a tabloid newspaper at the grocery store checkout counter knew that name: Lola Scott, the diva of daytime TV. She starred as Mallory Eden in a hugely popular soap called *Kings Road*. She'd been Evan's first big success as an agent, a model with minimal acting talent but with a body that sold advertising. Her transition into acting had been mishandled by a manager/boyfriend until Evan discovered her in some cheesy horror film and made her a daytime soap star. He'd negotiated a contract that allowed her to do an occasional film, most of which went straight to video. Many actors like my mother, who worked hard at their craft and struggled to keep their head shots on casting directors' desks, resented the breaks Lola Scott had been handed.

Having a porn credit in her résumé didn't seem like a very good career move—if the news got out, it could be damaging. I assumed the movie had been made before Lola got into "serious" acting, and maybe before she got into modeling. The big question was, why did Evan have the tape, and why here at this apartment? Why not lock it in a safety deposit box or, better yet, destroy it?

As the video played on, I noted that the bedside manner of the young and sensuous Dr. Luster was now on full display. I muted the heavy panting and substituted my own dialogue: "Nice doggie. Beg. Stay. Play dead." Finally, I turned off the VCR and slid the tape into the pocket of my vest, opposite the one that contained Evan's mail. The tape might not have had anything to do with Evan's death, but I was going to let Detective Green make that call.

I made one last pass through the main bedroom to make sure I hadn't missed anything else important. Again I noticed the dying roses. They seemed too poignant to ignore, so I took the vase to the bathroom and filled it with water from the sink tap, knowing that the gesture was futile but hoping it would extend their life by a few hours. While I was there, I went through the drawers in the cabinet. Most of the stuff—shaving cream, aspirin, and toothbrushes—I threw in the trash can under the sink. Several towels were piled up in the bathtub. A couple of white terry-cloth robes were hanging on the back of the door. I folded them in a neat pile on the toilet seat, ready to transfer into Rose's boxes.

I returned the flowers to the bedside chest and was walking back down the hallway toward the living room when I glanced up and saw the front door. It was ajar. I tried to remember if I'd locked it. I was sure I had, which meant that someone other than Monique had a key. That could include any number of people: Evan's friends, lovers, drug dealers, or his killer. I assumed that the members of the latter two categories would be happy to send me into the afterlife limbo with Evan without batting an eyelash.

A moment later, I heard the unmistakable sound of a closet door sliding on its track. It was coming from the second bedroom. It was time to get the hell out of Dodge.

I had just bolted for the front door when something that felt like a freight train hit me between the shoulder blades. My arms flew in the air in an attempt at balance, but shoes bogged down in carpet defeated the effort. I crashed to the floor. I tried to scream but couldn't. The freight train yanked me off the floor by my vest, struggled to turn me over but managed only to wrench my back. I groaned and put my arms over my head to defend the same lame brain that had gotten me into this mess.

Something ripped. Fabric. I floated for a moment before landing face-first on the carpet. Everything grew still except for the floor, which vibrated against my cheek from the force of heavy footsteps pounding toward the exit. Just before the door slammed shut, I looked up and caught a glimpse of a heavy square-toed black boot with a strap and buckle. Embedded in the leather on the side was a silver medallion the size of a quarter.

My back hurt. My cheek stung from carpet burn. I lifted my head and rolled to a sitting position, fighting to calm the tremors vibrating every nerve ending. I looked myself over to make sure I was all in one piece. I was; my fleece vest was not. One pocket had been ripped off and was lying near my purse a few feet away. Aside from that, everything looked okay except for one thing: Lola Scott's porn video was gone, along with Evan's mail.

-10-

i sat on the living room carpet in Evan Brice's apartment, waiting for my hands to stop trembling. The freight train hadn't been inside when I arrived. I would have noticed. He'd probably entered while I was folding towels in the bathroom. My purse was still sitting by the door, which meant he'd probably come specifically for the video or the mail. If he came for the video, he must not have known it was hidden in the chest of drawers. He probably came on a fishing expedition, hoping the police hadn't discovered it when they searched the apartment. If he came for the mail, I couldn't imagine why.

I tried to recall what letters had been in my pocket. There was a notice from the gas company, but I assumed that if they had issues with Evan, they would simply turn off his pilot light. Ditto for other bills. Deadbeat did not justify dead meat. Nothing else in the pile struck me as earth-shattering.

I had to notify Detective Green about the theft, because it might have something to do with Evan's death, but I felt safer making the call from my car. Whoever had attacked me was likely long gone, but just the same, he had a key and could come back at any time.

I touched my cheek. It felt as if several layers of skin had been scraped off, but I couldn't worry about that now. I grabbed my purse and the loose vest pocket and cautiously opened the door before venturing into the hallway.

When I got to my car, I threw the pocket on the passenger seat. The tear looked clean. I didn't know how to fix it, but hopefully somebody else would. Neither Pookie nor I had ever owned a sewing machine. In my mother's world, sewing machines were symbols of the oppression of women. Right now they seemed more like symbols of a thirty-dollar repair bill at the dry cleaner's.

I used my cell phone to call the number for Pacific Station's detective squad. After waiting on hold for what seemed like an eternity, I finally heard Detective Green's voice on the other end of the line. He listened to my story without comment. When I was finished, he asked if I'd been injured. I told him no.

"I'll send a black-and-white to take a report, but it may take a while."

I was stunned by his nonchalance. Maybe he thought his case against Cissy was so airtight he didn't need any more evidence, especially if it contradicted his theory.

"Don't you want to come over in person and look around?" I said. "You know, check for fingerprints or something. What if this video is connected to Evan Brice's murder? You *are* looking for his killer, aren't you?"

For a moment there was silence on the line. "Yes, ma'am, I am—his and a few others, last I checked." There was a defensive tone to his voice, as if I'd just accused him of sitting on his duff all day, eating bonbons.

"Have you interviewed Monique Ruiz yet? I suppose you know she worked for Evan Brice. She also had a key to his apartment and left town around the time he was killed. Doesn't that sound a little suspicious?"

"In a homicide investigation, everybody's movements are suspicious." The implication was, *even yours*, but he didn't say it.

"That doesn't exactly answer my question, does it?"

"We've talked to the Ruiz girl. She has an alibi. It checks out."

This conversation was going nowhere. I certainly didn't want to sit around Evan's apartment waiting to explain my qualms to a couple of skeptical patrol officers. I told him that.

"Why don't you come to the station?" he said. "I'd like to ask you a few follow-up questions anyway. While you're here, you can file a robbery report."

It was at least a compromise, so I agreed. When I walked into the lobby fifteen minutes later, two uniformed officers were at the front desk. One was listening intently to a telephone conversation. The other was taking a report from a woman whose personal computer had been stolen from her desk at work.

When the officer concluded his call, he turned his attention to my report. He was meticulous about details, so it took a while. When he was finished asking questions, he led me through a door off the lobby, into a rabbit warren of small rooms that emptied into a hallway bisected by a low wooden bench. Bolted to the bench was a long metal bar, which held sets of handcuffs attached by a length of chain. We continued through a steel door into the back parking lot. He pointed toward a double-wide trailer next to a cinderblock wall, where the homicide unit was temporarily housed, and told me Detective Green was waiting for me. Something about the way he said that was unsettling.

I headed up the portable steps of the trailer, past a Bankers box marked "Burn." I found Moses Green alone, sitting behind a desk, wearing a crisp white shirt and a burgundy knit tie that sported a gold Brooks Brothers sheep-in-a-sling emblem. When he saw me, he stood, silently staring at the abrasion on my face. He motioned for me to take a chair across from him.

"Just so you know," he said, "there's no smoking allowed in here."

"I don't smoke."

"Good. Me, neither. I quit a couple of years ago after I started getting winded picking up the Sunday paper from my driveway." He settled back into his chair. "So, how's the weather out in Malibu?" His tone was polite and chatty.

"About like here, I'd guess."

He nodded. "I bet it's nice living at the beach."

"It can be."

Why the small talk? I wondered if maybe he was trying to lull me into forgetting that I was at a police station, being questioned by a homicide cop.

Green adjusted his tie and referred to some notes in a file folder that was sitting on his desk, next to his black briefcase. "Like I told you on the phone, I have some follow-up questions about the statements you made to me yesterday. I wanted to give you a chance to clarify them."

The way he phrased his statement made it sound as though he'd caught me in a lie, and he was giving me one last chance to fess up. That irritated me, but I didn't call him on it.

"Ask away."

"Yesterday you said you hadn't seen the victim's wife in years. At the time, I got the impression the two of you had a falling-out. Now I find out you're helping her dismantle the crime scene."

I felt my jaw muscles tighten. "It's not a crime scene anymore."

"Right. I guess my question is really about your current relationship with Mrs. Brice. How would you characterize it?"

There was no easy answer to his question. The word "friend" definitely needed a modifier: former, estranged, old, false. Green's sympathetic expression made me wonder if he understood my labeling dilemma.

"We have a shared history," I said. "She asked for help; I said yes."

He nodded, as if he understood. "It's standard procedure in this type of homicide case to ask the spouse to take a polygraph. Cecelia Brice refused. Why do you suppose she isn't willing to eliminate herself as a suspect in her husband's death?"

The telephone on a desk across the room began to ring. It was loud and annoying. Green made no attempt to answer it. A few moments later, it went silent again.

"Maybe she thinks you're taking the easy way out by pinning the murder on her."

"We don't 'pin' anything on anybody. We collect evidence and let the chips fall where they may."

"And these chips—are they falling near anybody else?"

Green hesitated before answering. "No."

He blinked a couple of times, allowing me a first-rate view of those long eyelashes. They made his eyes look soft and compassionate. I wondered if he knew the effect they had on women.

"You know," he continued, "in a way I feel sorry for Mrs. Brice. She put up with a lot from her husband—

drugs, money problems, other women. Sometimes a person can take just so much before they snap. It can happen so fast they don't even have time to think. They just pick up the nearest thing that causes damage and start thumping away." He paused for a moment to judge my reaction. "You say you have a history with Mrs. Brice. What would it take to push *her* over the edge like that?"

"We've been down this road before, Detective. I told you yesterday, I don't know."

"I was hoping you'd have done some thinking about the question since then." He paused. "And the penalty for withholding evidence in a homicide investigation."

The air in the trailer suddenly seemed warm and oppressive. "You asked me to come in for a follow-up interview. This feels more like an interrogation."

Green didn't respond. Once again he referred to the notes in front of him. "A night clerk at the Oakwood Market on Pacific claims the victim came into the store at about one a.m. on the morning he was killed. He bought a bottle of champagne and a six-pack of Coke. Both were still in the brown grocery bag on the kitchen counter when we arrived at the scene. Champagne. Now that sounds like a party. What do you think he was celebrating?"

"Beats me."

"Come on, Ms. Sinclair, you're a smart person. Take a wild guess."

"What good does that do?"

"Think of it as brainstorming."

I rolled my eyes. "Okay, fine. What kind of champagne?"

He looked surprised but referred to his notes and called off a French label, which I knew sold for about twenty-five dollars a bottle. I was somewhat familiar with the Oakwood Market, because I'd shopped for Rose's groceries there. It was a small neighborhood place, so I assumed that that particular champagne was the priciest brand they carried.

"Evan just got out of rehab. He wasn't doing drugs, so he probably wasn't drinking, either. A single bottle of champagne isn't enough for a party, so I'd say he bought the Coke for himself and the champagne for somebody else. He had an argument with his wife earlier that day. I think he regretted it and was taking the champagne home to her with an apology. What do you think of my theory?"

He frowned. "Interesting."

"But not what you wanted to hear, right?"

He studied me for several moments without responding. "You ever think about irony, Ms. Sinclair?"

"Sometimes. Why?"

He leaned forward in his chair. "When I was a kid, my grandma had a fancy porcelain horse on her dresser. I wanted to play with it so bad I could taste it, but my grandma, she said, 'No, Moses. That's not a toy. You go playin rough with that pony, you gonna break it all to pieces.' Well, when you're three, you don't want to listen to 'no' from an old woman. One day when she was out in her garden pulling weeds, I climbed up on a chair and got that horse. On the way down, it slipped out of my hands and broke into a million pieces on her linoleum floor. I never forgot that. I not only betrayed my grandma, I also destroyed the one thing I wanted most."

"I guess there's a point to your story, Detective Green."

"Yeah, I guess there is. Sometimes you think you can have it all, but you end up with nothing. Cecelia Brice took your man, because she wanted him. She betrayed a friend. Now it looks like she also destroyed the thing she wanted most. What do you think of *my* theory?"

"I think it needs work."

He shook his head as if he regretted ever saying I was smart. "You're a better friend than she deserves, Ms. Sinclair. Tell you what I think: Mrs. Brice went to her husband's apartment that night. She found him getting ready to romance another lady. She figured enough is enough. If she can't have him, nobody can. She grabbed a kitchen knife and got in a lucky blow right off. Or maybe the victim was so shocked to see his wife with a weapon in her hand, he didn't put up much of a fight. There weren't many defensive wounds. It looks like she caught him completely off guard."

"And what evidence do you have against her? Eye-witnesses? Bloody fingerprints? Anything?"

"I can't discuss the evidence. Let's just say we're putting our case together. I was hoping you could help us with that."

"I thought I *was* helping. I just told you a man broke into Evan's apartment and stole items that may relate to his murder. That didn't seem to grab your attention, so I assume you only want evidence that points to Cissy Brice."

He no longer looked sympathetic, just irritated. "You know better than that."

"Do I?"

Green looked tight-jawed and frustrated. "We investigate all leads, including those from well-meaning citizens like you."

Moments later he told me he was finished asking questions. He said he'd get a copy of my report from the front desk. If he had any questions, he'd call me. For now, I was free to go.

As soon as I got to the car, I called Cissy Brice. I wanted to find out if she knew who else had keys to

Evan's apartment. I also wanted to warn her about Green's growing suspicions. Her machine answered. Discouraged, I left a message and headed for home.

A dull gray marine layer hung over the Pacific Ocean like a dingy sheet. A Norah Jones CD played on the car stereo as I drove along the coast highway. Norah's sultry voice acted as a balm, until I felt almost whole again. I probably drove too fast, but traffic was light and speed made me feel in control. It also got me home in half an hour instead of forty-five minutes.

When I arrived, I found Pookie sitting outside on a deck chair, looking uncharacteristically drab in a baggy gray sweat suit. She was flipping through an old textbook of mine entitled *Financial Management: Theory and Practice*. My mother's choice of reading material may not have seemed odd to folks who didn't know her, but it seemed more than odd to me. Before meeting Bruce, the only thing she'd ever calculated was her numerology life-path number. I should have felt good that she was expanding her horizons, but I didn't. I felt only a sense of impending doom.

Muldoon was in his regular spot on the chaise longue, using his cashmere sweater as a pillow.

"Where's Bruce?" I asked.

"Meeting with the trustees." Pookie didn't take her eyes off the book.

"You didn't go?"

"I wasn't invited."

"That sucks."

She shrugged, but I could tell that not being included bothered her. She closed the book without marking her place and turned toward me. "My God! What happened to your face?"

"I fell."

"Tucker?" Her voice was high-pitched and filled with concern.

Muldoon detected the anxious tenor in her voice and let out a questioning whine.

"Don't worry, I'm okay. I just need some ice."

She followed me inside and sat on the living room couch, letting the soft pillows surround her like a cocoon. Muldoon settled in next to her because the couch was within striking distance of the refrigerator, and he sensed by the edgy tone in her voice that comfort food might be in his future.

While filling the ice pack, I told her about my run-in with the freight train and that the detective in charge of Evan's murder investigation didn't buy my theory that the robbery was connected to his death. She listened but didn't say much. Her eyes were closed as if she was pretending that the ugliness of the world would disappear if she couldn't see it. Pookie had never been the type of mother who soothed my bumps and bruises with TLC and homemade brownies, but her laissez-faire approach to mothering had made me self-sufficient, for which I was grateful.

I sank into an adjacent overstuffed chair and put the ice pack on my cheek. "Tell me all the dirt you know about Lola Scott."

She looked at me suspiciously. "Why?"

"Just curious."

She bit her lip and thought for a moment. "I can't. I promised Bruce."

"Relax, Pookie. The gossip Nazi is at a trustees' meeting, remember?"

I had hoped that by reminding her of Bruce's slight it might trigger some of her vintage spunk, but it didn't.

"I wish you'd give him a chance, Tucker."

I couldn't fault my mother for trying to be a good person, but I would have felt better if the decision to give up gossiping had come from her, not from a guy who had the analytical instincts of a canned ham.

"I'm trying," I said.

She was still sitting on the couch as I went outside to get Muldoon's sweater from the deck chair. I took it and the ice pack and retreated to my bedroom. True to form, Muldoon followed the cashmere. I punched up the bed pillows, leaned back against my grandma's wrought-iron headboard, and pressed the ice against my face. Muldoon took another nap. I thought I'd rest for a minute, too, and wait for inspiration. None came. A few moments later, I heard a heavy sigh. I glanced up and saw Pookie standing in the doorway.

"You want what I know or what I've heard?"

Yes! I thought. *The old Pookie is back.*

"Both."

She came over and sat on the edge of the bed. "Okay. Remember that biker film I mentioned the other night? I told you my friend Sheila Mayhew did the makeup. Well, Lola Scott was the star of that picture. Sheila says Evan came to the set a few times. He and Lola would go into her trailer and have these loud arguments followed by even louder makeup sex. She said that Winnebago rocked like a ten on the Richter scale."

That was some monumental screwing. I thought of the sheets on the bed in Evan's apartment and wondered if they had been bought at Lola Scott's behest. Except that didn't make sense. Lola was a big star. If she wanted a romantic rendezvous, she'd simply book a room under a fake name at the Peninsula Hotel in Beverly Hills.

"Okay," I said. "They were having sex. So what?"

"No. Evan was having sex. Lola was making love."

"How do you know it wasn't love for Evan, too?"

"Hello? Where's the little cynic I raised? It's like this, sweetie. When Evan got out of rehab, he dumped Lola. The end."

"Why?"

She shrugged. "Who knows?"

"How did Lola take it?"

Pookie gave me her earth-to-Tucker look. "She didn't exactly confide in me, but I imagine she took it the way any woman would have. She wanted to cut off his little winkie."

I thought about that for a minute. "Maybe she didn't stop with his winkie."

Pookie's eyes got big. "See? I knew I couldn't trust myself. Bruce was right all along. This is exactly how gossip gets out of control."

Pookie was probably right. Floating the notion that Lola Scott had anything to do with Evan's death might be interesting, but it was pure speculation, and probably dangerous speculation to boot. Still, in a homicide investigation, everyone is a suspect, including the diva of daytime.

"What would happen to Lola's career if the public found out she'd done a porno film?"

"Tucker, why are you asking all of these questions?"

I had no choice; I had to tell her about the videotape. When I did, the news didn't seem to surprise her.

"Ordinarily, doing porn wouldn't matter for somebody like Lola Scott," Pookie said, "but lately she's been trying to sell herself as a serious artist. I hear she's taking private acting lessons from the coach du jour, plus she just hired a top-notch PR firm to put a positive spin on her career."

"And now she'll be hiring a new agent as well."

Pookie shot me a warning glance.

Nobody was taking my suspicions seriously, and that irritated me. If nothing else, Lola Scott was a person of interest. Maybe Detective Green was overworked and didn't have time to do the necessary legwork, but somebody had to do it. For Cissy's sake, somebody had to do it now. As reluctant as I was to get more involved in her troubles, I decided to check into the Lola Scott angle, at least until Cissy could be persuaded to hire a lawyer to manage her defense. After all, I'd researched hundreds of strategic plans for all kinds of businesses; I could certainly collect a few tidbits on a high-profile actor like the venerable Dr. Luster.

"So how can I get in touch with Lola-baby?" I said.

"Are you out of your mind? First of all, I don't know her, and second of all, what are you going to say? 'Hey, Lola, Pookie Kravitz thinks you killed your agent because of some porno movie you did when you were still jailbait.' I'd never work in this town again."

"You won't work again in any case. You gave up acting. Remember? For Bruce."

Her facial muscles went slack. "I can't tell you anything more."

"Then maybe Sheila Mayhew can. How about giving me her number?"

Pookie stood and put her arms out like a cop stopping traffic. "No more negative gossip. I'm taking Deepak Chopra and some bath salts, and I'm going to soak away any memory of this conversation."

So much for the old Pookie.

When Muldoon heard the bathroom door close, he seemed conflicted. On one hand, he loved to lick bathwater off legs. On the other, there was cashmere and the hope of greasy food if he stayed with me. I asked him if he thought one little telephone number was too much to ask of Pookie. He cocked his head and whined, which meant he expected compensation for siding with me. My fans were few and far between these days, so I went into the kitchen and got him a turkey hot dog from the refrigerator, because I didn't want any debt to him hanging over my head.

I should have dropped the whole Lola Scott thing right then and there, but I couldn't. I had to find out if she had a reason to want Evan dead, not to mention if she was to blame for screwing up a perfectly good vest. Maybe I'd confront her with my knowledge of the tape and wait to see if sweat beaded on her upper lip. First I had to find her.

I considered finagling tickets to a taping of *Kings Road*, but I wasn't sure if soaps used live audiences. After coming up with a series of less than brilliant alternatives, I decided my best chance of locating Lola was through Sheila Mayhew. If my mother wouldn't give me Sheila's telephone number, I'd have to find it another way. Luckily, that wasn't going to be difficult.

Despite Pookie's recent efforts to master the semi-annual compounding of bond values, she wasn't exactly on the cutting edge of high finance or high technology. No Palm handheld computers for her. She still used a leather Coach address book she bought in the early eighties, which was at this moment sitting on the kitchen counter. Feeling only slightly guilty for invading her privacy, I thumbed through it until I got to the "M's."

Sheila Mayhew was what you'd call a vagabond. Her address had been crossed out and reentered five times in the years my mother had known her. As far as I could tell, she was currently living in Studio City. I called the number labeled "cell." To my amazement, she answered on the second ring. After accepting only the briefest of introductions and the skimpiest of explanations why I wanted to speak with her, she surprised me further by inviting me to meet her the following afternoon in Whittier, where she was doing makeup for a low-budget film about a couple of vampires who decide to leave the life and move to suburbia. It sounded like the perfect vehicle for Lola Scott, so I was disappointed to learn that she wasn't in the picture. Just as well. If Lola was involved in Evan's death, I didn't want to tip her off that I was hot on her trail and that the police would soon be, too. All I needed was a little more evidence to convince Moses Green.

-11-

f Muldoon had bothered to ask, I would have told him I hadn't slept at all that night. Yet if pressed, I couldn't have accounted for every moment between the times I heard Pookie and Bruce arguing and the aggressive knocking on the front door that awakened me the following morning. The knocking was too early for UPS. Jehovah's Witnesses and door-to-door solicitors usually came in the afternoon and always gave up after a couple of taps went unanswered. I assumed that Pookie and Bruce had gone out for a makeup walk and forgot to take the house key.

At the first hint that an intruder had breached his perimeter, Muldoon bolted from the bed, barking with the zeal of a tent preacher. I pressed the pillows to my ears against the din and stretched my legs toward the place where he'd been lying, feeling the warmth of body heat and cashmere. Lately, the pup had been sleeping all night on my bed. I assumed he'd discovered, as Pookie had, that Bruce's deviated septum produced a sound that was not conducive to a good night's rest.

I opened one eye and glared at the clock—7:45 a.m. I'd overslept. I wasn't scheduled to meet Sheila Mayhew until one; however, Eugene was coming over at nine, and before I left the house, I had to call the Holiday Inn's catering department and hammer out a muffin strategy for the focus group's morning coffee break.

I forced my toes from the warmth of Muldoon's nest and swung my legs over the edge of the bed, aiming my feet for the slippers I'd left on the floor the night before. The shock of warm soles against cold tile signaled that my slippers were gone. Muldoon had probably commandeered them to use as enemy operatives in his commando games.

My back was stiff from my encounter with the freight train the day before, and when I brushed my fingers across my cheek, I felt what was undoubtedly a nasty abrasion. I grabbed a bathrobe from the closet and made my way toward a window at the side door, angling the shutter slats upward.

Woolly gray fog had smothered the morning sun, but I could clearly see a woman standing on my deck. She was in her late twenties, with dark hair and pleasant features. Her arms were crossed over a fussy gold crest on the breast pocket of a navy blazer that looked expensive but too small for her. She was looking downward, scowling at powdery sand coating a pair of hiking boots that were poking self-consciously from the narrow legs of her trousers.

I grabbed Muldoon's collar with one hand and used the other to ease open the door. The woman tensed at the timbre of Muldoon's bark, backing away until the deck's railing stopped her. As a courtesy, I scooped the pup into my arms and spoke muffled reassurances until his fury was reduced to an anxious wiggle.

Seeing him contained, the woman curled her mouth into a wary smile. "I didn't think anybody was home."

Her enunciation was exaggerated, as if she thought I might be foreign or deaf, or perhaps her carefully cultivated speech was meant to disguise the fact that she was the first generation out of the barrio.

I raised my eyebrows. "If you didn't think I was home, why'd you keep knocking?"

Again the woman stared at her shoes. "Sorry if I bothered you. My name is Marta Cruz. I work for the *Valley News Now*. I wanted to ask you a few questions about Evan Brice."

Muldoon was right. Our perimeters had been breached. I wondered how this woman had connected me to Evan. Maybe she'd been among the mob of reporters in front of Cissy's place and had somehow learned my name. At least she wasn't from the *Los Angeles Times*. But any reporter at my front door was bad news.

"How did you find me?"

"I can't reveal my sources, just like I can't tell anybody else what you say to me. I'm doing an article about Mr. Brice's murder. I want to get to know him better to make my story more interesting."

Her attempts at information gathering seemed clumsy. I didn't know how the woman would ever make it as a reporter, a career in which it seemed the odds of survival, never mind success, were against you. However, her question was intriguing enough to keep me from slamming the door in her face.

"What do you want to know?" I said.

"Was he a man of his word?"

At first I was startled, and then suspicious. She should have been asking the same questions the police had asked: When was the last time I'd seen him alive? Did he have enemies? Which one of them may have wanted him dead?

My tone was cautious. "Depends on what you mean by 'man of his word'."

"I mean, if he made a promise, would he keep it no matter what?"

"Why are you asking me?"

Without hesitation she said, "Because he loved you once."

The pulse pounded in my ears as I thought about where she'd gotten her information and what she hoped to gain by it.

"If you don't mind me saying so, Ms. Cruz, you sound more like a jilted lover than a reporter. What's your scam?"

Her tone was indignant. "I was *not* Mr. Brice's lover, and this is no scam. I just wanted to talk to you. I thought you could help."

"Help with what? Your Pulitzer Prize–winning exposé on the Brice murder? Frankly, Marta Cruz, I think your story is full of shit."

I moved to close the door, but a hiking boot shifted quickly to block the way. Muldoon resumed barking and nearly slipped out of my arms.

"Get your foot away from my door—now."

A flush of embarrassment burned her cheeks, as if some deeply ingrained civility was warring with her role as hard-nosed investigative reporter. On the other hand, maybe she was just uncomfortable getting caught in a lie. She moved her foot but stood her ground, watching me. For a moment I thought she might try another approach— like the truth—but she didn't.

"I was wrong," she said, turning to leave. "You're no help at all."

Moments later I watched as she fought her way through the dunes, slipping and sliding until she reached the road. She paused only occasionally to brush the wet sand from her clothes. She obviously hadn't seen the public easement on the south side of Mrs. Domanski's house, though I wasn't surprised. My neighbor nurtured the trees along the path with fertilizer spikes to discourage such access to her front yard.

At least Cruz had had the presence of mind to wear the right shoes. It almost seemed as if she knew she'd need them to negotiate the sand, almost as if she'd been to the beach house before. Great! Just what I needed—my very own stalker.

I felt unsettled about Cruz's appearance at my door. I didn't know what she was up to, but I was going to find out. I'd never even heard of the *Valley News Now*. Of course, there were dozens of neighborhood newspapers across the Southland that nobody had heard of. They reported on Friends of the Library book drives and local crime statistics and survived by publishing weekly grocery ads paid for by the big chains.

I was willing to bet that covering celebrity murders was not the usual fare of the *Valley News Now*. If so, I couldn't imagine what had driven one of their employees to hunt down a minor player in Evan's life at 7:45 in the morning. Maybe she'd set her sights on grander ambitions than selling grocery coupons for a throwaway rag, and thought I fit into her plan—that is, if anything she'd told me was the truth.

It was just after eight when I dialed directory assistance and got a number for the *Valley News Now*. I was disappointed when the woman who answered the newspaper's telephone confirmed that Marta Cruz was on their payroll. At least that part of the reporter's story was true. However, she balked when I asked if Cruz was assigned to cover Evan

Brice's murder. Frustrated, I hung up and logged on to the paper's Web site. The only accessible information was an array of classified ads and an invitation to download a fifty-cents-off coupon for an economy-size bottle of Mr. Clean.

Other than Cissy Brice and Claire Jerrard, I couldn't think of anyone who still remembered or cared about my college romance with Evan. It seemed ridiculous to think either of those two had leaked information to the press. Maybe Detective Green had blabbed, but I didn't think so. He hadn't even been interested enough in me to ask Pookie to verify my alibi for the night of Evan's murder, as he said he would.

The tile floor was cold. So were my feet. During my first winter in the house, I'd vowed to install wall-to-wall carpeting by spring. Then the rains came. After warring for a few months with gritty beach sand, which inveigled its way into everything, I decided to stick with tile and area rugs just as my grandmother had done. Of course, Anne Sinclair could have afforded to replace ruined carpet after each season, had she chosen to do so. I couldn't even if it meant cold feet, because my financial future was still too iffy.

I went in search of my slippers, finding one under the living room couch and the other out on the deck. As I headed down the hall, I glanced toward the bedroom where Pookie and Bruce slept. The door was open, the room empty. That was odd. I wondered where they'd gone.

I quickly showered, dressed, and slapped on some concealer to camouflage the abrasion on my face. Eugene would be here soon. He was a worrier, and I wanted to avoid explaining what had happened. Unfortunately, the concealer only made the abrasion look crusty. I washed it off and instead arranged my hair so it covered my cheek.

I went back to my office and called the Holiday Inn

catering director, managing to broker an optimal muffin arrangement for the focus group's morning coffee break in five minutes flat, a record for me. She even sweetened the deal with some free orange juice. In the not too distant future, I'd have to report my progress to Marvin Geyer. I wasn't looking forward to that. The guy had the disposition of an arthritic cat. How he'd managed to survive in business all these years was a mystery to me. Several times I reached for the receiver to dial his number. In the end I couldn't bring myself to make the call.

Instead I made a quick call to Regent Rentals and arranged for them to pick up the furniture in Evan's apartment. The first available appointment they had was the following Tuesday. Not surprisingly, they also confirmed that the bed in Evan's master bedroom wasn't theirs. I could have discovered that for myself if I'd checked the contract more carefully. Cissy would have to decide what to do with the bed. I suspected she'd want to donate it to charity along with everything else. Next I called the battered-women's shelter to arrange a pickup time for the boxes of bathroom and kitchen items.

I still had a few more minutes before Eugene arrived, so I logged onto the Internet and Googled Lola Scott, searching several Web addresses that popped up, including a movie trivia site. There I found a list of films with unfamiliar titles dating back four or five years. From a brief bio, I learned that Lola was seventeen when she started modeling and eighteen when she appeared in her first horror film. Two other films followed before Evan took charge of her career.

I also searched the archives of *Variety* for any articles about Lola published within the past six months. I found several. A headline dated just days before Evan's death read, SCOTT, AGENT REEVALUATING PAIRING, followed by,

"It appears that one of Hollywood's more successful agent/client teams may be on the rocks, with Evan Brice and TV soap star Lola Scott considering an end to their six-year relationship." I clicked on the title of the article and waited for the full text to appear but was disappointed to discover that it was available only to subscribers.

I'd scrolled down a few pages and was about to log off when a teaser for another article caught my eye. It had been posted only the week before and read, "Lola Scott has committed to joining Grant Medina in Square-rigger's 'Pagan Dreams,' a drama to be directed by Richard Burnett and produced by P. J. Chien and his Square-rigger Productions. Filming begins June 30." Again, the complete text was unavailable.

I thought, wow. No wonder Lola hired a PR firm to position her as a serious actor. Considering her questionable talent, getting a starring role in a Richard Burnett picture was a big coup. I wondered what Evan had done to close *that* deal.

Burnett was known as an actor's director because of his ability to transform mediocre performers into Oscar contenders. He was also considered one of the hottest directors in Hollywood. Not only had both his last two films scored big bucks at the box office, but each had also garnered Best Actor nominations for its respective stars.

I had only two questions: Why had Evan and Lola severed their relationship just when her career was heading in a more promising direction? And did the breakup have anything to do with the porn video I'd found hidden in Evan's apartment? I wondered if Cissy Brice could answer either of those questions. Perhaps I should ask her before I came to my senses and realized that skirting around a murder investigation could be more than a little dangerous.

-12-

t exactly 9:00 a.m., Eugene Barstok arrived to help me with the focus group. Before opening the door, I made sure my hair was still draped over my facial abrasion.

Eugene was standing on the deck, holding a plastic bag. He was dressed in a heather-colored cable-knit sweater he'd made himself, and the beige corduroy pleated trousers he often wears to add bulk to his slim build. His right wrist was wrapped with an elastic bandage.

Eugene is in his mid-twenties, with big, blue eyes that could disarm almost any cynic. He's five feet five or so, with sandy-brown hair, which he keeps cut short because of a cowlick that refuses to be tamed. Today was no exception. A few unruly hairs were standing at attention on the crown of his head.

A broad smile made his oval face seem round. "You are *not* going to believe what I found. It's too perfect." He bustled past me into the house.

"Don't make me guess. I've had enough suspense for one morning."

He reached into the plastic bag—with his left hand, I noted—and pulled out a box. "Tah-dah!"

He put the box on the breakfast bar, ignoring my puzzled frown. Inside were file folders that sported a royal blue and white hibiscus pattern. He grabbed one and canted it beneath his eyes, like a geisha seducing a client with her fan.

"Hawaiian-motif file folders! Didn't I tell you they were perfect?"

They *were* perfect, not to mention hilarious.

"And . . ." He stretched out the word for a second or two. "I have an idea. Ever since we talked yesterday, I've been obsessing about your muumuu dilemma. At three o'clock this morning I finally figured it out. The problem is, they're unfashionably voluminous. So what do we do? We downsize them, make them shorter and slimmer—you know, more like a cheongsam. We market the new version as trendy beach wear. Maybe we even add a coordinating tote bag with an edgy logo and give the line a name—something that pops, like 'Hula Bitch.' Then we watch Mr. Geyer ride the retro wave back to profitability. What do you think? It's good, right?"

I had to admit it: In a quirky way, the concept had potential. Still, Mr. Geyer was set in his ways. He might not be open to the idea, even if it meant saving his business. Eugene didn't buy that argument.

"That's ridiculous. When your baby's in jeopardy, you'll do anything to save her." Moments later, his enthusiasm faded to concern. "What's wrong?"

"Nothing. It's a great idea."

"No, I mean what's wrong with your face. It looks scratched."

I reached up to touch my cheek and realized my hair was no longer covering the abrasion. I didn't want to dampen Eugene's mood by telling him about my troubles. On the other hand, lying to him would never work. His bullshit meter was hypersensitive.

"I think you'll need to sit down for this one."

Eugene followed me into the living room. I sat on the couch next to Muldoon. Eugene settled into the easy chair. I told him about Evan's murder, closing the Venice apartment, and finding the Lola Scott porn video. When I got to the part about being attacked by the freight train, Eugene's face blanched.

"You could have been killed."

"But I wasn't."

"But you could have been. Why did that ox have to hurt you? Why didn't he just hide in the closet until you were gone? I'll tell you why—low id control. You can't trust a person like that, and you can't predict what he'll do next. What if he comes looking for you again? This is serious, Tucker. I think we should leave town for a few days."

"I can't do that, Eugene, but I promise I'll be more careful from now on."

He pressed his lips into a hard line. "You always say that."

"This time I mean it. Okay?"

It seemed as if minutes passed before he spoke again. "Was it scary?"

"Kind of. Getting attacked isn't my idea—"

"Not that. The porn video. I heard Lola Scott has so much cellulite on her butt she uses a body double for all her close-ups."

I couldn't help it. I laughed. "I'll let you know if I ever get an up-close-and-personal look at her derriere. Enough gossip. Let's get to work."

I gathered the focus group paperwork and put Eugene

to work at the breakfast bar, labeling and organizing. I went to my office alcove to make a few calls, trying without much success to get some new business out of some old clients. Frustrated, I decided to take Muldoon on a short walk, but after a few minutes the cold March air began seeping through my sweater, so I lured him back inside with the promise of microwave popcorn.

At 9:45 a.m., Cissy still hadn't returned my call from the day before. At the risk of being a pest, I called her number again. This time Jerome answered. He told me she'd taken Dara to the carousel at the Santa Monica pier for an hour or so. After that, he didn't know where she'd be. I wondered if they'd made it past the gate without the media following them.

I hung up and tried her cell phone. A computer-generated voice told me her mailbox was full, probably jammed with calls from the press. I couldn't wait any longer. I decided to drive to the beach and find her.

There was still no sign of my mother or Bruce. I had no idea when they were coming back, so I grabbed a sweater and asked Eugene to look after Muldoon. I told him that if I wasn't back by the time he finished work, he should lock up the house and take the pup to my neighbor's place. Mrs. Domanski was always game for Westie-sitting.

Thirty minutes later I was driving along Pacific Coast Highway toward Santa Monica, one of a series of seaside communities strung together along the California coastline like train cars in a child's pull toy. From PCH I headed up the California Incline and found a parking spot in a two-hours-free city lot. I walked toward the pier through Palisades Park, a narrow greenbelt on the cliffs overlooking the Pacific Ocean, detouring around a homeless man who lay huddled on the grass beneath a stained mattress pad. Across the highway in the parking lot below, two cyclists leisurely rode along the bike path past a young man practicing turns on his Rollerblades.

Finally, I spotted what I thought might be Cissy's green Jaguar. When the crosswalk light chirped at Colorado Street, I headed down the ramp past henna tattoo artists and vendors selling maps to the stars' homes. A group of eager children formed a line in front of the slate blue and taupe carousel building, but none of them was Dara. I waited through several revolutions of brightly painted horses before I was satisfied that Cissy and Dara weren't inside the carousel building, either.

Just beyond the Boathouse Restaurant, I walked down the wooden steps to a pathway that led to a rickety sea-foam green lifeguard station boarded up for the winter. It was quiet on the beach except for the roar of a jet taking off from LAX. The fog was burning off. A flock of gulls had nestled quietly in the dry sand, soaking up warmth from the sun.

I found Cissy sitting on an aluminum folding chair in front of the lifeguard station, reading from a small hardcover book. She glanced up frequently from the page to watch Dara stomp on bubbles in the foamy surf a few feet away. I emptied the sand from my shoes and called Cissy's name. She looked up, startled. When she closed the book, I could see from the cover that it was a collection of haiku poetry. That surprised me.

"I didn't know you liked haiku," I said.

She shrugged. "I found it on Evan's nightstand. It's not very good. It doesn't even rhyme."

"Some people consider haiku the highest form of poetry."

"Well, I don't know what all the fuss is about. They talk about frogs or the moon and then it's over."

I could have told her that it wasn't as simple as that. If I remembered correctly, there were a lot of rules in haiku. You were allowed only three lines of verse, each required a specific number of syllables, and you had to include one of the seasons in there somewhere. Only there was no point in pontificating, because after today Cissy would probably never look at the book again.

"At least this haiku stuff doesn't pretend to be about a picnic in the country, and then you find out it's really about death and how your life is crap and nobody cares."

I understood why she didn't want to deal with hidden meanings right now. She was the prime suspect in a murder investigation that could take away her freedom and deny Dara her only remaining parent. In my head I thought of a haiku for Cissy:

> Life grows more complex
> when the Spring sun shines brightly
> on the cold handcuffs.

Cissy's breathing was deep and controlled as she watched Dara scamper back and forth between the surf and the dry sand, daring the waves to douse her bare feet in chilly salt water. Dara picked up what looked like some kind of shell. She proudly held it up for her mother's approval, until she noticed me watching and turned shy. She lowered her head and began to brush sand from the shell's surface, as if nothing else in the world existed.

We watched her play at the water's edge for a few minutes, avoiding the issue on both our minds. We talked about bacteria levels in the water, and a trip to the Long Beach aquarium she and Dara had recently taken. I waited for a lull in the conversation.

"I was at Evan's apartment yesterday," I said.

She seemed pleased. "Good, you got the key. Thanks a million, Tuckie. How's the little Ruiz girl doing anyway?"

"I don't know. I didn't see her."

She frowned. "What do you mean? I thought you said you got her key?"

"I did, but not from Monique. I think she's avoiding me."

Cissy looked as if she'd judged my efforts and found them lacking. I hardly expected her to fall all over me with gratitude, but her irritation seemed odd, even if she was under pressures I couldn't begin to understand.

"Did Evan ever have any break-ins at the apartment?" I said.

"It's possible. It's a bad neighborhood. Why do you ask?"

"A man came in while I was there. He stole some mail and a videotape."

Her eyes darted back and forth as if she couldn't process what I'd just told her. "That doesn't make sense. Who'd want to take stuff like that?"

"I don't know, but whatever he was after, he wanted it pretty badly."

Her gaze settled on the abrasion on my cheek. "Oh, my God! Is that why your cheek is all screwed up? Oh, Tuckie, I'm so sorry. I should never have gotten you involved in this mess."

Her angst seemed sincere. On the other hand, maybe she was just trying to manipulate me into feeling sorry for her. If so, it wouldn't be the first time.

"Do you have any idea who'd want Evan's mail? I can't remember what all was there, but I think there were a couple of bills; one was from the gas company."

She shook her head. "That can't be right. All our bills go directly to our business manager. When Evan was doing drugs, he got us into big financial trouble, blowing all kinds of money on jewelry and boob jobs for women he didn't even know. If I hadn't taken away his credit cards and his checkbook, we would have lost everything."

I was sure there had been statements in that stack of mail, but it didn't seem important enough to quibble about. There were many weightier issues to discuss, like Evan's relationship with Lola Scott. I suspected that the news would come as no surprise to Cissy. If people in the industry like my mother knew about the affair, she must know as well. Still, I decided to start with the easy stuff first.

"Did Evan ever discuss his work problems with you?"

"Sometimes. Why?"

"I'm just curious why he and Lola Scott parted company."

Cissy's lips pinched together in a hard line of distaste. "Because she's a slut. Evan should have left her in the gutter where he found her."

"It seems odd, that's all. Evan arranges the coup of the century by getting Lola the lead in a Richard Burnett picture. If things go well, she gets Oscar buzz, which is very good for everybody. So why would he dump her?"

"Because the woman is toxic."

Perhaps Cissy was right, but agents didn't have to like the actors they represented. Evan had an office overhead to support. It seemed like a poor business decision to get rid of a cash cow like Lola Scott merely because she was toxic or even because his love affair with her had cooled.

"There must have been more to it than that."

"What more do you want?" she said. "Evan pulled out all the stops to make Lola a star, but do you think she appreciated it? No. She even had the gall to ask him to waive his commission on Richard's picture. Can you believe it? Everybody in this town thought she was a joke until my husband made them sit up and take notice."

"What happens to Evan's commission now that he's dead?"

Cissy looked surprised and then concerned. "It'll go to the agency and eventually to me and Dara."

"What if the Burnett deal falls through?"

"Don't talk like that, Tuckie. You're making me nervous."

A shrill scream and then a giggle interrupted our conversation. Our attention shifted to Dara. Score one for the Pacific Ocean. Her jeans were now soaked with water, and her ankles were wrapped in a tangle of greenish-brown kelp that had been washed ashore by the last wave. She picked up a kelp bulb with her fingertips and held it up high.

"Mommy. Looky here."

"Put that down. It's dirty."

Dara weighed her mother's advice before dropping the kelp and kicking to free her feet of the leafy debris. The movement managed only to expose something gray and feathery caught up in the snarl.

"Mommy. Mommy," she whimpered. "It's a birdie. It's hurt. Hurry."

The shift in her child's tone was subtle, but enough to trigger Cissy's internal mommy alarm. She bolted from her chair and rushed to her daughter's side, leaving behind a pair of fuchsia sandals adorned with floppy pink daisies. She unwound the kelp from Dara's feet and grabbed her wrist.

"Come on, sweetie. Get away from there."

Dara tried to pry her wrist from Cissy's grip with the fingers of her free hand.

"We can't go. It's hurt. We have to fix it."

Cissy knelt on the sand in front of her child. "No, baby, it's not hurt; it's dead. It's not going to feel anything anymore."

Dara stared at the bird for a moment. Slowly her expression of concern began crumbling until it became a portrait of pain and horror. There was one sharp intake of air before her small body collapsed into her mother's arms, and she began to sob.

When I couldn't deal with watching them anymore, I quietly turned to leave. Cissy sensed the movement and looked up. There was a look of panic on her face, as if she'd suddenly realized she was not well suited to the single-mother role she was now forced to play.

I felt sorry for her, but there was nothing I could do to help. Either she'd figure it out or she wouldn't. I gave her what I hoped was a look of support and headed back up the stairs toward the pier.

I'd almost reached the parking garage when my cell phone rang. It was Joe Deegan. He didn't sound happy.

"Your name came up in a conversation I just had with Moses Green. Remember him? The detective from *my* division who interviewed you two days ago about a love letter he found at the scene of a homicide. Is any of this sounding familiar?"

"Are you asking as a cop or a friend?"

"Don't bullshit me, Stretch. It pisses me off."

"It wasn't a letter. It was a poem, and I can explain."

"Oh, I'm sure you can. I just want to know why you didn't explain yesterday when you were here. Just what the hell are you up to?"

I counted to ten before answering, because I didn't want this to turn into an argument. "Look, Deegan, I'll explain everything, but not on the phone." I tried to drum up a teasing tone to my voice to defuse the situation. "So, you want what I've got, or not?"

Normally Deegan would have made something out of my choice of words. Not this time. He was obviously not responding to my mojo.

"I'll be at your place around six," he said.

"You still remember how to find it?"

"Some things you just don't forget."

I preferred meeting Deegan in neutral territory, away from Pookie and Bruce, but I didn't want to antagonize him further, so I said okay. Besides, I had to get off the telephone, because I didn't want to be late for my meeting with Sheila Mayhew.

All the way to Whittier, I thought about my life and how little harm would come to me if I went back to it and forgot about the whole sorry mess surrounding Evan's death. In a few hours I'd tell Joe Deegan everything or nearly everything that had happened to me in the past few days. Maybe the confession would be cathartic.

However, there would be some things I wouldn't tell him, even though I could dredge up the words if I tried. I wouldn't tell him what it felt like to lose somebody you cared about to violence, or how it would be for Dara to grow up with a well-meaning but less than perfect mother. I'd even listen patiently to Deegan's lecture about leaving police work to the professionals, but in the end I knew, as he probably did, that I wasn't going to take his advice.

-13-

hittier is located about thirty miles east of the Pacific Ocean, in an area where smog layers replace marine layers. It's also the birthplace of Richard Nixon, but nobody holds that against it anymore.

Sheila Mayhew's vampire flick was being filmed on a quiet residential street a block or two off Norwalk Boulevard. I parked on a side street and made my way toward a motorcycle cop who was probably moonlighting. He checked for my name on a list and, after finding it, allowed me behind the barricade.

The center of activity was a small bungalow at midblock. The place had no landscaping to speak of, just a front yard choked by snake grass, brown from lack of water. The house was painted fish-scale green and had probably once been a pleasant but boring little square until someone tarted it up with a grandiose black wrought-iron fence and a pair of concrete lion sculptures, one on each side of the gate. The front door had been expanded to two doors and painted black, making it look like the maw of a largemouth bass. The fantasy may have been *Architectural Digest*, but the reality was more like *Field and Stream*. Still, it seemed like a good spot for a couple of vampires in transition.

Small clusters of neighbors stood on sidewalks and lawns, probably hoping to catch a glimpse of some big-name movie star. A dozen or so young people wearing sneakers and faded jeans milled around a row of trailers. I asked for Sheila Mayhew and was directed to the second trailer from the end. I made my way up the stairs, tapped on the door, and waited until I heard, "Come in. We're decent," before poking my head inside.

Sheila Mayhew was in her mid-forties, with chestnut-colored hair that looked chic piled up in an untamed twist atop her head. She wore cowboy boots with black tights and a low-cut spandex top so taut that it squeezed her breasts together into one massive lump. Her makeup was somewhere between glamorous and overdone and was complemented by brows that arched gracefully over her eyes like two well-groomed chinchillas. She reminded me of everyone's favorite aunt, the one who always brought you bags of those teeny tiny Avon lipstick samples and took you to get your ears pierced without your mother's permission.

Costumes, makeup, and script pages littered the trailer, but even amid all that chaos, Sheila looked serene as she applied the finishing touches to a set of fangs on a twenty-something girl vampire whose makeup was so convincing I found myself yearning for garlic.

"Sheila? I'm Tucker Sinclair. Pookie's daughter."

She looked as if she'd hit a wall trying to make that connection.

"I take after my dad," I explained.

Her face relaxed into a smile. "I knew you didn't get those cheekbones from Pookie. Even with contour she looks like Charlie Brown. What happened to your face?"

"Rug burn."

She smiled again. "I hope it was fun."

Just then the trailer door swung open, and a guy in his twenties, wearing chinos and a Hawaiian shirt, bolted through the opening. He had a baby face and a receding hairline. The incongruity made me think the stork had put him together on the Friday afternoon before a three-day weekend.

"Come on, Sheila," he said. "Enough with the fangs, okay? This isn't DreamWorks. This is real money."

"Don't worry, Danny, she's ready." Sheila put on a pair of glasses to inspect her handiwork. Then she pulled the towel from around the vampire's neck and scooted her out of the makeup chair.

Danny shifted his gaze toward me. His mood darkened. "Who the fuck is this?"

Sheila looked at me. Then she looked at Danny. "She's an extra."

"Shit, she's tall." He rubbed his eyes with the palms of his hands, as if his observation had suddenly made him tired. "Just keep her the fuck away from Derek."

"Sure, honey, you can count on me."

Sheila pulled me into the still-warm seat of the makeup chair as Hawaiian Shirt and the vampire disappeared through the door. She tucked a clean towel into the neck of my sweater and began looking through her makeup case.

"Danny out of Prozac?" I asked.

"Don't let him upset you, honey. He's a putz, but I forgive him because he's under a lot of pressure. Trust me, he loves his job as much as I love mine, and I'd do this for free if love bought kitty litter. Know what I mean? Anyway, I'm glad Pookie sent you over."

"Well, she didn't exactly send me over."

She patted my hand. "Sure, I understand. Gosh, you

have beautiful skin. It's almost a shame to cover it up, but Derek gets pissy when he finds strangers on the set. This'll give us a chance to gab. Besides, I work magic on rug burns."

She studied my face for a moment before starting to apply foundation with a tiny sponge. I winced when she got to the abrasion on my cheek, but didn't complain. Hopefully, she'd keep the makeup toned down. I didn't want some vampire slayer to get confused and try to pound a stake through my heart.

"I had dinner with your mom and Bruce a few nights ago. She's gaga over him. It's nice to see her so happy, don't you think?"

"Um . . . yeah, I guess so," I said. "By the way, Pookie said you just worked with Lola Scott. That must have been interesting."

Sheila shook her head in disgust. "If that girl doesn't take better care of her skin, she's going to look old before she's thirty."

"She must be pretty broken up over Evan Brice's death."

"I think her new boyfriend has done a lot to ease the pain. Jeez, I don't know what she sees in him. The guy looks like he makes a living fencing stereos, but don't tell anyone I said that. I have three kitties who expect me home every night."

"How long has she known him?"

"She met him on the set. He was an extra, just like you."

Sheila had obviously lived too long in fantasyland, but I didn't want to break the mood by reminding her that I was only pretending to be an extra.

"Lola's not the type who can go without a man," she went on. "She just doesn't get it. Sex isn't everything."

"So what's she up to now?"

Sheila had drifted into a Zen-like state of dabbing and brushing and lining, so she sounded distracted when she answered. "Advance promo for her new film."

"Pookie said she'd just wrapped some motorcycle picture."

"Uh-huh. *Born to Ride*. There's a big to-do next week in Hollywood—a charity ride-a-thon, I think. She's also scheduled for a photo shoot at that biker bar at the top of Mulholland. Her people asked me to do makeup, but obviously I'm here, so they got somebody else."

I knew the place she was talking about. It was called Clancy's Cantina. It wasn't exactly a bar, more like a café.

"Lola must really like your work."

Sheila smiled. "Yeah, she's already booked me for the Richard Burnett picture. She knows she has to look good, because this could be her big break. I had to juggle a couple of other jobs, but it worked out okay."

"Does it make any sense to you that her agent would drop her as a client on the brink of a breakout performance under a director like Burnett?"

"Honey, I've worked in this business long enough to know you can't figure anybody out, but I'll tell you one thing: Lola was a bear to work with on that last picture—tense, angry all the time. By the time we wrapped, everybody wanted a break from her. Evan Brice, too, I imagine. He came to visit her on the set a few times. The two of them were always at each other's throats."

"What were they fighting about?"

"Who knows? Maybe the relationship just stopped being fun, or maybe he decided to cool it for the sake of Lola's career. If Richard Burnett had known those two were screwing, he'd have never given her that part. He's the biggest prude in town."

That was interesting news. If Burnett would be upset by an affair between his star and her married agent, how would he react to Lola's porn movie? Burnett certainly created an incentive for both Evan and Lola to keep that video a secret. Again, I wondered why the tape was hidden in Evan's apartment, and from whom.

Before I could say anything more, the trailer door flew open. It was Danny again. His face had turned an unhealthy shade of purple, and the pulse in his temple was throbbing.

"Sheila, get your ass out here—now. Mandy got a caramel stuck on her fang, and the whole fucking denture is lying on the sidewalk. Derek's ranting and we're sitting on our asses, sweating away dollars."

Sheila winked at me. "Sure, honey, be right there."

Danny left, and Sheila quickly threw a few items in a hard cosmetic case. When she was finished, she handed me a mascara wand.

"You'll have to do this yourself," she said.

"When will you be back?"

She shrugged. "I'm not sure, but better not hang around waiting, because, you know, Derek and all."

As she hurried toward the door I said, "Sheila, wait. When is Lola's photo shoot?"

"Some time this week, I think. I didn't pay much attention. Why?"

"It's a long story."

There was a look of uncertainty on her face. "Maybe another time, then. I have to go." Just before she left, she added, "Oh, and thanks for the chat, Tucker. I know you'll learn to love Bruce. It'll mean so much to your mom. And who knows? You could end up with a new daddy."

My jaw muscles tightened. I wondered if my mother had encouraged Sheila to have this girlie-girl talk with me. If so, I hate that kind of behind-the-scenes influence peddling, but at least it explained Sheila's willingness to speak with me.

After Sheila left, I sat in the makeup chair for a few minutes, trying to figure out why Lola Scott, who could have her pick of the litter, would choose a loser for a boyfriend. Maybe, as Sheila had implied, the guy was good in bed and that was enough. Or maybe Lola suffered from repetition compulsion when it came to making bad decisions.

After I'd waded through all the rationalizations, justifications, and speculations for even caring about the answer to that question, the truth came down to this: The one thing I hated worse than being manipulated by my mother was giving up. I had to know the truth. I'd set out to find Lola Scott, and I wasn't going to cave in until I found her, even if all I netted from the effort was a free makeover.

I grabbed a mirror to see what Sheila had done to my face. The good news: My bruise was almost completely camouflaged. The bad news: I looked like Toulouse-Lautrec's date for the Moulin Rouge. Unfortunately, I didn't have time to transform myself back into boring Tucker, so I quickly applied mascara as instructed and removed the towel from around my neck. When I was sure no one was watching, I ran down the steps of the trailer and headed for the car.

At the moment, my only path to Lola Scott was through one of the public relations events Sheila had mentioned. The ride-a-thon was a week away, which was too long to wait. That left only the photo shoot. I considered trying to wheedle the date and time out of Lola's new agent, but even if I'd known who it was, the tactic was iffy at best. On the other hand, somebody at Clancy's might have some information and might be more than delighted to share it with the new and improved Moulin Rouge Tucker.

As I checked for directions in my *Thomas Guide*, the inch-thick L.A. County map book for the directionally impaired, an ominous warning flashed through my head: Good makeup does not a convincing motorcycle mama make. Quickly, I swept my concerns into a back corner of my mind, started the engine, and headed toward Clancy's Cantina.

-14-

forty-five minutes after leaving Sheila's makeup
trailer, I was making my way through the Santa
Monica Mountains on the narrow, winding Mulholland Highway. I put the Boxster through its paces, racing
past sheer cliffs and around blind curves, slowing only to
dodge rock slides that had spilled onto the road.

I hadn't been in this area since high school, when a
friend and I had set out on a mission to find real bikers
after renting a video of *The Wild One.* In the intervening
years, the area had become less boondocks and more
Beverly Hills in the mountains. Old horse ranches and
trailer parks now mingled with luxury homes, and professional landscaping intruded on native pine, sage, and
chaparral. Pretty soon, along with the Extreme Fire Danger and Horse X-ing signs, Caltrans would be posting
signs for another danger: urban sprawl.

A distant hum quickly grew to a roar. I glanced in my
rearview mirror and saw a motorcycle bent to the road,
rounding the corner in defiance of gravity. The driver,
who wore a helmet that looked like a turtle's shell, nodded his appreciation when I slowed the car so he could
safely pass. Moments later, three more bikes came from

behind me and roared up the hill. Clancy's had to be close by.

At the crest of the next rise, the café came into view, along with at least 150 immaculately groomed motorcycles standing handlebar-to-handlebar in the hard-packed dirt parking lot. There were the requisite Harleys, both production and chopped, but also some Suzukis and Ducatis. The riders milling around outside were an eclectic group, from tattooed and pierced outlaw types to computer nerds faking a sick day.

There was no room for my car, so I drove up the road about a quarter mile and parked on the narrow gravel shoulder near a sign that read, "No Stopping Any Time." I walked back toward the café, accompanied by a persistent fly buzzing around my face, obviously intrigued by the mix of aromas from Sheila Mayhew's cosmetics bag.

Clancy's Cantina was a shit-kicking kind of place with distressed-wood siding, a front porch, and a hitching post that looked authentic. A rusty miner's cart was parked near the entrance. Next to it stood a mountain of a guy somewhere in his forties. He wore jeans and a black leather jacket over a T-shirt that sported a picture of a skull on the front. His stringy brown hair was pulled back into a ponytail and harnessed with a leather thong at his massive neck. A scruffy Fu Manchu mustache partially obscured the lower half of his face but not enough to hide pleasantly symmetrical features. That face, coupled with a spare tire around his waist, gave him the look of a former high school football jock gone to seed. The fat roll was still Schwinn-size, but if he didn't switch to lite beer soon, it would be moving into Harley territory before you could say "Jenny Craig." He continued smoking his cigarette, drinking his beer, and watching me without expression as I walked past him on my way to the front door.

The interior of the café featured a small bar, which was separated from the eating area by partition walls and a center hallway. The place looked as if it had been designed by trailer trash with lottery money. Everything that wasn't draped in crimson velvet was smothered with phony Wanted posters and other Western memorabilia from yon years of yore. I half expected Miss Kitty to greet me at the door with an enthusiastic howdy, which would have been a refreshing change from what you heard in most trendy L.A. restaurants: "Hi, I'm your waiter, but what I really want to do is direct." It was an old L.A. joke, but there was still some truth to it.

As it turned out, seating was self-service. The only available booth in the café featured a prime view of a stuffed armadillo in a glass case—an effective enough appetite suppressant that I opted to sit at the bar, which was empty except for three guys drinking together near the back wall. Two were of indeterminate age, but at least forty. The youngest was twenty-something, my height—five-nine or so—and well muscled from years of lifting weights, hopefully not in the yard at San Quentin. He had a mustache and goatee and wore a black leather skullcap over what looked like a shaved head. All of them appeared to be a little rough around the edges. I was willing to bet they all owned weapons and knew how to conceal them. I set my purse on the floor next to the barstool but wrapped the strap around my ankle a couple of times for security. Then I waited.

The bartender was a woman in her late thirties with frosted hair, cut in a shaggy style that should have been mothballed along with Marvin Geyer's muumuus. She had on a pair of tight jeans and a sleeveless denim vest that showed she had taken her *Biceps of Steel* workouts seriously. She was wiping glasses and chatting with the Three Musketeers, but a jukebox playing country and western music was drowning out their words. When she noticed me, she looked annoyed that her high-level meeting had been interrupted. Eventually she sauntered over to take my order: a cup of coffee, which she served in a dented blue metal cup that looked as if it had been bouncing around too long in some drover's saddlebag.

"I haven't been here since high school," I said.

Her expression was deadpan, her tone sarcastic. "And yet, we're still in business. Amazing."

I smiled to let her know I hadn't taken offense. "Anybody ever tell you that you look like Farrah Fawcett?"

She continued wiping water spots off a pilsner glass. "You're shitting me, right?"

I shrugged, ignoring the sarcasm. That comparison ploy usually works as an icebreaker in L.A., but obviously this bartender was in that minuscule percentage of restaurant personnel who weren't pursuing a career in show biz. The bartender already seemed suspicious, so I couldn't just come out and say I was looking for Lola Scott. Before I could think of another approach, she said, "Enjoy the java," and retreated to the end of the bar.

That was a bad sign for Moulin Rouge Tucker. As I sat there sipping bad coffee and trying to come up with a way to win her over, I felt a blast of hot air detonate on the back of my neck. When the odor finally reached my nose, it registered as multiple beers on an empty stomach, and a three-pack-a-day cigarette habit. I swung around to face the source and nearly flattened my nose on Fu Manchu's fat roll.

He placed his empty beer bottle and his forearm on the bar, leaning in close enough for me to hear the rattling wheeze in his chest as he breathed. His proximity was intimidating. I could only hope he wasn't the type who heard voices in his head telling him to rid the world of tall, thin, heavily made-up women with brown hair and a slightly crooked eyetooth.

"Hey, pretty lady. You look like you could use some company."

My mouth opened, and I prepared to set him straight. He seemed to read my mood, because his expression transitioned from self-satisfaction to self-doubt. It was a subtle change, but I took it as a hopeful sign. Since I'd gotten nowhere with the bartender, I decided to stifle my rebuff.

"Why not?" I said.

His body relaxed. He slipped onto the barstool and gestured toward the bartender. "Don't take nothing Mavis says too personal. She's got man troubles, and it makes her bitchy."

I nodded in sympathy. "Don't we all."

"That's kinda hard to believe. Good-lookin lady like you." He paused to study my face. "I don't remember seeing you around here before."

Small talk, I thought. This was good. "It's been a while . . . so, what kind of bike you ridin?"

A broad smile spread across his face. "Shit, the only kind. A Harley. Screamin Eagle Deuce. I'd take you for a ride, but she's in the shop."

"Nothing serious, I hope."

"Nah, just a scratch or two. Laid her down horsing around. My fault, but it happened on the lot, so Universal's paying for it. Guess I lucked out."

"Universal, as in Studios? Are you a stuntman?"

"I wish. Maybe I'd a made some money. As it was, I didn't break even for the two days I took off work."

I thought about asking him what he did for a living, but I was probably better off not knowing.

"What's the name of the film? Maybe I'll go see it."

"Born to Ride."

My jaw tingled. "The new Lola Scott movie?"

"Yep. That's the one. Me and half the regulars in here was extras." A puzzled frown creased his forehead. "The picture's not even out yet. How come you know about it?"

I didn't want to arouse his suspicions, so I lied. "Actually, I'm doing Lola's makeup for a photo shoot here this week. I dropped by to make sure I could find the place."

"No, shit? I'll be here, too. I just hope my bike is ready by then."

Rats! I'd just finessed myself out of a chance to meet Lola Scott. There was no way I could show up now and risk being exposed as a fraud.

"So, what time is your call?" I said.

"Seven, but shit, with Friday traffic, I gotta roll out of the sack at four just to make it here on time."

"It's none of my business, but are you Lola's boyfriend?"

He laughed. "Hell, no. That's Jakey. Poor bastard. Lola's a fine-looking woman, but she's even bitchier than Mavis. When Lola says jump, Jakey says how high—or else. I saw her thumping on him out front yesterday. Mavis had to break it up."

"What set her off?"

"Shit, man, I don't know. What sets any woman off?"

"You couldn't tell what they were arguing about?"

He lowered his voice. I leaned in closer. "Jakey was probably just screwing up again. Whatever he did, Lola didn't like it."

"Lola runs the show, huh? Maybe Jakey's a little starstruck."

"Nah, that ain't it."

"Hey, Bo, you just warming that chair, or you drinking beer?"

It was Mavis. I'd been so intent on listening to Bo dish dirt on Lola and Jakey, I'd almost forgotten about her. In the interim, a dark cloud of discontent had rolled onto her face.

"Sure, Mavis," Bo said. "Set me up again, and while you're at it, bring a Corona for Lola's makeup gal here."

The atmosphere grew tense as the three guys at the end of the bar turned in unison and stared at me.

"You talking shit again, Bo?" she said.

"Nah, Mavis." He sounded hurt, as though he'd gotten the wrong end of the stick again. "Just keepin' a pretty lady company, that's all."

Mavis crossed her arms tightly across her chest and turned toward me. "What's your game, girlfriend?"

Apparently, I waited too long to answer, because the next thing I heard was the sound of wood scraping against wood as the youngest of her drinking buddies pushed back his barstool and stood. Bo's body stiffened. The acrid odor of sweat and fear now mingled with the smell of beer and cigarettes.

Muscle Boy strolled over and sat on the barstool to my left, sandwiching me between him and Bo. He wagged his index finger at me and said, "Oh, what a tangled web we weave, when first we practice to deceive." On the surface his tone was casual, but underneath there was an undercurrent of menace.

I tried to keep things light. "You the in-house poet?"

He smiled. It made me cringe. Then he grabbed my

hair at the crown and pulled. I yelped and reached up to pry his hand away.

"Let go, shithead," I said. "That hurts."

Somewhere behind me furniture toppled. I heard Bo say, "Come on, man. Don't do that."

Muscle Boy ignored him. He jerked my hair again. It hurt, but this time I didn't cry out. "This is how it is," he said. "We cleared everybody who's coming here on Friday, including the makeup gal, and you're not her. So what are you up to?"

Here's what I was up to: the maximum reading on my panic meter.

"That's enough." It was Mavis. She was still holding the pilsner glass but looked as if she was getting ready to smash it on the bar and grind the shards into somebody's face, maybe even mine. "I think she gets the point."

The poet looked annoyed with the interruption. It took a second and louder "I *said,* I think she gets the point" from Mavis to convince him that the fun was over. He gave my hair one last yank before letting go. Several people from the café had left their tables and were standing around like spectators at a train wreck. Bo stood near an overturned barstool a few feet away, flanked by Mavis's two other bar buddies. They weren't touching him, but the tension was palpable. Bo seemed big enough to take out both of them with one punch, but his body remained rigid with indecision.

After what seemed like an eternity, Mavis said, "Sit down, Bo. I'll buy you a beer."

My breath didn't return to normal until Bo finally righted the overturned barstool, and the three men went back to their drinks. Mavis gave me a look that said, get out while you still can. *That* I understood, but if she thought I got the "point," she was wrong. I had no idea what had just happened, or why. All I knew was, my lungs felt compressed by the weight of many bad decisions.

I reached down to get my purse. That's when I noticed Bo's boots. They were black, square-toed jobbies with a buckled strap and a silver medallion riveted to the leather. They looked like the pair worn by the man who'd attacked me in Evan's apartment. My heart pounded so hard in my head that I could barely hear.

Bo ignored the draw Mavis set at his place on the bar. Instead, he walked around the partition wall and headed toward what had to be the restrooms. I made a pretense of leaving, but at the last minute I ducked around the wall and followed him. I found him standing in front of a vending machine in the hallway, trying to buy a pack of cigarettes. The machine apparently wasn't cooperating, because he gave it a hard kick, frustrated that it kept rejecting his torn dollar bill.

"Nice boots," I said.

His voice was low and dull. "You better split, pretty lady, before you get us both in real trouble."

"Where did you get them?"

He hesitated and then glanced down the hall to make sure Mavis and the boys weren't anywhere near. "Why do you want to know?"

"Maybe I'm just trying to have a conversation." When he didn't respond, I went on. "Look, Bo, they're just boots. What's the big deal?"

He made several more unsuccessful attempts to feed the dollar bill into the machine. Finally he sighed as if he'd decided to settle a debt.

"They're from the movie. We was supposed to be part

of an outlaw motorcycle gang. Jakey got Lola to pull some strings, and they let us keep the boots."

"Does Jakey have a pair, too?"

"Hell, we all got a pair."

"Why is Mavis so prickly about Lola Scott?"

He looked around again, nervous. "I don't know. Maybe because Jakey's her ex."

"And she's upset with Lola Scott because Lola stole her husband?"

"Shit. You don't know nothing. Nobody steals from Mavis unless she wants it that way. If anything, she's just trying to protect Jakey."

Now *I* was frustrated. "Protect him from what?"

"Do me a favor. Get the hell out of here before somebody rearranges that pretty little face of yours." His words were more warning than threat.

When I turned to leave, he was still hunched over the cigarette machine. He wouldn't look at me, but he mumbled something I couldn't quite make out.

I paused for a moment. "You say something?"

"I'm on parole," he said a little louder, "or I would a helped you."

He jammed the ratty dollar bill into the machine again, but it came back out. That's when I reached into my purse and pulled out a newer bill. I didn't approve of his smoking, but I couldn't stand to see him fail one more time.

I decided to exit from Clancy's before Muscle Boy came barreling around the corner on his way to take a whiz and found Bo and me talking. As I stepped onto the porch outside, I heard what sounded like a blastoff at Cape Kennedy. My startled shriek was obscured by the sound of dozens of motorcycles roaring to life. Almost immediately, they began peeling away one by one like flies off road kill. I sprinted back to my car and locked the door, looking over my shoulder to make sure no one had followed me.

I glanced across the street at a vacant lot next to the café. Above, a hawk circled and then dived. I diverted my gaze because I didn't want to see some bloody little field mouse that just moments before had been thinking he had a future in this town.

For the second time in as many days, I'd escaped a predator. I hoped the mouse had fared as well. Unfortunately, neither of us could survive on luck alone. I wasn't sure what that meant for the mouse, but for me it meant that all the way from Las Virgines to the coast highway, I kept checking my rearview mirror to make sure I wasn't being followed.

-15-

It was dark by the time I got home. As expected, Eugene's car was gone from the driveway, but surprisingly, so was Pookie's. That troubled me. My mother had never been one to provide a detailed itinerary of her movements, but technically I hadn't seen her for twenty-four hours. It was unusual for her to disappear for that long without telling me where she was going. Bruce didn't own a car, so I assumed they'd left together.

The house seemed eerily quiet as I searched unsuccessfully for any notes from her. I told myself that she and Bruce could have left before I got up this morning, and come home and left again in the time I'd been away. That calmed me enough to go next door to retrieve Muldoon. The little guy was technically my mother's responsibility, but he and I had grown closer during the couple of months my mother and Bruce had been traveling. I worried about him, so at times like these I appreciated Mrs. Domanski's free pup-sitting services.

By all appearances, Mrs. D. was already well into her third martini when she answered my knock. Thanks to her largess, Muldoon now had a new tug toy that looked like a floppy purple ponytail tied in the middle. Her words were a little slurred, but I gathered that she'd had the toy delivered from the market with her weekly gin supply. I thanked her and headed home with the pup in tow.

Once inside the house, I walked into my office. It was immaculate. Eugene had labeled all the muumuu folders and filed them in my desk drawer. He'd also emptied my wastepaper basket and dusted the desktop. I was probably hallucinating, but the windows looked cleaner, too.

Deegan was due at six. That was dinnertime. I wondered if I was expected to feed him. I'm not much of a cook; the kitchen was Eric's domain when we were together. After we split, I'd bought a lot of cookbooks and marked numerous interesting-looking recipes with Post-it notes. Despite my good intentions, none of the pages had any greasy butter stains on them, just those Post-it notes wagging like mocking little tongues from dozens of untried recipes for turkey wing ragout and trout meunière.

The fact was, I wasn't a big eater either, which meant there wasn't much food in my refrigerator. To remedy that, Muldoon and I made a quick trip to the Trancas Market for some Brie and a box of heart-shaped crackers. By the time I'd finished shopping, my cart also included a salmon fillet big enough for two, and enough romaine, Kalamata olives, and pecorino cheese to make a salad. As an afterthought, I threw a bottle of champagne into the cart, because it's about the only alcohol I like to drink.

At 6:15 the doorbell rang. Deegan stood under the light on the deck, in a dark blue business suit. The top button of his cream-colored shirt was undone, and a jazzy blue and gray tie hung loose and casual around his neck. He smelled good, too, like clean sheets hanging on an outdoor clothesline. In his hand was a white paper bag.

When he saw me, he frowned. "What the hell happened to your face?"

So much had happened since morning that I'd almost forgotten that Sheila had given me the Moulin Rouge makeover.

"Get a life," I said. "It's makeup. What's in the bag?"

He guided me into the house and under a light in the kitchen to get a better look. "It's takeout," he said, setting the bag on the counter. "As I recall, you're not exactly Julia Child. And I'm not talking about the makeup. I'm talking about what it's trying to cover up. Who's been pounding on you?"

"I fell." He wasn't buying that even as a joke, so I added, "Want some champagne?"

He crossed his arms over his chest and waited, as if he were trying to figure out what I was up to. "If that's what it takes to get the story."

Muldoon looked as if he might shred Deegan's pant leg, pawing for attention. The two of them hadn't seen each other in a while, but they'd been pals once, and the leg-lifter never forgot a scent. When Deegan finally squatted down to pay homage, Muldoon rolled on his back and allowed his stomach to be patted.

I popped the cork on the champagne and put the cheese and crackers on a Lucite platter, which had been a wedding gift from my grandma and grandpa Felder. It was one of the few household items I'd kept after my marriage ended. The crackers looked a little forlorn sliding around on the oversized tray. Eric would have said there wasn't enough color, but I doubted Deegan would notice.

I didn't have a dedicated cheese knife, so I pushed aside a Martha Stewart hors d'oeuvres kit with remnants of the white Styrofoam packing material still clinging to the metal container and pulled out a set of decorative spreading knives with ceramic fruit basket handles. I stuck one in the middle of the cheese. Then I peeked inside Deegan's white takeout bag and found some kind of dreamy chicken dish and an Italian chopped salad. It definitely looked better than grocery-store fish frying in a peeling Teflon skillet, so I put the salad in the refrigerator to cool, the chicken in the oven to stay warm, and the salmon in the freezer to be forgotten over time.

Deegan had already removed his jacket and laid it neatly over the arm of my living room chair. He'd only been to my house once before, so if he noticed Bruce's feng shui modifications, he didn't comment on them. His eyes were closed, and his head was resting on the back of the couch. He looked tired. Muldoon was lying next to him with his head on Deegan's thigh. The pup's teeth were still clamped over the tug from Mrs. Domanski, and a pool of slobber was forming on Deegan's trouser leg.

When I set the cheese tray on the coffee table, Deegan opened his eyes. By the time I'd made a second trip to get the champagne bucket and glasses, he was at full attention and inspecting the spreader. He looked at me and grinned.

"Don't even think about giving me a bad time," I warned.

He held up his arms in a sign of surrender. "Did I say anything?"

I filled two glasses with champagne and handed him one. By rote I said a quick "Cheers."

Before the glass reached my lips, Deegan said, "Whoa! You call that a toast? You need to practice before the wedding so your ex doesn't think you're still pining away for him."

I wasn't in the mood to be teased. "I don't need any practice."

He shrugged. "I got the impression you want him to think you've moved on. Isn't that the reason you asked me to be your date?"

I tried for a shocked and dismayed tone in my voice. "You think I'm using you?"

His eyes crinkled in amusement. "Sure you are, but I wouldn't get in the car if I didn't think I'd enjoy the ride."

Deegan was right. In a way, I *was* using him, but there were other reasons why I'd invited him. The truth was, I liked him. He could be funny and warm. He was also old-fashioned and bossy, which was why nothing had jelled between us other than this off-again, on-again friendship. I might have taken his teasing come-ons more seriously, except that good-looking guys are never attracted to me. Mostly, I'm a magnet for octogenarians playing chess in the park, or teenage boys bagging groceries at Vons. When a guy like Deegan gives me that my-place-or-yours look, I always think he's hitting on the person who's standing behind me.

"Okay," I said, "so show me your version of a good toast."

He raised his glass and got an Oscar-caliber seductive look in his eyes. "To us."

I knew he was just joking, which produced an unexpected twinge of regret. Nevertheless, I delivered my response in a tone that was as dry as the Korbel. "Knock it off, Deegan. I'm not in the mood."

He laughed. "Which is why you didn't hear me say 'Happy anniversary, baby.'"

I raised my glass, smiling in spite of myself. "Skoal."

"So, where's your mom? I was hoping to meet her."

I told him I hadn't seen Pookie since she and Bruce argued the night before, and that I was worried.

All he said was, "It's only six-thirty, Stretch. They're probably at a motel making up. Why don't you give it a few more hours?"

"It's just not like her."

"Maybe not, but people do strange things when they're in love."

He paused for a moment, no doubt trying to interpret the look on my face. Worried? Annoyed? He must have picked up on my distress, because his expression softened. He patted the cushion next to him and said, "Come here."

It sounded like something he'd say to the dog, so I said, "I can hear the lecture from here."

A muscle in his jaw twitched. "Fine. Then stop stalling, and tell me what happened to your face."

I didn't want to wrinkle his jacket, so I moved it from the chair to my grandma's steamer trunk before sitting down. "It's a long story."

He pointed to Muldoon and the slobbery tug resting on his thigh. "Do I look like I have other plans for the evening?"

"No, but you may change your mind when you hear what I have to say. Deegan, we need to talk about Evan Brice's homicide investigation."

He didn't look happy about that. "You know it's not my case, and even if it was, I couldn't tell you anything."

"Just hear me out. Okay?"

He listened attentively as I explained about helping Cissy close the apartment, interrupting only to express his suspicions about her motives. He wanted to know why she'd asked me to lend a hand, instead of a family member or her insurance company. Of course, I'd wondered about that, too. I'd thought Jerome Fielding was the logical person for the job, until I saw him interact with Cissy. There was underlying tension between those two. In the end, their rapport, good or bad, didn't matter. I was convinced that the reason Cissy had asked for my help was because she wanted to reconnect me with her mother. My theory didn't rock Deegan's world.

"Look," I said, "I think Moses Green wants to nail Cissy Brice for the murder, because the wife is always the easy target. But he's on the wrong track. Cissy swears she's never even been to the Venice apartment. Besides, how could she stab Evan to death and not even break a fingernail? Think about it."

"I hate to tell you, Stretch, but women kill their husbands all the time."

Generalizing was getting me nowhere. I had to tell Deegan about the freight train attacking me, or I'd lose his interest. When I did, the look on his face reminded me of the presidents on Mount Rushmore: silent and stony. For the next few minutes, he asked me lots of questions about the guy's height, weight, distinguishing marks or tattoos, and about the clothing he had on, including those boots. He also asked me to tell him anything I could remember about the porn video and the missing mail. This was more like it. I found myself wishing Deegan were in charge of Evan's homicide investigation.

By the time I finished describing Bo, the crowd at Clancy's Cantina, and that the distinctive boots my attacker wore could be traced directly back to Lola Scott and her boyfriend, Deegan was rubbing his temples as if he were trying to contain a monster headache. Even Muldoon sensed the tension and retreated to the opposite end of the couch.

"I can't prove it was Jakey who stole Evan's mail and Lola Scott's porn video," I said, "but who else could it be?"

Deegan paused for a moment, as if considering his next statement. "Did you ever consider that Cissy Brice might be lying to you?"

"She may be lying but not about killing Evan. I think she's innocent. If you have proof to the contrary, tell me. I can keep a secret."

I studied his face but got nothing from it. He'd make a good poker player. "All I can tell you is what's been officially released to the public."

"Okay, I can work with that."

According to Deegan, on the night Evan died, he attended an open-mike poetry reading at Poet's Corner, the same coffeehouse in West Hollywood I'd learned about from Claire Jerrard. He ate chicken and a salad at about seven p.m. and left the café at around eight. The coroner estimated the time of death sometime between midnight and three a.m. I waited for Deegan to mention Evan's trip to the market that night, but he didn't bring it up. Obviously the police were holding back some facts, because according to Moses Green, Evan was alive and shopping for champagne at one a.m. That narrowed the time of his death to between one and three a.m.

Deegan paused for a moment, watching me intently. "That poem Brice wrote to you. It was pretty steamy. The guy obviously had a thing for you. Was it a two-way street?"

I bristled. "It was until he dumped me for my best friend."

"Cissy Brice?"

"The one and only."

Deegan didn't speak for what seemed like a long time.

When he did, his voice was soft. "Your so-called friend did you a favor. From what I've learned about Evan Brice, you'd have thrown your life away trying to save him."

Maybe he was right, but I didn't feel all that lucky right now.

"She didn't do it, Deegan. You couldn't possibly understand, but I know she'd never take Dara's father away from her."

"I don't get you, Stretch. The woman steals your man, and you still try to help her. Why?"

"It's complicated."

"Try me. You may be surprised just how much I understand."

I paused, debating the wisdom of telling him more, but eventually I did.

"Evan called me the night he died. I didn't pick up the phone. If I had, maybe I could have saved him. That one decision may have left Dara fatherless."

"You talk like everything that's happened to the whole Brice family is your fault."

My chest felt tight. "In a way, it is."

He paused for a moment, watching me. "Come on, Stretch. You look like you could use some fresh air. Let's go for a walk."

Muldoon heard the word "walk" and began barking so enthusiastically, he was nearly levitating. It was chilly outside, so I loaned Deegan one of Bruce's down jackets. He kicked off his shoes and socks and rolled up his trouser legs. The three of us headed to the beach, carrying the sack of food, the champagne, and an old blanket. A few yards away from the house, we spread the blanket on the sand, and with Muldoon huddled between us, we ate chopped salad and what turned out to be chicken tetrazzini.

I don't recall exactly what we talked about at first— movies we'd seen or books we'd read. All I know is, at some point I told him about Frank Jerrard's death. How he'd called me the day he died, just as Evan had. Frank had insisted I write down several recipes, the ones he made for Claire every Sunday, which was his night to cook. At the time, I thought it was weird. I was impatient to get him off the telephone. As it turned out, I should have listened more carefully to the tension in his voice. Shortly after he replaced the receiver, Frank Jerrard stacked his neatly folded clothes on the dresser. He grabbed a pillow from the bed to muffle the sound, stepped into the shower, and put a bullet through his head.

Deegan listened to my story without comment. I was grateful he didn't put his arms around me and say, "I'm so sorry. Let me give you a big hug." He must have sensed that trying to take the edge off my guilt would have been a mistake. I thought more of him for knowing that.

"I keep thinking those recipes were his way out," I said. "Maybe he hoped I'd tell him that the world couldn't survive without his stuffed pork chops, and he'd have a reason to live. Instead, I told him I had to study for a chemistry exam. Because of me, Claire doesn't have a husband, and Cissy doesn't have a father."

"Don't tell me they blamed you for his death."

"No. They didn't. I blamed myself. The Jerrards were like my second family. Frank was the father I never had. I felt so guilty, I didn't even tell Claire about his call. I still have his recipes in an old cigar box in the closet."

"You were just a kid, Stretch. Even if it happened now, how could you possibly know what was on his mind?"

"Eighteen's no kid, and I wasn't some sheltered West-side ingenue, either. I'd seen things in my lifetime. Besides, the warning signs were in neon. Maybe if I hadn't been so caught up in worrying about college and getting a summer job, I would have noticed."

It's amazing how sharply focused hindsight had become after twelve years of adjusting the lens of my memory. I knew that Frank Jerrard had invested heavily in a gas-and-oil limited partnership that was being challenged by the IRS as an illegal tax shelter. There were lawsuits, which had generated hefty attorney's and accountant's fees. The Jerrards stood to lose big-time if things didn't go their way. Living on the brink of financial ruin was a situation my mother and I knew all too well. We'd always managed to land butter side up. I had assumed that Frank Jerrard would, too, because he was strong and smart and deserving. I'd been wrong.

His slide into depression had begun with cocktail hours that lasted through four martinis instead of one. Eventually, he had stopped smiling, working, and trimming the hedge. The hedge. That's when I should have known something was terribly wrong.

Deegan and I stared at the water, taking turns petting Muldoon. Deegan refused a second glass of champagne because he was driving. That didn't stop me from having a refill and then another. It wasn't a particularly good idea, because I wasn't used to drinking. After the third glass, I was feeling no pain, or almost none. Deegan suggested we go back to the house. My response came out sounding something like "sheowsnlikeaplaaan."

Deegan washed the dishes while I put away the cracker tray and the fruit basket spreaders. At about nine-thirty I walked him to the door. He paused at the threshold, watching me. His jacket was slung casually over his shoulder. I dread the end of evenings when you've had too much to drink and no opportunity to check for lettuce leaves stuck between your teeth, when a man is standing in the light of your doorway, and you have no idea what might happen next. I decided to defuse the situation.

"Can't you convince Green to be more open-minded about Cissy Brice?"

"Moses is a good cop. He doesn't need counseling from me." He tenderly brushed his fingers over the bruise on my cheek. "You know, Stretch, punching out bad guys in biker bars is a dangerous game. Do yourself a favor and me, too. Stay out of it. I'd hate to miss our wedding date because something bad happened to you."

He turned and started down the steps.

"Who was the woman in the car with you yesterday?"

He looked back, puzzled. Then a lopsided smile appeared on his face. "Ah, you mean Candy."

"Is that a name or an endorsement?"

"A name."

"For now."

"That's right, Stretch. For now."

"She your new partner?"

"Nope." He turned and headed for his car.

After Deegan was gone, I felt unsettled. I'd given him intimate details about my life, but as usual, he hadn't told me squat about his. Worse yet, the only information he'd shared about Evan Brice's homicide investigation was already part of the public record. At least I knew Evan had eaten at Poet's Corner the night he died. If nothing else, the information would help me piece together the last hours of his life.

Deegan had warned me to stay out of the investigation, as I knew he would. What I'd failed to make him understand was that I couldn't turn my back on Cissy Brice. Despite his admonition, I was going to push ahead until I got somebody to listen to reason.

-16-

bout twenty minutes after Deegan left, the telephone rang. It was Pookie.

"Where in the hell are you?" I said.

"In Vegas."

"And that would be because . . ."

There was a long pause, followed by a girlie-girl squeal. "Bruce and I got married."

My throat felt dry. All I could manage in response to her announcement was a breathy, "H-h-a-h-h-h."

"It was so amazing, Tucker. Wednesday night Bruce and I had this huge fight. We went for a ride to cool off. Before we knew it, we were in Sin City. So we thought, what the heck, let's take in a couple of shows and play the machines. We stayed up all night, got polluted, and then we got naked—"

"Whoa, Pook! Too much information. I get the picture."

She laughed. "I just wanted to let you know. We'll be home tomorrow."

I didn't say anything for a moment, because I was thinking, and because Pookie was babbling on about winning a sixty-five-dollar jackpot while playing the slots. It's not that I felt slighted because my mother didn't invite me to her wedding. In fact, I was relieved that I hadn't been there. Watching Bruce become my stepfather wasn't on my all-time great things-to-do list. On the other hand, I wanted to be objective, so I floated the theory that I was jealous Pookie had found someone to love, while I was still sharing my pillow with a dog. Except that I knew it wasn't true. I loved my mother. I wanted her to be happy, but sometimes I also wanted her to be an adult. This was one of those times. I waited for a lull in her monologue.

"You know, Pookie, I don't think it's a good idea for you and Bruce to live here anymore. You're big kids now. It's time you two got a place of your own."

"We're looking, sweetie."

"Not hard enough."

"I know it's a little crowded, Tucker, but it won't be much longer—really. Bruce and I want to find just the right place. That's not as easy as you think. Mrs. Gwee is working at it, but she has other clients—"

I interrupted. "Why don't you send Bruce to live with Mrs. Gwee for a week or two? That should fire up her work ethic."

There was silence, followed by a sigh. "I'm sorry Bruce annoys you, Tucker. I hope in time—"

"Pookie, can't you see you're making a terrible mistake? He's not right for you. You could do better."

There it was. Out in the open. Maybe it was blunt, but if anybody other than Tucker B. Sinclair needed to keep her eyes wide open about men, it was Mary Jo Felder Sinclair, aka Pookie Kravitz. I figured my mother needed a wake-up call. I was just doing the dialing.

There was a lengthy pause. "I'm sorry you think I'm such a failure, Tucker. I love you." She hung up before I could respond.

THE FOLLOWING MORNING I woke up with a well-deserved champagne headache. While searching through my purse for aspirin, I found the key chain I'd taken from Evan's apartment. More of the beads had slipped off, which made the flower look slightly bedraggled, as though petals were missing. I knotted the loose threads together to hold the remaining beads in place, imagining Dara's delicate hands laboring over the design with the help of her teacher. I attached the key chain to my own as a reminder to give it to Cissy.

I dumped the loose beads in the garbage, on top of what remained of the white tetrazzini sauce from last night's dinner. The specks of red and green looked like those tiny candies you sprinkle on desserts. They reminded me of when I was in first grade and Pookie brought cupcakes to school to celebrate my birthday. It must have been during one of our grimmer financial periods, because she'd thinned out the white frosting to make it stretch and used sprinkles left over from some long-forgotten Christmas. Not only did the cupcakes taste awful, they looked awful, too. I still remember how humiliated I felt when my classmate Ronnie Horn told everybody that the frosting looked like bird shit. Hopefully, at this very moment the IRS was auditing his tax returns.

Predictably, Eugene called right at nine. He was still concerned about my safety, but it hadn't blunted his enthusiasm for the Hula Bitch line of products for Mr. Geyer's mail order catalog. I told him I'd pitch the idea as soon as an opportunity presented itself. When I broke the news that I didn't have any more work for him to do, he seemed disappointed but not breathless.

"How's Liza?" I said.

"Better. Thanks for asking."

"Is she well enough for Palm Springs yet?"

"I suppose, but we can't go now. I'm not going to desert you, not with a homicidal maniac on the loose. Plus, there's the focus group to worry about. I'd never leave you in the lurch like that."

" 'Homicidal maniac' is a bit extreme. The freight train was more like a burglar. And as far as the focus group is concerned, I'm pretty organized, thanks to you. I think you should go to the desert. It'll be good for you. Liza, too. All that hot, dry air will do wonders for her respiratory infection. Look, if I have a problem, I'll call the police. I promise. What do you think?"

"Here's what I think: We should all go to Palm Springs. You could stay in my friends' spare room. I'll sleep on the couch."

"I can't leave town right now, Eugene. Maybe when business picks up. But look on the bright side. Palm Springs is a great place to do resort-wear research. You could scope out Mr. Geyer's muumuu competition."

I waited through a long pause.

"Promise you'll call the police at the first sign of trouble?" he said.

"Yup."

There was another pause.

"You know I can tell when you're not being sincere. I can hear it in your voice."

"Your bullshit meter is top-notch, Eugene. Haven't I always told you that?"

It took several more minutes of gentle persuasion before he finally said, "I suppose a couple of days away from the smog couldn't hurt."

It wasn't until after we hung up that I realized he

hadn't mentioned knitting or carpal tunnel syndrome once during our conversation.

For the next few hours I worked on the focus group, tweaking the wording of my opening remarks and jotting down a few notes for an e-mail, which I intended to send to Mr. Geyer on Monday morning. By the afternoon, my mind felt dull. I decided to take a break and drive into Santa Monica to look for a dress for Eric's wedding. Muldoon looked eager when he saw me putting on my jacket.

"You can't go," I said. "You have to stay and guard the house."

That didn't meet with his approval. He dropped his tail and headed for his favorite hiding spot under my bed. Muldoon's funk made me feel guilty—not a state I liked to be in. Under pressure, I filled a small bowl with some leftover popcorn and slid it under the bed.

"If you tell Pookie I gave you this, it's over between us."

The sound of enthusiastic crunching assuaged my guilt long enough to get me to my car.

· · · ·

SANTA MONICA PLACE is a shopping mall in the downtown area that is anchored by two big department stores: Macy's on one end and Robinsons-May on the other. I walked each of the three levels, trying on outfits in every shop that carried formal wear, until I found a dress I liked. It was a little more orange than anything I had in my closet, but the style accentuated the few curves I had. I just hoped the message it conveyed to Eric and his bride was "hot babe moving on with her life" and not "Caltrans road crew flagging traffic."

With that task out of the way, I headed to the Third Street Promenade, a pedestrians-only boulevard peppered with trendy shops and outdoor cafés. I dawdled over a mochaccino at Starbucks, even though I knew that drinking it so late in the day would keep me awake. But it was Friday night, and I had no one to answer to but Muldoon.

It was after seven o'clock by the time I arrived home, juiced up by caffeine and consumed with buyer's remorse for buying a dress that made me look like an orange Popsicle. As I walked in the door, the telephone was ringing. It was Venus.

"Where have you been?" she said. "I called earlier, but nobody answered."

"I already have one cranky mom, Venus. I don't need another."

"Listen up. Turn on the TV—channel six. There's something you gotta see. And use the remote, because you need to be sittin down for this."

The tension in her voice was contagious. "Shit! Did the police arrest Cissy?"

"Turn on the tube, girl, before I lose my patience."

I carried the telephone into the living room and flipped on channel six as directed. The tabloid show *Celebrity Heat* appeared on the screen. The program was in the final minutes of a segment about dogs on diets.

"What's the deal?" I said defensively. "You think Muldoon is *fat*?"

Venus didn't have time to answer, because the chunky-pups segment ended, and a clip of me arriving at Cissy Brice's house appeared on the screen. The image was accompanied by a voiceover: "Explosive new details uncovered in the murder investigation of Hollywood talent agent Evan Brice. Who is the mystery woman in his life? Her identity revealed after the break."

My heart was pounding as I sank into the couch. I remembered the *Celebrity Heat* van parked outside Cissy's house the day I was there, and Darcy Daniels asking me a question, which I hadn't even answered. I didn't have any idea why the show was focusing on me. It must be a slow news day.

"They've been playing that teaser ever since I turned on the TV," Venus said. "What's going on?"

"I have no idea."

Venus and I stayed on the line through a poignant interview with the East L.A. parents of a young man killed in a drive-by shooting . . . through another commercial break . . . and one more teaser for the mystery woman segment. Each delay hiked my blood pressure. Finally, the program's host appeared on camera. He was a fresh-faced black guy in his late twenties with skin that looked as if it had been polished with Pledge.

"*Celebrity Heat*'s investigative reporter, Darcy Daniels, has recently uncovered the identity of a woman seen arriving at the home of Hollywood agent Evan Brice just a day after he was found slain in a gang-infested Venice neighborhood."

"Uh-oh," Venus said. "I don't feel good about this."

The camera cut to Darcy, standing outside the gate to Cissy Brice's house. She had a microphone in her hand and an *ultra*serious look on her face, as if she were a hard-nosed investigative reporter prowling the war-torn caves of Afghanistan instead of loitering in an upscale neighborhood in Benedict Canyon.

Even in her official *Celebrity Heat* windbreaker, Darcy didn't look hardened by anything more serious than the minimum required balance in her checking account. Granted, it was difficult to look like a seasoned journalist when you had lips so glossy and puffed up by silicone that they looked like two blimps flying in formation. I noticed that those lips were also tempting targets for the wind, which was whipping her mane around, causing wisps of hair to catch in the sticky gloss. She brushed away the hair sandwich and leaned conspiratorially toward the camera. Clearly the gesture was meant to seduce the audience into thinking she was entrusting them with some sensational secret. I waited impatiently to hear what it was.

"*Celebrity Heat* was first to break the story about the gruesome murder of successful Hollywood agent Evan Brice. Now in a stunning new development in the investigation, we have uncovered the name of the mystery woman seen entering the victim's house shortly after he was found bludgeoned to death . . ."

"Bludgeoned?" Venus said. "I thought you said he was stabbed."

"S-h-h-h! I can't hear."

"She is businesswoman Tucker Sinclair, who was involved in another recent murder. Now, only four short months later, someone else close to this woman has met with violent death." Darcy turned away from the camera and dramatically pointed toward the entrance to Evan's driveway. "The man who once lived behind these gates . . ."

"Whoa!" Venus said. "Check out the camera angle. Makes Darcy's ass look like a double-wide."

"Venus!"

"Okay, okay."

Darcy went on. "Sinclair and Brice were once lovers. Our sources tell us the couple had planned to marry, but Brice, a notorious womanizer, left her at the altar for his current wife, who is also a suspect in his tragic death. So why are the wife and the other woman meeting just hours after . . ."

While Darcy Daniels blathered away, they replayed my arrival at Cissy's house over and over: The Boxster drives up the road; I lean out to speak with the rent-a-cop; the gate opens; I drive through the gate. In reality, the whole episode must have taken all of thirty seconds, but the way they spliced the tape together, it looked as if they had documented a road trip across the Australian outback.

Unfortunately, Darcy had more to say. "As we previously reported, Tucker Sinclair was linked to another grisly murder last November. Now she's back in the news, threatening to send the Brice investigation into a tailspin. With the police no closer to an arrest, we turn our focus to the spurned lover. What is the story she has yet to tell? Stay tuned for exclusive coverage in the days ahead."

Spurned lover? Give me a break! Darcy Daniels's breaking news was nothing but lies and innuendo. How long had they been playing this crap? I felt not only angry but also embarrassed, violated, and more than somewhat frightened because not only would my friends and family learn about this, but clients would, too, not to mention the police.

"What are you gonna do?" Venus said.

"I don't know."

"Maybe you should call that lawyer of yours. Tell him he needs to scare the shit out of these people."

"Shelly has his hands full fighting off my aunt Sylvia. Besides, I can't afford to give him any more billable hours. I'm already supporting two of his ex-wives. I'll just contact the station myself. Tell them to back off."

Venus let out a hoot of fake laughter. "Honey, *Celebrity Heat* is sacrificing your reputation to sell ass wipe. You think they're gonna stop just because you say 'pretty please'?"

"Maybe not, but it's worth a try."

After we hung up, I let my anger carry me away to the far reaches of my memory. Who could have fed Darcy Daniels all that baloney? I ran through a list of suspects, including Cissy and Claire. After careful elimination, there was only one name that remained: Marta Cruz, the reporter from the *Valley News Now* who had come to my door asking questions about my relationship with Evan. Maybe providing false information to *Celebrity Heat* was her idea of career development. I'd sensed from the get-go that Cruz had come to the house with a hidden agenda. I didn't know what her game was, but maybe Darcy Daniels did.

I looked up the number for *Celebrity Heat* on a list of TV show contacts Pookie kept by the telephone. I dialed, and following a brief runaround, I was connected to one of the show's producers, an aggressive kid named Jason-something who probably hadn't even been born when everybody in the world was wondering who killed J. R. I told him Darcy had gotten it all wrong in her report. I'd been at the Brice home at the request of the family—okay, so it was a minor lie—and I wanted a retraction of their salacious story.

Jason interrupted me rudely. "Our information came from a reliable source."

"Which one? *Yellow Journalism for Dummies*? Did you actually pay somebody for those lies or did you make them up yourself?"

"We don't pay for information," he said. "Look, if you want to set the record straight, I have a proposition for you. Sit down with Darcy Daniels for an exclusive interview. You pick the place. Sound fair?"

"Not only does that *not* sound fair, Jason, it sounds like you want a lawsuit on your hands for defamation and slander."

"Whatever. Call if you change your mind."

Before I could ask about Marta Cruz, the line went dead. Venus was probably right. Maybe it *was* time to call my lawyer, even if it meant dipping deeper into my dwindling savings. Before I made any rash decisions, I decided to wait until I no longer felt like throwing something at the TV set. I didn't want Muldoon to freak out. He hated loud noises.

Then I thought . . . *wait a minute . . . where's Muldoon?* True, he didn't always come to the door to greet me, but he generally wandered out from wherever he'd been napping long before this.

I called his name. No Muldoon. I searched every room in the house and checked all the doors and windows. Nothing had been disturbed. I ran next door to Mrs. Domanski's to see if somehow I'd spaced out and forgotten that I'd left him there. No dice. I started to panic. I ran up and down the beach, calling his name. I knocked on doors, searched along the highway. I called the local pound, left messages every place and with everyone I could think of. I couldn't find him anywhere. As much as I hated to admit it, there appeared to be only one explanation for Muldoon's disappearance: I'd been so preoccupied with my own problems that I hadn't seen him slip past me when I opened the door to leave for the mall.

For most of that night I sat on the couch in front of the TV, because silence brought only unbearable images of Muldoon, alone and frightened. At some point I fell asleep, clutching his yellow cashmere sweater.

-17-

the first thing I did when I woke up the next morning was to create a missing-pup flyer. I scanned into the computer my favorite picture of Muldoon sitting in front of the Christmas tree, wearing a green velvet jingle-bell collar. His eyes were bright and alert because I'd been holding a turkey leg over my head when I took the shot. Beneath the photograph, I typed in text that I hoped was a plaintive but not maudlin narrative highlighting all the little guy's good points.

Unfortunately, Muldoon hadn't been wearing his collar or ID when he went missing. He didn't like the feel of it around his neck, so I only made him wear it when he was out on an official walk. That was a huge mistake. To compensate, I added a list of contact numbers, including my cell phone number. I took a couple of dozen flyers and drove around the neighborhood, posting one on every telephone pole, storefront, and road sign. It was Saturday, so I hoped people would be around to see them.

By the time I'd finished posting the flyers, it was only eight a.m. While I waited by the telephone for someone to call about Muldoon, I tried to figure out who Darcy Daniels's "source" was. Marta Cruz may have funneled information to *Celebrity Heat*, but that didn't explain where she'd gotten it.

My romance with Evan had been common knowledge among our college friends, but there were only two other people who knew he'd asked me to marry him: our best friends, Cissy Jerrard and James Brodie. We'd sworn them both to secrecy because I didn't want news of the engagement to reach Pookie. She didn't like Evan. I knew she'd be upset, but I thought I could soften her attitude. The plan was this: Evan had proposed in early November. We wanted to announce our engagement at a New Year's Eve party we were planning, which meant I had less than two months to make my mother love Evan as much as I did. Not much time, but I was sure I could pull it off.

In early December I'd planned a romantic dinner to celebrate the one-month anniversary of our still-secret engagement. It was going to be just the two of us, a surprise for Evan. I opted to hold the event at his apartment because it had a real kitchen, instead of at mine with its hot plate and refrigerator that looked as though it had been purchased at a Motel 6 yard sale. All four of us had classes scheduled that morning. My last one was at eleven. I calculated I'd still have enough time to prepare the food and decorate in the afternoon. To help, Cissy volunteered to take Evan to the county museum to see a special exhibit of Impressionist art, so I could work in secret.

Unfortunately, I've never been much of a cook or an event planner. At the last minute, I panicked. The decorations seemed trite, and the menu too complex. I didn't think I'd be able to pull off a party, even a small one, in such a short amount of time. I decided to skip my morning classes and throw myself into the preparations.

At about nine-thirty a.m., with my arms loaded with groceries, I slid my key into the lock of Evan's front door. The first thing I saw were clothes scattered all over the living room floor. Evan had never been a neatnik, but still, that seemed odd. Then I heard groans. My mind raced. I imagined Evan lying on the floor injured, maybe bleeding to death. My adrenaline surged. I bolted down the hallway and nearly tripped over Evan and Cissy, going at it on the gold shag carpet. What hurt most was that they couldn't even make it to the bedroom.

I'm not sure what happened next. All I remember is confusion, shouting, followed by overwhelming feelings of anger and humiliation. I also remember Evan's socks, because that's all he had on. Black socks. Cissy, my best friend since high school, my soul sister and confidante, just sat there looking merely surprised that she'd been caught.

In the days that followed, Evan tried repeatedly to apologize, but any capacity for forgiveness I may have once possessed had retreated into a dark, impenetrable jungle. After a while he stopped seeking absolution. My anger eventually subsided, and I began the mourning process. The following June, I graduated from UCLA. With that passage I was able to brush the memory of my failed relationship into a dark corner of my mind the way Pookie had always taught me to do.

I suppose other people may have learned about Evan and Cissy's affair, but not from me. I hadn't told a soul. I sincerely doubted that Cissy had, either. She hated being put in a bad light. As for Evan, he was no longer talking to anybody. That left only James Brodie.

The three of us—Brodie, Evan, and I—hung out together back in college. In the beginning, Brodie had been just another fresh-faced kid from one of those Midwestern "M" states: Michigan, Minnesota, Missouri—I couldn't remember which. He'd once told me he'd fallen in love with California at age twelve while on a pilgrimage to Disneyland with his family. Years later, as a student at UCLA, he'd completed his transformation from transplant to native son. He let his hair go wild and become bleached by the sun. He'd let his Midwestern inhibitions go, too. In winter Brodie was a ski bum, in summer a beach bum. Finally, he dispensed with those limiting adjectives and became simply a bum for all seasons, the embodiment of the California dream, or so he thought.

At some point I'd brought Cissy into our circle, hoping she and Brodie might hit it off. They never did, but she began hanging out with us, usually for activities that scored high on her genteel-o-meter. The rest of the time she preferred shopping at Saks Fifth Avenue, while Evan, Brodie, and I spurred one another into doing fun but dangerous things, like parachuting out of airplanes and scuba diving too deep, too long. Then Brodie and Evan began experimenting with drugs, and something shifted. Things weren't fun anymore, only dangerous. I was amazed any of us had survived those years.

Brodie had obviously maintained contact with Evan. If he was at Poet's Corner the night Evan died, he may have also been one of the last people to see him alive. I wanted to know if he'd talked to the press about me, and why, because my reputation and quite possibly my livelihood were at stake.

To get my mind off Muldoon's disappearance, I began searching for Brodie. First I did the obvious thing: I checked several telephone directories I keep for use in my consulting work. Brodie wasn't in any of them. That didn't surprise me. Nobody in L.A. had a listed telephone number. I have this theory that the phone company makes up all those names in the white pages just so they can sell ads in the yellow pages.

After a few minutes I grew restless. Once again I checked my voice mail, hoping somebody had found Muldoon. There were no messages. I walked out on the deck and scanned the beach. No Muldoon. I called his name. Nothing. Discouraged, I went back inside.

I logged onto the Internet and Googled Brodie. The search produced dozens of links. Some of the Brodies I found were historical figures; others were linked to genealogy sites. One of the addresses directed me to the *Los Angeles Times*. I clicked on it and found an amusing article about baristas in L.A.'s hippest coffee shops. James Brodie was listed as the author. I wasn't sure if it was the same Brodie I knew back in college, but I had to start somewhere. I called the *Times*, but the operator couldn't find a listing for him on the roster of employees.

It was difficult to concentrate. I couldn't stop thinking about Muldoon. I took another break and called Mrs. Domanski to see if she'd heard anything that sounded like barking. She had, but it was only Mr. D., throwing a tantrum when he discovered they were out of cocktail onions. Regrettably, that kind of barking didn't count. She promised to call me immediately if she heard anything.

Without much enthusiasm, I went back to the computer and wandered onto the UCLA alumni Web site. Brodie wasn't listed in their directory, even though I was sure he'd graduated. Eventually I found him in the unlikeliest of places, as an attendee at a yoga retreat held in Mexico about six months before. I knew it was the right guy when I noticed the middle initial: "X" for "Xavier." There was a contact number with a 323 area code, presumably for the convenience of other participants who might want to debate the merits of Ashtanga versus kundalini over a wheatgrass cocktail. I switched to another Web site that featured a reverse directory, and found Brodie's address. I jotted down the information but decided against calling him. It was possible he wasn't eager to speak with me, either. Better to drop by unannounced.

There was still a small window of opportunity between the two rush hours, so I decided to chance the freeway. First I made sure my cell phone was charged up. Then I dropped my torn vest at the dry cleaner's for repairs and headed east on the 10 Freeway, toward downtown L.A. Unfortunately the exit I planned to take was closed for construction. I detoured onto the 101 and exited at Echo Park. I backtracked on Sunset Boulevard, driving west past low-slung buildings swathed in colorful Mexican murals.

In that part of town, the store signs read "El Rancho" and "Carnicería"; the car radios crooned ballads in Spanish; the dusty, downtrodden houses had barred windows, each with a story to tell but probably not to me. As I approached Hillhurst, the barred windows had all but disappeared. By the time I reached the stately houses lining Los Feliz Boulevard, the only bars left were wet bars protected by elaborate security systems.

Brodie lived in a residential neighborhood in the Hollywood Hills just south of Griffith Park, where W. C. Fields allegedly once stood on the front lawn of his neighbor, Cecil B. DeMille, and pitched gin bottles through De Mille's front windows. I took a meandering road up the hill to Woking Street. From a distance, it looked as if somebody had taken a giant peashooter filled with houses, and blown. Only the strong stuck and took root. I followed the loop of a narrow one-way lane that looked like a private driveway. Up there you could see the city from end to end, simmering in soupy smog. Only the tops of skyscrapers pierced the opaque sky, as if they were straining to catch a breath of fresh air. Parking was limited, but I managed to find a spot in front of a massive Tudor residence. Hanging from the surrounding brick wall were iciclelike Christmas lights. Apparently even rich people are too lazy to take them down after the holidays.

Brodie's house was a white Spanish bungalow with a flat roof and small front porch and looked as if it had once been the caretaker's cottage for a hacienda farther up the hill. There were trees in the area but none in Brodie's yard. The stucco house stood bare and exposed. A row of terra-cotta pipe tiles at the roofline provided the only break of color in a sea of white.

The shutters were closed. The house looked deserted. I knocked several times, but no one answered. Frustrated, I called Brodie's number and listened to the recording on his message machine: "Hark! What news from yonder city breaks? Is it from the east and Jamie is not home? Forsooth! I am sick and pale with grief to have missed your call. Please leaveth a message."

Brodie had obviously graduated from the Evan Brice School of Poetry. William Shakespeare must be turning in his grave. I'd just said my name after the beep when I heard a man's voice on the line. "Tucker? Man, is that really you?"

"Hey, Jamie, you're home."

"Yeah, hiding from my fans. Where are you?"

"Standing on your front porch."

He sighed. "Shit! Hold on a minute."

I was holding my breath, not knowing what to expect as the door opened. Standing before me was a trim, thirty-year-old man wearing beige chinos and a white Oxford shirt, both neatly pressed. His feet were bare. His hair was still that familiar strawberry blond but cut short now. Everything else seemed familiar: blue eyes, red-head's fair and freckled complexion. He'd grown a mustache and goatee since I'd seen him last. The facial hair helped camouflage his boyish looks.

"Sorry I didn't answer the door," he said. "I haven't felt much like talking to anybody."

He motioned me into a clean and spare living room featuring hardwood floors, no rugs, white walls, and a few pieces of essential furniture, including a couch, two chairs—also white—and a side table with a telephone sitting on it. I wondered what had happened to James Brodie in the intervening years to strip his life of color.

While he was opening the shutters to let in some light, I asked him if he worked for the *Times*.

He looked surprised. "Actually, I'm freelance. About once a month I write a humor piece for the Calendar section."

"What do you do the rest of the time?"

His expression was deadpan. "It takes me that long to find L.A. funny."

I sat in one of the white chairs, wondering if Brodie owned this place. If so, cracking jokes once a month must pay well. The house was small, but property in this neighborhood was pricey.

He disappeared into the kitchen but returned shortly carrying a wicker tray that held a matte brown teapot with a bamboo handle. An earthy, sweet fragrance meandered from the spout as he poured tea into two matching cups.

I noted that he was not of the school that believed in straining the leaves before pouring. They floated on the surface of the liquid like pond scum.

Brodie sat down on the couch across from me. "I'd like to think you've been pining away for me all these years," he said, "but I guess you're here about Evan."

"I want to know who killed him, Jamie."

He sighed and shook his head. "I wish I knew."

"Have the police interviewed you?"

"A couple of times. I told them everything I know."

Apparently that included everybody Evan had ever met, partied with, or slept with. When Jamie hadn't remembered names, he'd given descriptions. He acknowledged that the police had asked questions about Cissy, but they had seemed equally interested in Evan's drug connections and his women friends.

"Evan always had girls after him," he said, "wanting him to make them stars. At first he loved the attention. After he got sober, it depressed him. Shit, man, most of those girls weren't ever going to make it in the business."

"So he let them down gently by screwing them?"

Brodie let the teacup warm his hands for a moment before he spoke. "Look, Tucker, I know it's hard for you to understand, but present company excepted, those girls were just sex to him. All of them, even Cissy—at first, anyway."

"Lola Scott, too? Just sex?"

He rolled his eyes to dismiss that notion. "No, not Lola. Sparks flew in both directions. It gave me a hard-on just watching the two of them together. Lola's a fox, and from what Evan told me, she knows the difference between erotic and kinky and can play it either way."

"So what broke them up?"

Brodie swirled the floating debris in his teacup. "You might say Lola rose to the highest level of her incompetence. Some of the things she did on her way up came back to bite her."

"You are talking about the video?"

He frowned. "What video?"

"Never mind. Go on. Why did they break up?"

His stare was probing, as though he preferred hearing my story to telling his. Eventually he decided it wasn't worth the wait.

"Lola Scott thinks she's Sarah-fucking-Bernhardt. She was always pressuring Evan to find projects 'worthy' of her talent. He didn't think she was ready for the big time. He suggested she take some acting lessons. That just pissed her off, so he decided to give her what she wanted. Evan had to jump through hoops for Richard Burnett, but he finally got her a starring role as the hooker-with-a-heart-of-gold in *Pagan Dreams*. So what was Lola doing while Evan was finessing the coup of the century? She was sneaking around behind his back, negotiating a picture deal with some Italian so-called producer who promised to cast her as Eleanor of Aquitaine in a remake of *The Lion in Winter*. Lola Scott as the new Hepburn? Now, *that's* funny. Anyway, when Evan found out, that was it. He fired off a fax and canned her ass. She went crazy, but it was too late. He was finished with her."

"You think she went crazy enough to kill him?"

He thought for a moment. "No. In her own narcissistic way, she loved Evan. It didn't stop her from screwing him over for the sake of her career, but I don't think she would physically hurt him."

I wasn't so sure about that but dropped the subject for the moment.

"Were you at Poet's Corner with Evan the night he died?"

He nodded.

"So that was the last time you saw him."

Jamie covered his face with his hands. "Man, I thought you knew." He sighed again; then he dropped his hands and looked at me. "Evan and I were supposed to meet on Monday to talk. When he didn't show up, I called his home, his office, his cell. I couldn't find him anywhere, so I went to the apartment. The door was unlocked. I found him in the kitchen. There was blood everywhere. Man, I'll never get that picture out of my head for as long as I live."

"He called me just hours before he died, Jamie. Why?"

"I don't know. Something was eating at him, but he wouldn't talk about it. He wanted to work out the details first. He said once he got everything clear in his mind, he'd tell me everything. I got the impression he knew something that was going to sink somebody's boat. Whatever was bothering him, he took it to his grave."

I doubted that but didn't tell Brodie. More than likely at least one other person knew about Evan's troubles: his killer.

"Aside from Lola, was Evan still involved with other women?" I said.

Brodie paused, as if looking for some way to avoid answering the question. "I don't know. Maybe. But he hadn't mentioned any names. Not for a long while."

"There's something you're not telling me. What?"

"Look, Tucker, I'm just guessing, but I think he did something shitty to somebody. It made him feel real bad, and it wasn't just lip service to satisfy some twelve-step sponsor. He was hurting, man."

I wondered what that something could be. Maybe

Evan had second thoughts about firing Lola Scott. Perhaps he felt guilty because he'd threatened to use the porn video to ruin her career as payback for the Italian producer stunt.

"Do you think he was upset about Lola Scott?"

"I doubt it. Evan was done with her. Like I said, I'm guessing, but I got the impression Evan's problem wasn't going away without costing him money—lots of it."

"Maybe Lola was planning to sue him for breach of contract. You must have some idea what it was. Tell me, Jamie, please."

He looked surprised and then skeptical. "Why are you asking all these questions, Tucker?"

"I don't know . . . for Dara, I guess." And Claire and Frank and Evan, too, but I didn't say that, either.

"Evan's kid? I don't get it."

"I think the police are about to arrest Cissy. That leaves Dara holding the bag for everybody's mistakes. I won't let that happen."

"What if Cissy did it?"

"What if she didn't?"

Brodie ran his fingers through his hair and then blew out all the air in his lungs in one big sigh. "I don't know if it means anything, but just before he went into rehab, Evan had a big party at the apartment, with lots of booze and drugs and people who all wanted a piece of him. Back then he wasn't exactly conscientious about keeping his social calendar straight. From what I heard, he invited several ladies to be his date that night. Two showed up. One was so embarrassed she left in tears. The other one freaked out. Called him a few choice names. Dumped a glass of wine on his shirt. I heard Evan was so stoned he hardly noticed. A couple of guys hustled her out of his place before the neighbors got pissed off about the noise and called the cops."

Having been discarded by Evan myself, I could sympathize with the feelings of betrayal those women must have experienced. I wondered if he'd really been too high to remember inviting them or if he'd done it on purpose, to entertain his guests with a catfight. It was sad to realize how much of Evan's life had been devoted to drugs and lies. I couldn't help wondering if that devotion had caused his death as well.

"I need names," I said.

"I only know one: Amy Lynch. Evan never mentioned the other woman's name. I hear she was a mousy little thing with a deer-in-the-headlights look, definitely not his type."

"Where can I find this Amy Lynch?"

"I'm not sure. I think Evan met her in a hotel bar. She was a cocktail waitress or something, but he told me she quit right after that to work in a nail salon. Last I heard, she was hustling ice cream at Ben and Jerry's in Brentwood."

"Amy sure changes jobs a lot. She must be an actor."

Jamie smiled. Then he shifted his gaze to the cup in his hand, as if he was revisiting some private moment. "I have a friend who reads tea leaves. She thinks they're a window to the soul."

"Is she any good?"

"Not very, but I keep hoping she'll get it right. It would make everything so much easier."

For a while we said nothing. I helped him take the tea set back to the kitchen, where I noticed a small statue of the Buddha—the young one, not the fat one—on the cabinet near the toaster. Resting on his upturned palms like an offering was what looked like a piece of torn lace, maybe from the edge of an old pillowcase.

"You know," he said, "I almost looked you up after you split with Evan, but it seemed like a shitty thing to do . . . you know . . . because he was my friend."

"Yeah, that loyalty issue is tricky, all right," I said. "I'm just curious, Jamie. How much sleep did you lose over not telling me Evan was screwing my best friend behind my back?"

His face reddened. "You didn't need me. You found out on your own."

"The hard way."

This time his smile was thin and resigned. "I can see now that you and I didn't stand much of a chance."

"About as much chance as Lola Scott as the new Hepburn."

There was a moment of uncomfortable silence, as if he didn't know what to say but didn't want me to leave, either. Finally he walked with me to the porch.

"By the way, Jamie, did you ever tell anybody that Evan and I were engaged?"

"No. Why?"

"Just curious." I turned to leave.

"Good luck to you, Tucker."

"Yeah, Jamie. Good luck to you, too."

He stood on the porch watching me until I slid into the front seat of my car. Then he went back inside. As soon as he'd closed the door, I used my phone to check both my cell voice mail and my home message machine for any word about Muldoon. Zilch. To take my mind off what was beginning to feel like a hopeless situation, I called Ben & Jerry's. When I asked for Amy Lynch, I was told she'd moved on to greener pastures. It was too late to find her without doing some research, so I headed for home.

When I arrived, I made another round of calls to local shelters and the neighbors. No one had seen Muldoon. In desperation, I listed him on a Web site dedicated to missing pets. At the moment, there was nothing else I could do but wait and hope.

At about nine p.m. I was sitting on the couch, holding Muldoon's cashmere sweater and trying to divine some cosmic clue about his whereabouts, when the telephone rang. It was Joe Deegan. There were sounds of music and voices in the background, as though he was at a party.

"We have to talk." His tone was edgy.

"Okay. Shoot."

He hesitated. "In person. Tomorrow."

"I may be busy tomorrow."

"I'll be at your place around ten."

I heard a woman's voice in the background. It was both whiny and seductive. "Who are you talking to?" she said to him.

He lowered his voice and added, "Make that noon."

He hung up before I had a chance to tell him Muldoon was missing or to ask if the woman's voice belonged to Candy. Maybe I'd pose the question in person tomorrow. He might be in a better mood to answer it. The problem was, I knew I wouldn't be in a better mood to ask it.

-18-

The following morning, there was still no word on Muldoon. I tried to call Venus for solace, but she didn't answer the telephone. Eugene wasn't picking up, either. I assumed he was on his way to the desert.

I still had to find out how Darcy Daniels had gotten intimate details about my relationship with Evan Brice and why she had twisted and embellished the facts to make her coverage of his murder investigation seem even more salacious. I had already eliminated Jamie and myself and probably Cissy as the source of the leak. Perhaps Evan had told somebody. If so, it was going to be a difficult if not impossible task to find out whom he had told, much less why. Maybe I should accept Jason-the-twit-producer's offer to do an exclusive interview with Darcy Daniels. I could use our meeting as a ploy to turn the tables and interview her. The idea was perilous at best. At worst, it could be a total disaster, but avoiding risk had never been my strongest trait. On the other hand, it was Sunday. Jason and Darcy were probably too busy doing brunch, or each other, at some trendy Beverly Hills hotel to make interview appointments with the subject of yesterday's news. I decided to sleep on the idea.

My house had always been my refuge, but now I

couldn't stand the thought of being there without Muldoon. My cell phone number was listed on the missing-puppy flyer. It was also registered with all the nearby shelters and posted on the missing-pet Web site. Everybody was looking for him. There was nothing more I could do.

Deegan wasn't due to arrive at my place until around noon. If I sat around the house waiting for him, I would only get more depressed. As much as I hated the thought of going back to Evan's apartment, I had to finish packing. I gathered up some old newspapers from my recycling bin in case I needed to wrap any glass and headed for Venice.

When I arrived, the Latino's black Honda Civic was taking up two spots in front of Evan's apartment building. As usual, I had to leave the Boxster in the parking lot down the street.

I was nearing the front lobby when I noticed somebody squatting next to the Honda's front tire. I heard s-s-s-s-t and saw the car's front end list to port. A moment later, the culprit stood. It was the woman I'd seen shouting at the Honda's owner earlier in the week. She was wearing the same pair of rubber flip-flops and that red kimono—silk, I guessed. Resting against her leathery brown chest was some kind of necklace that consisted of a black silk cord strung with six small cubes, each engraved with a letter. Together they spelled "Brenda." When she realized she'd been caught vandalizing somebody's car, her self-satisfied smile turned into a defensive glower.

"Damn punk," she said.

I wasn't sure if she was talking to me or just muttering to herself, so I said, "Beg your pardon?"

"It's bad enough he leaves his car here for days. He doesn't even live in the neighborhood. Seventy-two hours. You're not supposed to park on a city street any longer than that. Now he's taking up two damn spaces. Where does he expect the rest of us to park, huh?"

I gave her a perfunctory nod. "Yeah, it's a bummer, all right."

She watched me carefully for a moment, perhaps judging whether I was friend or foe. "I've seen you around lately. You moving into the neighborhood?"

I was reluctant to tell her anything, so I just said no, that I was visiting a friend. Without another word, she turned, and with a swish of red silk and the slap, slap, slap of the flip-flops against her heels, she crossed the street and walked up a flight of stairs. A bicycle was chained to the railing at the top of the landing. As she passed it, she caught her robe on one of the pedals. There was a ripping sound. She lifted the hem of the kimono and ran her hand gently over the damaged silk before she opened the door to her apartment and disappeared inside.

I suspected that the owner of the Honda was going to be colossally pissed off when he saw the flat tire. I didn't want to be hanging around when it happened, so I made my way up the stairs to the third floor.

When I walked into Evan's place, the smell of industrial cleaners lingered oppressively in the still air. I opened the windows to let the sea breeze freshen the room while I wrapped and loaded kitchen items—wineglasses mostly—into the boxes I'd gotten from Rose. At the last minute, I decided to launder the towels and sheets before giving them away. I made several trips between the apartment and the washing machines in the basement until everything was clean. I'd finished in the kitchen and

was getting ready to make a trip to the Dumpster to toss
the food from the refrigerator when I heard a loud sound
from outside in the hall.

My heart pounded as I tiptoed up to the peephole and
cautiously looked out. The Latino was banging on
Monique Ruiz's door with his fist, which made the
buxom-woman tattoo on his biceps jerk suggestively. He
was wearing a white short-sleeved shirt with red, orange,
and yellow flames licking upward from the hem toward
his chest. The stubble on his head was glistening with
what looked like sweat. Obviously, he'd just discovered
the flat tire. I couldn't see his face, but I suspected that his
wide, sensuous mouth was now distorted by a scowl. I
wondered who he was. The boyfriend?

A moment later, a fragile-looking young woman appeared at the threshold. Before I could get a better look,
the guy pushed past her into the apartment and slammed
the door closed.

If he was Monique Ruiz's boyfriend, at least it would
explain why he left his car parked for days on the street:
He was living at her place, at least part of the time. I wondered what her parents thought of the arrangement. Not
much, I suspected.

I opened the door wide enough to hear loud voices
coming from inside Monique's apartment, but I couldn't
make out the words. I was about to go over to see if she
was all right, but almost immediately things quieted
down. I wanted to talk to her, but I didn't want to get in
the middle of a lovers' quarrel, so I went back to my
packing.

When I finished, I decided to check in with Rose. She
greeted me in a snappy pair of red pedal pushers and a
red, white, and blue stars-and-stripes blouse.

"What was all that noise I heard a while ago? I'm still a little jumpy because of Mr. Chatterton."

"Monique Ruiz had a visitor, her boyfriend maybe. I think he had a flat tire and wasn't too happy about it."

Her face lit up. "I hope she brings him over. She keeps promising to introduce us, but I guess he travels a lot. She tells me he's a good man, though. That's a high compliment coming from her."

Granted, I'd had limited exposure to the guy, but Rose's upbeat description didn't quite fit with what I'd observed of his behavior. Maybe I'd caught him on a bad day. Actually, by now it was more like a succession of bad days. On the other hand, there was no point in trashing him in front of Rose, so I shrugged off her comment. We visited for a few more minutes before I got up to leave.

On my way out, I collected the mail from Evan's box. When I stepped out onto the street, I saw Monique's boyfriend standing by his Honda, staring at the flat tire. The wraparound sunglasses covered his eyes but not the tops of his brows. They were pinched together in a frown. His anger had faded, leaving only confusion, as if he didn't know what to do next. I felt sorry for him, so I walked over and asked if he had a spare.

He looked up, startled. "Yeah, but it's flat, too."

"I think you can buy some emergency inflator stuff. It comes in a can and pumps up the tire long enough for you to drive to a service station. There's a tire store over on Marine. Maybe they carry it. If you want, you can use my cell phone to call them."

After I said it, I realized he probably knew about the tire store, since Monique worked there.

He smiled, exposing white, even teeth. "Nah, that's okay. Somebody's picking me up."

"Sure?"

He nodded. "Yeah."

Maybe I'd misjudged him. He seemed nice enough. Perhaps Brenda's antics had temporarily pushed him over the edge.

When I arrived home, the place was eerily quiet. I missed Muldoon, and I missed my mother. Mostly, I missed somebody to talk to. Even Bruce was looking good to me right now. At about a quarter after noon, there was a knock on my side door. I opened it to find Deegan looming over me, with his hand resting on the doorjamb above my head. He'd cut himself shaving and looked as if he'd dressed in a hurry. His expression was a mixture of wariness and fatigue.

"Rough night?" I said.

He ignored my comment and walked past me into the kitchen, where he leaned against the counter. His legs were crossed at the ankles, and his arms were crossed, too. As body language goes, his was on the negative side.

"So," I said, "to what do I owe the pleasure of your company?"

"Moses Green tells me you've been dogging his investigation. Every place he goes, you've been there first. He isn't happy about that."

"If he'd do his job right, I wouldn't have to help him."

"Have you ever considered that there's more to this case than you know?"

"Don't be ridiculous, Deegan. I realize that. But since you won't tell me anything, I'm forced to find out for myself."

"I told you before—"

"Yeah, yeah, yeah. It's a secret. Well, I know a few secrets, too. For example, there's a girl named Amy Lynch who may have had a grudge against Evan for a stupid party stunt he pulled before he went into rehab. There's another girl—currently nameless—who probably feels the same. I also know that Lola Scott was double-crossing Evan and went crazy when he dropped her off his client list. There's more. Should I go on?"

"You're off base, Stretch."

"Tell me why."

"Give it a rest or Green is going to come down on you like a ton of bricks."

I felt my face grow warm. "Did he send you here to threaten me or was that your idea?"

"He thought you'd prefer hearing the message from me."

"Well, you were both wrong. I don't like being threatened by anybody, but especially you."

Deegan looked up at the ceiling and sighed in frustration. "Use your head. You're no longer just helping out a friend. You're interfering with a homicide investigation. If you screw up Green's case, your lover's killer is going to get off scot-free."

Something about the way he said that irked me. "*Former* lover. I told you, we broke up ten years ago. And I'm getting sick and tired of everybody hinting that we were back together again."

"It's my job to ask questions."

"Not of me. This isn't even your case. And who I sleep with is none of your business. I didn't ask where *you* spent last night, did I? You're just using Green as an excuse to needle me about Evan Brice. Why?"

He paused for a moment, studying my face. "I saw you on TV last night. You're very photogenic."

It felt as if all the air had been squeezed from my lungs. Deegan had to be talking about *Celebrity Heat*. Ei-

ther they'd rerun the Friday night program or they'd uncovered new information. I didn't want to know the particulars at the moment. Imagining them was enough.

"I didn't know you watched that kind of crap."

"I don't. I just happened to be in a room where a TV
was on."

"And what room was that?"

He didn't answer.

"Why don't you ever answer my questions?"

"Like I said, my job is to ask questions, not to answer
them."

Frustrated, I walked over and plopped onto the couch.
He followed me but kept his distance at the opposite end.
We sat like that for what seemed like a long time.

When he spoke, his voice was soft. "Look, I'm just
trying to protect you. Interfering with a police investigation is against the law. Since the Department doesn't
allow me to associate with ex-cons, I'd hate for that to be
the reason I couldn't see you anymore."

It was a feeble attempt at a joke, but I didn't like his
attitude. "I don't need your protection. I can take care of
myself."

He sighed and rested his head on the back of the couch
as if weighing his response. His expression was grim.

"Okay, then, here's the deal. Stay away from this investigation, or I'll personally find some way to throw
your ass in jail."

I bolted off the couch. "Don't try to intimidate me,
Deegan. It won't work. I've seen you on the dance floor
after a few Tequila shooters, and believe me, nothing
scares me anymore."

His eyes narrowed into a look that *was* intimidating,
even though I would never have admitted it to him.

A moment later he stood. "Maybe we should talk again when you've cooled down."

"No. I think it's best we keep our distance from now on. That way, you can go protect somebody who needs protecting, and I won't have to worry about being hog-tied and thrown into the backseat of your detective car."

Deegan's eyelids blinked slowly several times. Without another word, he turned and walked out of the house, slamming the door with a force that rattled the windows.

-19-

for the rest of the day I hung around the house, waiting for any word about Muldoon. It was Sunday. People were out and about. Why hadn't somebody spotted him? By evening the telephone still hadn't rung.

I was a wreck. I had barely eaten anything in the past twenty-four hours. Not only had my stomach stopped growling, it had stopped whimpering. At about eight p.m. I went to my office alcove and logged onto my computer's e-mail program. I'd just sent Mr. Geyer a detailed summary of my progress on the focus group when I heard rattling at the side door. I sat motionless, listening, but all I could hear was the humming of the refrigerator.

I tiptoed toward a window next to the door and carefully tilted the wooden blinds to look outside. No one was there. I let out the breath I was holding. Stress was making me paranoid. As I headed back to my computer, I heard scraping against the wood deck and saw the knob on the French door slowly turn. My pulse raced as I grabbed a cheese board from the kitchen to use as a weapon and headed toward the door. In one quick motion, I pulled back the curtains. Standing on the deck, wearing a pair of baggy overalls and a sheepish grin, was my mother. I felt relief then anger as I opened the door.

"Why are you creeping around in the dark?" I said. "You scared the shit out of me."

"I knocked at the side door, but I guess you didn't hear me."

"Why didn't you use your key?"

"I forgot it. Besides, I don't live here anymore. Remember?"

I was about to give her one of my responsibility lectures when I realized she didn't know Muldoon was missing. I felt horrible. She'd entrusted him to me. I'd failed them both.

"Pookie, something horrible has happened."

"Don't tell me you went to see Lola Scott. Sheila told me you'd been pumping her for information. What's wrong with you, Tucker? Why do you have to meddle in everybody's business?"

"I'm not meddling. I'm helping."

"Helping who? Cissy Brice? Save your energy. That girl doesn't have enough insight to appreciate your help. Let her solve her own problems."

"That's your answer to everything, isn't it, Pookie? Do nothing and hope things work out."

"I didn't come here to argue. I came to pick up my curling iron."

"Muldoon is missing," I blurted out.

She cocked her head. "No, he's not."

Obviously, she was in denial.

"I came home Friday night, and he was gone," I said. "I don't know how he got out. I've looked everywhere, put up flyers, everything. I can't find him. I don't know what else to do."

"Look, Tucker, he's not missing. When I called you from Vegas Thursday night, you seemed really upset. I discussed things with Bruce, and we decided to get up early on Friday morning and drive back to L.A. When we got here, you weren't around. Muldoon was alone, so we took him with us. He's fine."

A whole range of emotions coursed through my mind: confusion, relief, and finally anger. "I almost had a heart attack worrying about him. Why didn't you leave me a note?"

"Because last time we talked, you said you wanted us out. Well, we're out. All of us."

"Where is he now?" I said.

"In a kennel. Bruce and I are staying at a hotel. Muldoon will join us in a couple of days when we find a place to live."

I pictured Muldoon in a dark room, huddled on a dirt floor against the steel bars of his cage, terrified by the unrelenting howls of hundreds of pit bulls.

"How could you take him out of his home and leave him with strangers? You didn't even take his cashmere sweater."

"Look, Tucker, what's your problem?"

My voice felt strained. "I want him back—tonight."

She paused, weighing my anger. "This isn't about Muldoon, is it?"

In a flash of clarity, I realized she was probably right. This conversation was no longer about the abandonment issues of a scruffy white dog. But I was on a roll. Nothing was going to stop me now.

"I'll tell you what this is about. Muldoon deserves to be more than an afterthought. At least leave him here until you find a proper home."

"And *you* can give him a proper home? You're making

him fat with all the junk you feed him. It's just as unhealthy for a dog to be overweight as it is for a human being. And you let him hang his head out the car window. What happens if a bug flies in his eye? There could be permanent damage. Plus, you're always gone, and you leave him with that alcoholic neighbor of yours. God knows what could happen to him there."

"At least at the end of the day he knows I'll be home, instead of shooting craps in Vegas."

Pookie looked crushed. She didn't speak for the longest time. Finally, she gave me the name of the kennel and retreated to what had been her bedroom only two days before, presumably to look for her curling iron. I probably should have tried to patch things up before I left to get Muldoon, but I was too angry. Instead, I grabbed a jacket and stormed out of the house.

When I arrived at the parking lot of Fuzzy Friends Kennel, it looked neither fuzzy nor friendly, and the tinkle bell on the front door did little to alter my first impression. It was a cavernous place with cold, dank concrete floors. The acrid smell of urine didn't help the ambience, either. Behind the front counter were rows of built-in cages occupied by all types of kitty cats. I looked up to see a round-faced red and white tabby with folded ears, meowing plaintively as if to say, "Get me the hell out of this dump."

The attendant was in her early twenties. She wore jeans and a sweater, both black. Her hair was black, too, dyed a dull, opaque shade not found in nature. Her eyes were lined with red pencil, and what I initially took for a lisp turned out to be a tongue stud. I assumed she was either a goth princess or the snake god of some West African voodoo cult.

She seemed irritated that I had interrupted the TV program she was watching. When she sensed that I had the potential of becoming her worst nightmare, she agreed to release Muldoon. She sauntered into the back room and moments later returned, dragging him by the neck with his leash.

"Let him go."

Her face puckered petulantly. "I'm not supposed to."

"I *said*, let go of the damn leash!"

At the sound of my voice, Muldoon looked at me as if I was some kind of traitor. It was almost more than I could take. I sank to my knees and called his name. Slowly he walked over close enough so I could put my arms around him. He buried his nose in my armpit as if he hoped that kennels didn't exist if you couldn't see them.

On the way home I let Muldoon hang his head out of the window—just this one last time, I thought, just to cheer him up. Unfortunately, it wasn't enough, so I also stopped at McDonald's and bought him a Quarter Pounder with cheese. He seemed to feel better after that, but it was only a temporary fix. Tomorrow I'd have to do better by him.

When we got home, Pookie was gone, and with her, all hopes of patching together our dysfunctional little family. Everything I did lately turned to shit.

• • •

MONDAY MORNING I awoke to the glorious sound of a dog snoring. When I sat up to have a look, Muldoon issued a warning growl to let me know he was on my pillow again. I massaged his forehead and headed for the kitchen to make some coffee. He followed but seemed disappointed that breakfast consisted of a small ration of Pookie-approved vegetarian Zen dog food and a bowl of fresh water.

"I'm sorry, little guy, but as of now you're on a diet."

He plopped his butt down and stared at the bowl. I left him there to reconsider the cuisine while I went online to look for doggie day care centers. I called and interviewed several proprietors until I narrowed the choice to one: Hannah Mills of Le Bon Chien. There was only one glitch. She wouldn't accept Muldoon until she assessed his ability to "interface" with his fellow canines. I was amused by her attitude but agreed to drop him off for a playdate and an evaluation. Hannah made it clear that I was not invited to stay. Getting Muldoon into doggie day care was shaping up to be more of a contest than getting him into Harvard. With his appointment at Le Bon Chien set, Muldoon settled in for a nap on the couch. I went into my office to search for Amy Lynch.

Brodie claimed that Evan had met her while she was working at a hotel bar. That certainly didn't narrow the search. It was impossible to call all of them. Even if I got a break and found the exact hotel, with all the scams and lawsuits, companies no longer gave out references on former employees, let alone personal information like telephone numbers or forwarding addresses. Checking ice cream parlors seemed like a waste of time, too. I doubted she'd take a job at another one. Cherry Garcia was pretty much at the peak of the frozen milk products hierarchy.

According to Brodie, Amy had also worked in a nail salon. Unless she was an administrative employee, she had to have a license to do that sort of work. On a whim, I dialed the number for the agency in Sacramento that regulates cosmetologists and, to my surprise, came away with Amy Lynch's telephone number. A very accommodating roommate advised me that Amy was currently working as a receptionist for a company called Premier

Temps. I finally spoke with her there, offering a made-up story about collecting anecdotes from Evan's friends to use in a eulogy I was giving at his memorial service. Without hesitation, she agreed to meet with me.

After showering, I put on a business suit—something professional but not too corporate. Unfortunately, Muldoon interpreted all the activity as a sign that there might be a walk in his future. I had to watch how I handled the situation, because the little guy had longstanding abandonment issues, which hadn't been helped by his stay at the kennel from hell. I certainly didn't want to trigger an episode. When I asked him if he wanted to go for a ride in the car, he responded with the kind of joie de vivre only a Westie can generate.

On the way to the day-care center, I put the top down on the Boxster and gave him a pep talk about how to put his best paw forward, but he seemed to prefer listening to the wind in his ears, not to me. I dropped him off in the front lobby of Le Bon Chien and headed for Mid-Wilshire.

-20-

id-Wilshire is a commercial strip along Wilshire
m Boulevard just west of downtown L.A. where the
buildings are generally ten stories or so and the homeless share the sidewalks with lawyers, insurance executives,
and secretaries eating hot dogs from street vendors' carts.
The buildings to the north and south of the boulevard are
what you might call an architectural free-for-all: aging
apartment houses, small shops, and single-family homes,
many of which date back to pre–World War II.

Premier Temps was located in a building several
blocks east of Western, between two of the city's art deco
masterpieces: the former Bullocks-Wilshire department
store and the aqua and bronze Wiltern Center. I parked on
a side street and made my way up to the building's third-
floor hallway, checking each door until I spotted the Premier Temps sign.

The moment I stepped into the small reception area, I
was assaulted by the scent of somebody's fruity perfume.
Sitting behind a desk flanked by a couple of wilted palms
was a striking young woman with shoulder-length blond
hair. Her skin looked fresh and dewy, as if she'd just been
hand dipped in a vat of Kama Sutra oil. I could almost

feel the skin on my elbows molting in protest. A plaque on the desk read Aimée Lynch. I wondered if that was the spelling on her birth certificate or if it was some recent affectation. A woman wearing a sari stood in front of the desk, holding a piece of paper on which numerous words had been circled in red.

"It's okay," Amy said, patting the woman's arm. "Take a few minutes to study the ones you missed, and I'll test you again."

What masqueraded for business attire in Amy's world was a green jungle-print sarong with a coordinating sweater set. Surrounded by the forest green carpet and those palms, she looked like the guide for an Amazon adventure tour. When she noticed me standing at the door, she flashed a smile that was both dazzling and genuine. Her delicate features made her seem vulnerable, but the deep blue of her sapphire eyes kept her from looking inconsequential. I suspected she was the kind of woman that didn't inspire neutrality. Either you wanted to be her friend, her lover, her protector, or you wanted to draw a black handlebar mustache under her perfect little nose.

I waited at the door until the woman in the sari settled into a chair in a far corner of the room, hoping the fruity aroma would follow her. The closer I got to the reception desk, the stronger the scent became.

"Amy?" I said. "I'm Tucker Sinclair. I called earlier about Evan Brice."

Her smile faded. "Oh, gosh, I'm sorry. I know I promised, but can we possibly meet after work? Things are crazy around here. They're trying to fill a big order, and I have to cover the phones. Plus, I have to take my break at exactly ten-fifteen. The problem is, I called in sick yesterday, and I can't afford to get on the manager's bad side."

Her voice *did* sound nasally, which explained the heavy perfume. She probably had a cold and didn't realize that the smell was strong enough to fell a cheetah.

"I promise not to take much of your time," I said.

She hesitated, weighing her alternatives. Then she sighed. "Hold on."

She made a quick call, and shortly thereafter, a slightly androgynous young man with long, silky hair came bounding out of the back office with all the enthusiasm of an Irish setter chasing a mail carrier. As Amy brushed past him, she squeezed his arm and smiled. Her gesture was maternal, but he obviously didn't see it that way. He was practically panting for her.

Amy motioned for me to follow her, allowing me to get another up-close-and-personal whiff of her perfume. We passed through a large area where a half-dozen people sat at side-by-side desks talking on telephones. We ended up in a conference room, which had a window overlooking the boulevard. I sat in a chair at the table. As an icebreaker I asked how she'd first connected with Evan.

She hesitated. "I met him when I worked in hospitality."

That résumé entry was somewhat vague, but I assumed she was talking about her stint as a cocktail waitress. Of course, that could have been anywhere from the George V Hotel in Paris to the No-Tell Motel in Pacoima. It wasn't a crucial bit of information, so I decided not to pursue it.

"How long were you and Evan together?"

Her cheeks flushed with embarrassment. "The way you say that sounds like you think Evan and I were having an affair or something. We were just friends."

"Sorry, I didn't mean to imply . . . All I meant was, had you heard from him lately?"

"Actually, he called Friday night."

That surprised me. "What did he say?"

I probably sounded overly eager, because she looked at me quizzically. "You *are* writing a eulogy for his memorial service. Right?"

I cleared my throat. "Right." I should have come up with a rationale for my nosy questions, but it's hard to think clearly when you're holed up in a stuffy office with a woman who smells like Carmen Miranda's headgear.

She studied me for a moment before apparently laying her suspicions to rest. "He called to say he was sorry." I was about to say, "Sorry for what?" when she preempted my question. "One of the brightest stars in the universe was snuffed out when Evan Brice died. He graced us with his presence for such a short time, but he made a lasting mark on people he met in both of his worlds. In the world of poetry he made reality a dream. In the world of Hollywood he made dreams into realities for hundreds of his clients. The dark specter of death can never dim the brightness of his . . ."

Obviously, she'd done her Eulogy 101 homework. Nevertheless, I had to stop her before she damaged any brain cells—hers or mine.

"Wow, Amy," I said. "That's really . . . heartfelt."

Her face flushed again. "Thank you. I didn't mention it on the phone, but I'm a writer. I just took this job to get me through a rough spot."

"Seriously? What do you write? I mean . . . besides eulogies."

"Screenplays. I just finished a female buddy script I'm trying to get to Reese Witherspoon through an industry contact. If that doesn't work out, Reese's nanny is a friend of my hairdresser's cousin, so keep your fingers crossed for me."

She demonstrated how that might look by crossing her own fingers and looking hopeful. I wondered if there was a free hot-oil treatment in it for somebody.

"Hey, good luck with that," I said. "I mean it."

Amy hesitated for a moment before adding, "By the way, you have permission to use my name in the memorial program—you know, for a writing credit."

Granted, Evan's service, if there was to be one, would undoubtedly include a few Hollywood heavy hitters. Nonetheless, her blatant self-promotion startled me.

"Your generous contribution will be of great comfort to the family, I'm sure." I paused to come up with another plan of attack. "You know, it may sound morbid, but I just can't stop obsessing about what was going through Evan's mind in those days before he died. I think I'd feel better if I knew. Do you understand what I'm talking about? For instance, did you get any sense of his frame of mind from that last telephone call? How did he sound? Happy? Sad? Worried? Afraid?"

She paused for a moment, staring at me critically. Then she leaned back in her chair. "Yeah, that call was interesting, all right. First of all, I didn't think I'd ever hear from him again, so it was a surprise. He started off by apologizing for not connecting me to a producer friend of his at DreamWorks like he promised. I told him it wasn't too late: he could still make the call. This time he just changed the subject. So what, right? Evan Brice wasn't the first guy who broke his word to me. After that, it was just small talk. He asked if I'd seen this movie or that one. What did I think of the story structure? Who would I cast as the schlubby neighbor? I don't think he really cared what I had to say, and I told him so. Then he got weird on me. He started talking about God or whatever God means to you and how we should give up control to a greater power. He went off on a riff about why politicians have to lie to get elected and how the Catholic Church should stop obsessing about abortion and deal with more important issues like priests diddling little boys. That's when I started to wonder what he really wanted from me. Kind of like how I'm wondering right now about you." She leaned forward in her chair, her gaze fixed on me. "You're not writing any eulogy, are you? Who are you anyway? A reporter?"

"The temp business has made you cynical, Amy. Or did that happen in hospitality?"

She looked more hurt than angry. "Oh, for Pete's sake! Don't treat me like a dim bulb. I've been to enough funerals to know that no one wants you to say if the dead guy was afraid before he died. They only want to hear good things, even if they aren't true. Listen, I don't care about protecting Evan Brice's reputation. He did some bad things to me. If you wanted me to tell you that, I would have, but you should have been honest with me instead of making up stupid stories."

Perhaps I should have felt more sympathy for all the pain Amy Lynch had suffered at the hands of men in her life, but despite her dewy skin and alluring smiles, she wasn't 100 percent innocent—nobody was. For all I knew, Amy was using Evan to advance her writing career as much as he was using her—for what? Amy had denied having an affair with Evan, but she'd accepted an invitation to be his date at a party. Once they'd gone that far, it was difficult to imagine either of them passing up an opportunity for a few minutes of heady sex.

"I'm sorry," I said. "Maybe we should start over—"

She checked her watch and abruptly stood. "Maybe some other time. I have to get back to work."

Amy hadn't returned to her desk by the time I let myself out, because the panting hermaphrodite was still covering her phones. Even though I'd blown the interview, I felt grateful to be outside, breathing neutral air.

On my way back to the car, I thought about Evan's last conversation with Amy Lynch and tried but failed to draw any meaning from it. He'd chitchatted about films and casting choices but hadn't mentioned Lola Scott. It was impossible to know what had set him off about the church. Evan wasn't even Catholic. He'd been raised a Presbyterian, but he'd never attended any church during the time I knew him. On the other hand, maybe sobriety had deepened his thinking.

For now it appeared that Amy Lynch was a dead end. I was trying to figure out who might know the identity of Evan's other party date, when I heard a car door slam nearby. I looked up and saw Amy sliding into the passenger side seat of a vintage Mustang convertible parked across the street a couple of cars ahead of mine.

The Mustang's top was down, too. From what I could see of the man behind the wheel, he didn't look like anybody I'd waste another sick day on. As soon as Amy was settled in, he leaned over to kiss her. She immediately pushed him away, allowing me to catch a glimpse of his sharp, angular features. I noticed that his nose came to a point like a fox's. It took me a moment to realize who he was: Jerome Fielding, Evan Brice's personal assistant.

I waited for the Mustang to pull out into the flow of traffic. I planned to pull out, too, staying far enough behind so that neither would suspect that they were being followed.

there might have been an innocent explanation for why Evan's personal assistant and a scorned party date were kissing in a vintage Ford. It was possible Jerome was Amy's brother, except that his kiss wasn't a brother's; it was the kiss of a lover, or at least somebody who wanted to be one. In any event, after Jerome's first lip lock was rebuffed, he didn't try again.

I wondered why Amy was skipping work to meet with him. According to her, she'd called in sick the day before and didn't want to antagonize her boss by taking off more time, even to speak with me. Maybe something I'd said had upset her enough to ask Jerome to stop by and hold her hand. Only, how did he get here so fast? Then again, perhaps he was the reason Amy Lynch had to take her break at exactly 10:15.

We were parked on a side street, so traffic was minimal. There were no pedestrians except for a homeless woman pushing a shopping cart. She paused near my car to watch a couple of crows fighting over a spilled container of French fries in the middle of the road. When she turned her cart to get a better view, a wheel slipped into a crack in the sidewalk, which had been buckled by tree roots. I watched as she carefully readjusted her load of plastic bags, dirty blankets, and a fragile-looking black kitten.

I waited patiently for something else to happen, but the Mustang remained parked at the curb. The open convertible gave me a ringside seat to watch the conversation between Jerome Fielding and Amy Lynch. Too bad I couldn't hear what they were saying. The Boxster's top was down, too. I didn't want to get caught spying, so I scrunched low until I could just barely see over the dashboard.

Moments later, Amy handed Jerome a bulky padded envelope. I wondered what was inside. Some kind of payoff? More eulogies? Maybe it was Amy's movie script. She'd just told me she was planning to give it to an "industry contact." Jerome wasn't exactly that, but he'd certainly worked for one. Perhaps he'd mined a few leads of his own in hopes of earning more of Amy's kisses.

Ten minutes of watching two people chitchat in a car is a real snore, so I was surprised but relieved when Amy opened the door and got out. I waited until she disappeared around the corner. Then I strolled across the street to the Mustang, dodging the crows and the pecked-over French fries. I opened the passenger-side door. Fielding looked startled as I slid into the seat that Amy had just abandoned. The leather was still warm. The padded envelope was on the floor beneath my feet.

"Hey, Jerome. Cool car. Is it a sixty-six or a sixty-seven?"

He looked confused, as if he couldn't decide whether he should tell me to take a hike or ask me for a date to the Talbot-Lago exhibit at the Petersen Automotive Museum.

"Sixty-seven."

"Did you restore it yourself?"

"Reupholstering bucket seats isn't one of my gifts."

I nodded. "Yeah, I can identify. I once tried to make a slip cover for a wing chair. The thing ended up looking like a doghouse bagged for termites. By the way, I saw you talking to Amy Lynch. Have you known her long?"

He frowned. "Not very."

"I guess you met her through Evan Brice."

"That's right."

"His death was such a tragedy for everyone—you especially. I guess now that he's gone, you'll be looking for another job."

That assumption seemed to make him uncomfortable, because he looked away. "That's up to Mrs. Brice."

"Well, if you need a referral to a good headhunter, I can give you a couple of names." I dug out a pen and a business card from my purse. Then I picked up Amy's envelope on the pretext of using it as a lap desk. I ran both hands over the surface, trying to identify the contents. It definitely felt like sheets of paper as opposed to bundles of money. I jotted down a couple of executive search firms I'd worked with in the past, and handed him the card. He stared at the envelope on my lap as if he was afraid I'd leave greasy thigh prints on the manila.

"I'm sorry," I said, acknowledging his discomfort. "Is this something important?"

"No."

"Good. For a minute I thought it might be Amy's screenplay. She told me she was giving it to you. Did that guy at DreamWorks finally agree to read it?"

He paused a moment as if he wasn't sure how to respond. "No, I have a contact at Sony."

"Amy must be grateful. I hear Evan didn't have much success shopping it around."

The flush on his cheeks was the only break in an otherwise controlled performance. "Just so you know, Evan tried. No one was interested. He couldn't work miracles for everybody. The point is, he always gave it his best effort. Unfortunately, you seldom get credit for failure. Few people understand that."

"But Evan did?"

"Yes. He never set out to disappoint, but he had a lot of high-maintenance people to prop up, both at work and at home." The condescending tone of those last three words was unmistakable.

"I assume you're referring to his wife."

"Don't put words in my mouth, Ms. Sinclair. Of course, my first loyalty was to Evan, but I'm a professional. I've always extended Mrs. Brice every courtesy."

"I'm sure you have, Jerome. In fact, I assume your job includes extending courtesies to a lot of women in Evan's life. People like Lola Scott."

"My responsibilities were varied. That's why I got into this business. I like the challenge." He reached over and turned the ignition key. The engine purred to life. "You'll have to excuse me. I'm late for an appointment. It was nice seeing you again."

Again, his tone was even and his emotions controlled. I could only guess at what he was thinking. Unfortunately, asking him to enlighten me seemed futile. Obviously, I didn't have the necessary tools to pierce the armor of a professional personal assistant.

I put the envelope back on the floor where I'd found it, and got out of the car. Moments later the Mustang pulled away from the curb.

The crows were again squabbling over the French fries, holding their ground even as I put the top up on the Boxster.

It wasn't until the car edged into traffic that they flapped their wings and flew into the gritty Mid-Wilshire sky.

When I got to Western Avenue, I turned left toward South L.A. and the entrance to the 10 Freeway. On the way I tried to piece together possible scenarios that might have led to a liaison between Jerome and Amy. Amy had reason to dislike Jerome's boss, Evan Brice. I wondered if she'd disliked him enough to kill him. On the other hand, maybe she was using Evan's boorish treatment of her at the party to threaten him. He'd called in Jerome to negotiate a settlement. Only what was she threatening? Exposing Evan's drug habit didn't provide much leverage. That fact had already been made public. Ditto with his stint in rehab. From what I could see, all she had against him was his bad behavior. Big deal.

Then again, it was possible that Jerome and Amy found out about Lola Scott's porn video. The two of them cooked up a scheme to use their knowledge to coerce Evan into launching Amy's writing career. Evan found out that Jerome was involved in the conspiracy, and felt betrayed. They argued. Jerome killed him. Too bad Moses Green didn't have my keen imagination.

I was so caught up in my thoughts that I wasn't prepared when the guy in front of me braked at a yellow light. That was a flagrant disregard for L.A. road etiquette. Nobody stopped at an intersection until at least three cars had run the red light. I slammed on my brakes and was nearly rear-ended by a white van. The driver looked like a serial tailgater, because the van's grill was already smashed in from a previous accident. He also looked like a slob. From my vantage point, I could see that the dashboard was littered with stacks of envelopes and what looked like a crumpled license plate.

When the light turned green, I sped off, weaving in and out of lanes until I reached the entrance to the freeway, heading west toward Santa Monica. As I merged into traffic, I checked my gas gauge. It was less than a quarter full. I considered pulling off to fill up, but I thought I had enough to make it to a station closer to home.

I was about a mile from the transition to the 405 when I checked the traffic in my rearview mirror before changing lanes. That's when I noticed the white van behind me. Of course, white vans are almost as common in L.A. as Mercedes Benzes, but this one had a damaged grill and a crumpled license plate in the front window. I was sure it was the same one I'd seen earlier.

It wasn't unthinkable that we could be driving a similar route. After all, the 10 and the 405 are two of the busiest freeways in Southern California. But L.A. traffic generally flows like this: you get a few car lengths ahead; he gets a few car lengths ahead; you go fast; he goes slow; you go slow; he goes fast. No matter what, you both get to the same destination within a couple of minutes of each other. What doesn't happen is that for ten miles the same vehicle is still stuck to your tail like superglue.

At first I wondered if somebody from the media was dogging me to get an interview about Evan's murder. Unlikely. I didn't see any satellite equipment or cables mounted on the van's roof. It could be a case of road rage. I didn't remember displaying any egregiously bad manners—at least not today—but it didn't take much to annoy people. Maybe lingering too long at the green light had been enough. The third alternative? I was just being paranoid. I decided to test my theories.

If the guy was following me, I didn't want to lead him back to my house. I waited for a break in traffic and moved into the lane that merged onto the 405 Freeway, heading south toward San Diego. My pulse quickened when the van followed. As I neared Washington Boulevard, I moved over to the far right lane as if I planned to exit. So did the van.

I drove past the exit, frequently glancing at my rearview mirror to see if the guy was still on my tail. He was. My hands felt sweaty on the wheel. I told myself not to panic. While I was trying without much success to convince myself that everything would turn out okay, I drove past the exit that led to the police station where Deegan worked. I checked my gas gauge again. It was creeping downward. I decided against taking another exit. I didn't know the neighborhood and didn't want to take the risk of getting lost. At least the freeway was crowded with witnesses if things turned bad.

The traffic was heavy but moving. Just past the airport I calculated the holes in the flow and did the unthinkable. I stepped on the gas and shot across four lanes of traffic *and* the double yellow line of the carpool lane. I figured it would only be a matter of seconds before the California Highway Patrol pulled me over. My confidence disappeared when I noticed that the van had moved over, too. It was now cruising in the fast lane a car length behind me. Unfortunately, it was too far away to make out the identity of the driver.

I darted in and out of the diamond lane through El Segundo, Manhattan Beach, and Gardena, trying to draw attention to myself. It didn't work. I attracted a lot of rude gestures but no CHP officers. I'd always wondered why Deegan called the CHP the "Auto Club with guns." Now I knew. They were all back in the office, handing out road maps and booking cruises.

Luckily, the Boxster maneuvered better than a big, clunky van, but my wrists and shoulders were beginning to ache from my death grip on the wheel. The farther I got from L.A., the tenser I became. For what seemed like the millionth time, I checked the gas gauge and saw that the warning light had come on, indicating a low tank. I swore out loud, wishing I had a Prius.

I didn't want to run out of gas in the middle of a freeway lane. My car and I would end up looking like a sculpture at the Museum of Contemporary Art. On the other hand, I had to get away from this guy. I was getting dangerously close to Long Beach, a city crisscrossed with streets I couldn't even name. I had to get back to familiar territory. At the next exit, I flipped on my turn signal and maneuvered into the right-hand lane. The van followed. I took a deep breath and turned off onto the exit road. So did the van. My gaze flitted back and forth between the rearview and side mirrors, waiting, calculating before I spotted my salvation.

On the left side of the road was a rocky berm separating the road from the freeway. On the right side was a guardrail. The road sloped downward. Soon the berm would become too steep to navigate. All I cared about was waiting until it was too steep for the van but not for the Boxster. I slowed. The distance between us narrowed. My timing had to be flawless. At the last possible minute, I wrenched the wheel left and slammed my foot down hard on the accelerator.

Gravel pinged against the car's metal body as the car fishtailed and bumped across the unstable ground. The sound was deafening. For a moment, I thought I was losing control. I tried but failed to remember if you slowed down in a skid or sped up. Pookie had once dated a stuntman. He probably could have told me, but I'd barely bothered to learn his name.

Seconds later I was back on the freeway. I put my hand over my heart as if that might quiet the pounding. I was safe, but the car's wheel alignment was probably shot, not to mention the paint job. I glanced out the passenger-side window and watched as the van pulled to the shoulder of the exit road.

I took the next exit, driving around until I located a freeway entrance that would get me back to L.A. Just my luck—it was closed for roadwork. Near the intersection of a quiet little neighborhood, I pulled over and dug out my trusty *Thomas Guide* map book. I'd just pinpointed my location when the white van raced through the intersection in front of me. I was in unfamiliar territory, trying to evade a person or persons unknown, on a nearly empty gas tank. I crossed my fingers, hoping he wouldn't see me. Just then I heard the screeching of tires as he braked.

I made a quick U-turn and raced down the street, looking for a way out. That's when I saw the brick wall. The street was a dead end. Before I had a chance to do anything, I saw the van bearing down on me. I was screwed.

The van's driver slammed on his brakes and swerved to a stop in the middle of the street, blocking my exit. There was no way around him. The street was jammed with parked cars. Fences blocked most of the yards.

I locked my door, knowing it was a futile gesture. All he had to do was break the window and pull me out. Hell, all he had to do was shoot me. Either way, I was a goner—unless he wanted the car intact. Fine. He could have it. Except that I had a feeling he wanted more than that. I just didn't know what. For the first time, I wished

I had a weapon: a gun, a knife, or a large bull elephant with irritable bowel syndrome.

The van's door opened. A leg covered in blue denim emerged. A black military-type boot punctuated the leg. I couldn't see if the boot had a silver medallion on it, but even so, my mind buzzed with thoughts of renegade commandos, trained killers, and bloodlust.

Joe Deegan had once cautioned me to fight like hell if anybody ever tried to force me into a car. He said it was better to die fast than to suffer what probably came next. No wonder our relationship had never gone anywhere. While other couples were spending romantic weekends in Carmel, Deegan was lecturing me on the best way to die.

In any event, Joe Deegan was nowhere in sight. I was on my own. I depressed the clutch, slid the Boxster's gearshift into first, and poised my right foot on the gas, keeping my gaze fixed on the man's leg until another emerged. Finally, the driver's whole body came into view. He was wearing a beat-up olive-drab army jacket that looked as if it was a holdover from the Vietnam War. He stood around five feet eleven or so and looked fit. His short, sandy hair was turning gray, so it was hard to tell how old he was. I estimated somewhere between late fifties and geezerdom. Behind his aviator glasses, I assumed his eyes were as hard and unyielding as his body language.

Slowly he began walking toward me. I watched and waited. Then I let up on the clutch and pressed down on the accelerator. If the bastard came any closer, he was going to be sucking his dinner through a tube in the ICU.

- 22 -

y leg felt tense and tingly, poised on the gas pedal. I watched as the driver of the white van came closer and closer. I revved the engine. He stopped, reaching into his jacket pocket and pulling out something small and black. *Shit,* I thought—*a gun.* I dove for cover across the passenger seat. As I did, my feet slipped off the gas and clutch pedals. The car lurched and the engine died. No gunshots followed. That was good. Carefully, I raised my head far enough to peek over the dashboard. The guy was still standing in the same spot. He was smiling. I scrutinized the object in his hand and realized it was too flat to be a gun. It looked more like a wallet. That's when I knew I'd been living in L.A. too long. He flipped it open as a cop might. But he was no cop, and if he thought I was going to fall for some Tinkertoy fake badge, he was mistaken.

I rolled down the window and shouted, "Don't come any closer or you're road kill."

"Be cool," he said. "I just want to talk."

"Join Toastmasters."

"Look, it's not what you think. I'm a private investigator. Here's my license." Again, he stepped toward me, holding out the wallet.

"Stay where you are," I shouted. "Throw it over here."

He hesitated. Then he pitched the thing, but it fell short of its goal. I restarted the engine, inched forward, and cautiously opened the door. When I had the wallet in my hand, I once again locked myself inside the car.

The wallet contained a laminated card that appeared to be some kind of state document. It looked official, but I'd never seen a PI license before, so I couldn't say for sure. The name read: Charles John Tate.

I rolled down the window and stuck my head out. "Why are you following me?"

"A client of mine wants us to have a conversation."

"Why didn't you pick up the telephone and give me a call?"

"I was working up to that."

"How long have you been tailing me?"

"Couple of days."

"A couple of *days*? I don't believe you. I would have noticed."

He grinned. "Yeah, that's what they all say."

"Why did you pull that stupid freeway stunt? I could have been killed. Don't you gumshoes have a code of conduct?"

He held up his hands in a gesture of surrender. "Okay, in all fairness, you have a point. A freeway chase is probably not such a great idea, but old habits die hard. If I say I'm sorry, will you answer a few questions?"

"Not until you tell me who you're working for."

"No can do. That's confidential."

"I'm not telling you a damn thing until I know the name of your client."

While he paused to consider that, he rearranged rocks on the ground in front of him with the toe of his boot. Finally he said, "I'll tell you under one condition."

"No conditions."

"I don't think we should be shouting at each other on the street like this. Somebody's going to call the cops."

"That's even better."

"Look, there's a café down the road a ways. Tell you what. I'll buy you a cup of coffee. We'll talk about my client. If I get out of line, you can scream for help."

I hesitated going anywhere with him because I didn't trust him. On the other hand, I wanted to find out why he was chasing me down the 405 and if he knew the location of the nearest gas station. Finally, I agreed. Tate led me to a Shell station and waited in the van while I filled the tank and checked for gravel dings from the Boxster's recent mountain climbing expedition. Everything looked fine, at least on the surface.

Ten minutes later, I was sitting in a booth at Deanna's Diner, staring at Charles Tate's business card through the billowing steam of my coffee. The "T" in "Tate Investigations" had a Sherlock Holmes magnifying glass superimposed over it, making it larger than the rest of the letters. That wasn't exactly an original concept. He needed to hire me to create a corporate image with a little more pop.

"So, who's your client and what does he want with me?"

His ice blue eyes sparkled with a keen sense of mischief. If I'd gotten the impression from Tate's military jacket and boots that he was a burnt-out Vietnam vet, I was wrong. He looked alert and fully engaged. I suspected that if he hadn't seen it all, he'd at least seen most of it.

"I answer to everything but 'Hey, you,' but my friends call me Charley."

"I'm not your friend, Mr. Tate."

His grin was crooked and appealing. "Okay, have it

your way, Ms. Sinclair. Let's just say my client was clearing up a couple of issues when you showed up in the window of opportunity."

"That sounds about as clear as mud."

Instead of responding, he took a sip of coffee. I noted that he didn't slurp—unusual for a man.

"So what happened to your face?" he said.

I'd gotten so used to looking at my bruises and scrapes in the mirror for the past few days, I now took them for granted.

"None of your business."

He shrugged. "You look too smart to hook up with a guy who slaps you around, but I could be wrong. I still have friends in the Department. If you give me his name, I'll put a bug in somebody's ear."

"You were a cop?"

He nodded. "LAPD, thirty years, the last ten of it on the bomb squad. Personally I hate guys who beat up on women. If my buddies on the force can't do anything, I wouldn't mind taking a shot at the guy myself."

"Not literally, I trust."

Tate smiled. I was beginning to wonder if there was a required class at the police academy called Macho Bullshit 101.

"It wasn't a boyfriend," I went on, "at least not mine. In fact, I'm not sure who it was—yet. So, who's your client?"

I may have been mistaken, but I thought I saw his facial muscles relax. "Let's just say it's somebody in the public eye."

There were only two people in my life who fit that description: Darcy Daniels from *Celebrity Heat* and Lola Scott. I suppose Jason-the-twit-producer could have hired a PI to track me down, but his attention span didn't seem that long. That left only one other person.

"So let me take a wild guess," I said. "Your client is Lola Scott."

He looked surprised but dropped any further pretense of client confidentiality. "She heard you were pretty desperate to find her."

"So she hired a private detective to find me first? That doesn't make sense."

"Sure it does. People like her have to worry about your kind of persistence. With all the wackos wandering around, she didn't want to take a chance that you were one of them."

"Come on, Tate. Don't bullshit me. Do I look like a stalker? This is about the porn video. Right?"

He stared at me, frowning. "You watched it?"

"Yup, and it was pretty icky. I take it you haven't had the pleasure."

He shook his head. "I don't play in that sandbox."

"So what's Lola want with me? She got the tape back. Jakey saw to that. He *was* the one who attacked me, wasn't he?"

Tate leaned back against the leatherette booth and took another sip of coffee. "She'll pay your medical bills."

"In exchange for what? Dropping charges against her boyfriend?"

His jaw muscles twitched. "Among other things."

"Like what? Keeping my mouth shut about the videotape?"

"That and one more thing."

"Jeez, what else is there?"

He paused for a moment, as if he was reluctant to tell me. "She wants the bed."

"The *what*?"

"The bed in Brice's apartment. She bought it for him. Now she wants it back." Tate shrugged, clearly embarrassed. "Look, what can I tell you? The guy's death hit her hard. She thinks the bed will get her through the pain."

In a way, I wasn't surprised it belonged to Lola Scott. On the other hand, from what I'd learned about Evan's love life, Lola may not have been the only woman to frolic on those exotic sheets. I didn't understand why she'd want to be custodian of a piece of furniture with such a murky history.

"Okay," I said, "let's say I agree to give Lola everything on her wish list. Here's what I want in return: an interview."

Tate shook his head. "It ain't gonna happen. She's a mess right now."

"Let's put it this way, Charley. Make it happen."

He looked at me for a long time. Finally he rolled his eyes. "Stay put. I'll be right back."

Tate stood up, turned, and walked away. As he did, I saw him pull a cell phone from the pocket of his jacket. When he finally returned fifteen minutes later, the look on his face was a mixture of anger and menace. It wasn't directed at me, but it made me wonder if I should be more careful about what I asked for.

-23-

ccording to Charley Tate, Lola Scott had agreed to speak with me about Jakey and the porn video, but only if I would leave the diner immediately and meet her on the set of *Kings Road*. I agreed. Tate gave me directions to Sony Studios in Culver City and told me I was on my own.

As instructed, I drove to the Overland Boulevard entrance to the studio and spoke with the guard at the kiosk. After he found my name on his list, he advised me that somebody would meet me in the parking lot. A few minutes later I climbed into a golf cart driven by a young man who took me down a narrow street lined on both sides with large warehouselike buildings. He stopped at one toward the end of the row. Mounted above the door was a red police-type light. I followed him inside a dark room. Somewhere in the distance I heard the murmur of voices.

The young man pointed to an empty chair. "You have to wait with the atmosphere. The cast is getting notes. When they break, somebody else will come to get you."

The *Kings Road* "atmosphere," aka extras, were congregated in a back corner of the sound stage, reading or chatting in hushed voices. A woman in her fifties with a sweet, pudgy face was noshing at a table loaded with bagels, muffins, fruit, and soft drinks. When she noticed me, she popped a couple of grapes in her mouth and made a beeline for my chair.

"Hi, I'm LeAnn Bradley." Her mouth was still full of food. "You must be replacing Darlene. I told that girl not to bug Lola Scott, but she wouldn't listen."

"Lola sounds like a pill."

She nodded. "Aren't they all?"

For the next ten minutes, LeAnn regaled me with a list of every TV and film extra job she'd ever had, including some of her best scenes, which tragically had landed on the cutting room floor.

"Once I got special business on *Facts of Life* because I was standing next to Tootie, and they couldn't cut me out. I still get residuals. Don't you love the life?"

LeAnn eventually ran out of special-business tales and wandered back to the food trough. After making sure no one was watching, I maneuvered around a series of curtains. When the voices grew louder, I stopped maneuvering and started peeking.

A half-dozen people sat on director's chairs on a set made up to look like the living room of an upscale high-rise apartment. The floors were parquet, the decor sleek and modern. Several busts of unrecognizable old white men sat atop four-foot pedestals placed throughout the room. Floor-to-ceiling bookcases framed a fake window, through which the audience could see a backdrop of what looked like the Manhattan skyline. A painting of a distinguished older woman in a formal dress hung above the fireplace, which I assumed was also fake.

Lola Scott sat on the living room couch, staring

blankly into space. She was somewhere in her twenties. The white negligee she wore was filmy enough to reveal what was beneath all that fluff: the lean body of an athlete. Her blue-black hair was long, lush, and iridescent. I tried but failed to find a single flaw. She was a genetic freak, so perfect she looked computer generated.

A middle-aged man with thinning hair and probably the beginnings of an ulcer was referring to notes on a tablet attached to a clipboard. The director, I assumed.

"Your point is well taken, Lola." His tone was brittle. "Except Mallory Eden is not pissed off that her mother was just crushed by a garbage truck. She is heartbroken. I need you to tap into that inner pain."

The words were snide and meant to hurt. His intentions were not lost on Lola Scott. She seemed to be holding her breath. A moment later, her chin began to quiver.

"That's it!" the director shouted. "Okay, people, we've got tears. Let's take it from where Mallory throws the champagne glass into the fireplace."

Slowly Lola rose from the couch. "Excuse me. I'm going to my trailer."

With her negligee billowing like a cloud of mist, she walked off the set. The director collapsed against the back of his chair, put his finger to his temple, and pretended to shoot. I skirted around the fake living room and followed Lola out a door into the harsh sunlight.

"Excuse me, Miss Scott. I'm Tucker Sinclair. Charley Tate sent me."

As she whirled around to face me, each hair on her head floated out into the ether with a fluid motion that reminded me of a team of long-legged synchronized swimmers. The move had obviously been staged for maximum drama. Thick bangs nearly obscured her brown eyes, which were puddled with moisture. Instead of calling attention to the tears by wiping them away, she let them roll down her face. By the time they landed on the white negligee, they had gathered enough makeup to spot it with brown freckles.

"Bobby doesn't give me any credit for what I've done to make this show a hit," she said. "He's trying to kill me off. Everybody knows it."

I assumed that Bobby was somebody connected to *Kings Road*, the director perhaps, and that he wanted to kill her off the show, not literally kill her off.

"I'm sorry." It was all I could think of to say.

She began flapping her hands as if she were drying her nail polish. I suspected it was a tool she used to harness all those unwieldy emotions. "I'm sorry. I'm sorry. I have to go. You can come if you want."

I wanted. I slid in next to her on the bench seat of a golf cart parked outside the door of the sound stage. Lola turned the key. The motor purred, and the cart lurched forward. It stopped almost immediately in front of a trailer parked a hundred feet away. I guess walking wasn't in her contract.

I followed her up the steps and through the door of the trailer. Inside, sprawled on a couch, watching TV and drinking a beer, was a well-muscled guy with curly blond hair. He wore a white wife-beater undershirt that exposed beefy arms, one of which sported a tattoo of a coiled snake. I immediately checked out his feet. No boots with silver medallions, just athletic shoes—big ones. When the man saw Lola, he jumped up like a lonely lapdog.

"I'm cold, Jakey. Get me a robe?"

At the mention of his name, my heart produced an anxious thud. Jakey stared at me, too, as if I looked familiar, but he couldn't remember why. When recognition hit him, a dark, menacing cloud moved across his face.

"Shit!" he said.

Lola was too self-absorbed to pick up on the exchange. "Jakey," she repeated. "My *robe*."

He hesitated a moment longer before pulling out a long red bathrobe from the closet.

"Not that one, the white terry."

The muscles in his jaw twitched. Nonetheless, he went back to the closet and found the robe she'd asked for. Lola put it on over her negligee, while he dutifully returned the red one to the hanger.

"My face must be a mess," she went on. "Call makeup." Jakey turned to face the door. "No. Just get me some Q-tips and a jar of baby oil, and tell Jude to come by in fifteen minutes." He'd made it a couple of steps when she added, "Wait. Let Bobby stew for a while. Stay where you are. Don't do anything."

Jakey grew increasingly frustrated as Lola continued sending him to fetch things: bottled water, box of tissues, hairbrush. Maybe he was uncomfortable being ordered around in front of a woman whom he'd assaulted just days before. At some point Lola realized that he was glaring at me and, after a thoughtful moment, figured out why.

"Baby," she said tenderly, "I think you need a break. Why don't you go to Starbucks and get me a tall triple skinny dry cappuccino. Tell the barista to double-cup it."

Jakey looked conflicted, as if he wanted to get away from me but didn't want Lola to orchestrate his departure. I wondered how much further he could be pushed before he exploded. Apparently a little further, because he didn't protest—he just walked out of the trailer, slamming the door with barely contained rage. Great! Another guy in my life with low impulse control.

Lola wasn't looking so beautiful anymore. Tears had streaked her makeup. She'd wiped her nose on the cuff of the robe so that it no longer looked pristine and perfect. For what seemed like a long time, she didn't say anything, just stared at her reflection in a wall mirror as if she was mesmerized by the drama unfolding on her own face.

"Everything I do turns to shit," she said.

I could sympathize with that. "Maybe I should come back later."

She ignored my offer as if she hadn't even heard it. For a moment I wondered if she'd been rehearsing lines. Her voice was barely above a whisper. "Damn him. Why did he have to die?"

I assumed she meant Evan Brice, but trying to guess made me feel as if I were on some quiz show, filling in missing words in a sentence to win a new plasma TV.

She turned her gaze on me. "I just want to be at home in bed with the covers pulled over my head."

"Charley Tate told me you want the bed in Evan's apartment."

She nodded. "I know it sounds dumb, but it would make me feel closer to him right now. I've made so many stupid mistakes in my life . . ."

"You mean like making that porn movie?"

She looked at me warily. "Please, you can't tell anybody about that. I never thought I'd make anything of myself, or I wouldn't have done it. I was only sixteen. My parents had just kicked me out of the house, and I was broke. I met this guy named Stan at a party, and we moved in together. He convinced me the film was the answer to everything. We'd make some money, and I'd get experience in front of a camera. So I did it. A few months later I started getting bad feelings about it. I told Stan, and he promised to destroy all the copies. Copies, sure. He did that, all right. But he kept the master. Lying bastard. When I got the part in Richard's film, Stan saw my name in the paper. He called Evan and asked for a hundred grand."

"So you paid up?"

She nodded. "Evan was furious that I hadn't told him about the film. He came to the set of *Born to Ride* and told me to come up with the money. He'd arrange the rest. I was short of cash, so I asked if he'd advance me his commission on *Pagan Dreams* as a loan. He said no. We had this huge fight. I finally managed to get the payment together, and a few days later I gave it to Evan. He made the exchange with Stan."

"Why didn't you go to the police?"

"We couldn't. If Richard Burnett ever found out I'd done an adult film, I'd be stuck on this crappy soap forever."

Lola Scott had obviously had a tough life, but it was hard to feel too sorry for her. A lot of people would be thrilled to have a steady acting job, even if it was on a "crappy soap." I tried to look at life from Lola's point of view. In a dozen years, after multiple plastic surgeries had pulled her skin so tight that her eyebrows had merged into her hairline, she'd come to work one day and found out that the script called for a drop-dead gorgeous twenty-something newcomer to push her in front of a subway train. I couldn't fault Lola for developing a plan B.

"Look," I said. "I have to tell you the truth. The police already know about the video. They also have a description of Jakey and the boots he was wearing when he attacked me. Sooner or later, they'll find out about everything."

She closed her eyes and blew out a big breath of air. "Stupid jerk. I told him to go to the apartment and see if the tape was still there. That's all."

"Why did Evan have it at the apartment in the first place?"

"It was temporary. He didn't want to take it home or to the office, because he was afraid somebody would see it. He told me he was going to find a good place to hide it. He died before he could give it to me."

"Too bad Jakey didn't use better judgment."

Her expression hardened. "You're not going to cause problems about this, are you? Look, I'm sorry you got hurt. It's not my fault, but I'm going to write you a check anyway."

"I don't want your check. I want to know who killed Evan Brice, and right now I'm thinking it might have been Jakey. If he roughed me up, he might have done the same to Evan. Only Evan didn't end up hurt; he ended up dead."

"No." Her tone was firm.

"How can you be so sure?"

"Because Jakey was with me the night Evan died."

"And where was that?" I said skeptically.

"Rome. I went to meet somebody about a film role. I took Jakey along for the ride. We were both there when I got the news that Evan was dead."

That "somebody" was obviously the Italian producer James Brodie had mentioned, the guy who was going to make Lola into the next Katharine Hepburn. But Rome? She couldn't be talking about Rome-Rome. That was in Italy. Nobody flew to Rome-Rome to discuss a film role. They called or faxed or e-mailed. Sometimes they just said,

"You're beautiful, baby; don't change a thing. My people will call your people." Maybe Rome was some new housing project in Pacific Palisades. That was only a few miles from Venice. She and Jakey would have had plenty of time to drive to Evan's apartment and murder him.

"When I got the news," she continued, "I called Alitalia, and we took the first flight back."

Damn! Alitalia didn't fly from Pac-Pal, but it definitely flew from Rome-Rome. So she probably was in Italy. That was disappointing. Not only did she have an alibi, but Jakey had one, too. How many hours had I wasted on the goofy theory that Lola Scott had a hand in Evan's death? Too many. No wonder Moses Green had brushed me off when I confided in him. Deegan had warned me I was on the wrong track. I should have listened. Now Jakey and I had something in common. We were both stupid jerks.

"Where is the video now?"

"Destroyed."

"How do you know it's the only one?"

"Because Evan made Stan promise."

It was hard to believe she could be naive enough to think that a blackmailer wasn't going to come back for more money, but I guess she was accustomed to getting what she wanted. As much as I hated to admit it, I'd reached a dead end in my little investigation. Neither Lola nor Jakey could have killed Evan unless they'd hired out the job. That didn't seem likely. Lola appeared to be truly pained by Evan's death. On the other hand, maybe Stan the blackmailing porn producer had killed Evan. I thought about mentioning that theory to Detective Green but doubted he'd be interested.

Before I left, Lola agreed to send somebody to pick up

the bed before two p.m. on Tuesday, the day I'd scheduled the rental company and the charity pickups. I was relieved. By Wednesday morning the apartment would be empty, and I'd have fulfilled my promise to Cissy.

"By the way," I said, "Jakey took some of Evan's mail."

"I know. The stuff is at my house. It's mostly junk, but you can have it back if you want. I'll have him drop it by your place."

That was the *last* thing I wanted.

"Mail it to the Venice apartment. The post office will forward it to the right address."

As I walked back to my car, I found myself wondering why the police seemed to have eliminated Monique Ruiz and Lola Scott as suspects in Evan's death, but not Cissy. All three had alibis. Even though I still believed that Cissy would eventually be cleared, I couldn't chase away this nagging feeling that there were gaps in her story and missing words in her sentences. Maybe if I filled in the blanks correctly, I could win a new TV after all.

-24-

s soon as I left Sony Studios, I headed to West L.A.
to collect Muldoon from puppy day care. The traffic was moving at a glacial pace due to construction
on Olympic Boulevard. I couldn't tell what the road crew
was up to, but figured either it was tearing up a street that
had recently been repaved or else the city had finally
scraped together enough money to fill one of L.A.'s notorious potholes, several of which were large enough to
swallow Jonah *and* the whale. Whatever the case, the traffic jam managed to turn six miles into fifty minutes.

When I finally got to Le Bon Chien, I found Hannah
sitting on a couch in the dayroom, looking as if she'd just
found her goldfish floating belly up in its bowl. If Muldoon
hadn't been curled up next to her thigh, I might have worried. He glanced my way but looked as if he didn't have
the strength to move. All that "interfacing" must have
worn him out.

The room was filled with overstuffed couches and
chairs, playground equipment, and what looked like a
doggie treadmill. A dozen large canines, mostly retrievers
but also a standard poodle and a Great Dane, lounged on
the furniture. A disreputable-looking mutt was entertain-

ing himself by pushing a ball across the room with his nose.

"So," I said, "did Muldoon pass his D.O.G. exams?"

Hannah frowned as if she didn't appreciate my flippancy. "Please sit down."

I checked to make sure I wasn't crushing Le Bon Chien's resident flea circus before taking a seat on the couch adjacent to the one she and Muldoon occupied.

Hannah referred to notes on a tablet that was attached to a clipboard. "Sorry to say, we found that Muldoon didn't socialize well with his classmates." Her tone was solemn. "He seemed to prefer hanging out with the staff rather than with the other dogs. We often find this behavior in animals who are left alone a lot."

I felt my cheeks burn. "Did I mention that he's an only dog?"

"Yes," she said knowingly, "we're familiar with the syndrome."

Only-dog syndrome? Who knew? Frankly, I was a little put off by her attitude. She should have been praising Muldoon for his people skills, not criticizing him for his choice of companions. However, I swallowed my irritation because this whole day-care gig was important to the pup's mental health, not to mention my custody battle with Pookie.

"I'll admit he's alone too much," I said. "That's why we're here."

"Yes, of course, but you must also know we have dozens of applicants a week and limited enrollment. That's why we can afford to be selective."

I didn't like the direction this conversation was taking. Nonetheless, I smiled my most engaging smile. "Only the best and the brightest, right?"

As a reward for my finally getting it, she smiled back. "I knew you'd understand. While Muldoon is a very handsome boy, he would have spent the entire day curled up in my lap if I'd let him. That sort of behavior doesn't work here. He has to be a self-starter to make it at Le Bon Chien."

I stared at her in disbelief. "Wait a minute. You're *rejecting* Muldoon?"

"Don't think of it as a rejection—"

"You're rejecting *my* dog?"

"As I said—"

"I heard what you said." In my head I added: *And I think you're full of shit. In fact, screw Le Bon Chien. Day care my ass—the place is nothing more than a crappy, high-priced kennel. Muldoon is better off at home alone.* As much as I wanted to say all that out loud, I didn't, because a part of me didn't want to jeopardize the pup's chances to reapply after *le bon* Hannah came to her senses.

I waited for the catch—an offer to enroll Muldoon in some outrageously expensive remedial bonding therapy, perhaps—but none came. Instead, all Hannah offered was an image of a resolute young woman, staring at notes on a clipboard.

Finally I stood. "Come on, Muldoon. We're out of here."

The pup didn't respond. He just sat there looking at me with his big brown eyes. Uh-oh, I thought. Time to call in the big guns.

I looked him square in the eye. "You wanna go for a ride in the car?"

Bark! Bark! Bark! Bark!

That was more like it. Muldoon jumped off the couch, spun three quick circles in place, and headed for the door

as Warden Hannah frowned in disapproval at the din he'd
set off. Every dog in the joint was barking now. And who
could blame them? In the absence of tin cups to clank
along the bars, you work with what you got. Once in the
car, I lifted Muldoon's paw so we could high-five.

The pup was disappointed on the drive home when I
wouldn't let him hang his head out the window, but if he
was going to be my new partner, I had to set limits. There
was no time like the present to start. Besides, I had my
own disappointments to worry about. In the past week I'd
fought with my mother and alienated Joe Deegan, and
now, aside from Eugene and Venus, the only friend who
was still speaking to me had just been branded an un-
acceptable playdate at puppy day care. What more could
go wrong?

-25-

uldoon's kennel experience had left him smelling less than fragrant. He needed a bath. So on Tuesday morning I dropped him off at a grooming shop in Venice before heading to Evan's apartment.

I arrived just a few minutes after nine. The street was relatively quiet. Brenda the parking vigilante was out on the landing in front of her unit, glaring at the bicycle chained to the railing. Both its tires were missing. I wondered if Monique's boyfriend had finally exacted his revenge. I would have nodded hello to her, but she didn't look up.

The rental company was coming between ten and twelve to pick up the furniture. Representatives from the battered women's shelter had promised to arrive between twelve and two to collect the household items. I could have left the donation boxes out by the curb, but Lola Scott's people were coming for the bed sometime before two. Not that I was a wimp, but I decided to wait and let somebody else carry the stuff down three flights of stairs.

I made my way to the third floor, which by now I could have found blindfolded. I stopped in the hallway in front of Monique Ruiz's door. Green had verified her alibi for the night of Evan's death, but I still wanted to talk to her myself. Perhaps she knew something, even a rumor that she hadn't told the police but might tell me. I knocked on her door but got no response.

I wrote a note on one of my business cards, informing the rental company that they could find me at Rose's place. I tucked it into the seam of Evan's door and walked down the hall. When Rose answered the door, her hair was wet. A couple of brush rollers were hanging askew from the crown of her head. She looked disconsolate.

"My hair was looking a little frowsy," she explained. "I tried setting it myself, but I just can't do it anymore."

"Want me to give it a shot?"

Her face brightened. "If it wouldn't be too much of a bother."

I was a member of Generation Blow-Dry and didn't have a clue how to set hair. On the other hand, how hard could it be? All I had to do was roll it, dry it, and brush it into a neat little nuclear mushroom cloud.

Rose sat on a kitchen chair, offering advice on the finer points of curler placement. When I was finished, I gave the job a critical eye. It didn't look bad. I helped her tie what looked like an old rag around her head to keep the rollers in place. She told me it was a child's head scarf that had belonged to her daughter. As charming as that sounded, the scarf made her look as if she were on her way to thresh wheat.

At 11:15, the rental company movers arrived: two guys—one was black and the other looked Samoan. Both appeared out of shape but strong. They quickly loaded the furniture and left. At one o'clock, a couple of women arrived from the shelter. I helped them lug the boxes to their van. Finally, everything was out of the apartment except the bed. The place looked empty and sad. I realized this would probably be the last time I'd come here except to visit Rose.

At three o'clock I was still waiting for Lola's people to pick up the bed. By that time Rose's hair was dry, so I combed it out. It didn't look half bad. When four o'clock rolled around, I started to fume not only at Lola but at myself as well. I'd trusted her to show up as promised. I hadn't even asked for her telephone number. At four-thirty I decided not to wait any longer.

As I was leaving Rose's apartment, I heard voices through the flimsy door of Monique Ruiz's unit across the hall. It sounded like two women engaged in a high-octane dispute. I wondered who was giving her a bad time now. I decided to find out.

I knocked, and the voices stopped. A few moments later, the door opened. Standing in front of me was none other than the star reporter for the *Valley News Now*, Marta Cruz. She wore a tight purple skirt and matching vest over a long-sleeved lavender blouse with a collar that drooped over her chest like the ears of a basset hound. The getup looked cheerful and springy, but her scowl was as cold as winter in Buffalo.

For a moment, she blankly stared at me as if she didn't remember who I was. I took advantage of the lull to drum up a reason—any reason—why Cruz was in Monique Ruiz's apartment. After several hit-and-miss theories, only one survived the sniff test: She was badgering Monique for information for her newspaper article on Evan Brice's murder.

From somewhere inside the apartment I heard another voice. It was soft and tentative. "Who is it, Nonny?"

Nonny? Where had I heard that name before? Slowly

the memory came into focus. It had been recorded on Monique Ruiz's voice mail greeting. Later that same day her aunt, Estela Sandoval, had told me it was a nickname for Monique's sister.

How very convenient, I thought, and how very easy it must have been for a budding investigative reporter to gather information on a celebrity murder when her sister had a key to the crime scene. I wondered how many times Cruz had snooped inside Evan's apartment, and if that was where she'd found my name and address.

"Why didn't you tell me your sister worked for Evan Brice?" I blurted out.

Cruz's lips pressed together in an angry line. Before she could respond, Monique Ruiz appeared. I'd caught only a glimpse of her before through the peephole in Evan Brice's door. Up close, I saw that she was five feet three or so, with brunette hair and coffee-colored eyes, which were framed by carefully arched brows. Her features were small except for her lips, which were full and sensuous. Dark circles smudged the skin beneath her eyes, as if she hadn't slept well the night before. There was also a grayish cast to her face that made her skin seem washed out and dull. The dark circles and the dull skin gave me the impression she might be ill. Whatever she had, I hoped it wasn't contagious.

"Monique?" I said. "I'm—"

Before I could finish my sentence, Cruz tried to slam the door shut, but my foot was in the way. Instead of closing, the door bounced off my shoe like a boomerang, nearly smacking her in the face on the rebound.

"Nonny! What are you doing?"

"Go back inside."

"I told you before, stop telling me what to do."

It sounded like an old argument. I wasn't interested in the revival, so I interrupted.

"Monique, my name is Tucker Sinclair. I'm a friend of Evan Brice's. Your sister came to my house a few days ago asking questions for a newspaper article she's writing about his death."

The slow transformation of Monique's expression from surprise to alarm stripped her face of all color, even the gray. She turned toward her sister.

Cruz's jaw became rigid. "I did it for you, *mija*."

"No, not for me! You did it for your own self."

Monique darted back into the apartment. Cruz followed. I didn't want to miss the action, so I stepped inside, too.

The place was decorated in a style that could only be described as garage sale postmodern. The eclectic decor consisted of a small television, a chintz couch, and two mismatched chairs, worn from years of hard use. To the left I caught a glimpse of a small stove and refrigerator barricaded behind a three-panel divider made of azure crinkled plastic.

On a TV tray next to the refrigerator was an embroidered cozy that was draped over what looked like a toaster. It read, "Pop Goes the Toast." In the living room, a knitted afghan designed with a zigzag pattern of alternating royal blue and white yarn was draped over the back of the couch. Photographs from somebody's *quinceañera* were laid out on the floor, along with bits of colored paper and blank pages from a scrapbook. Nearby was a set of knitting needles that held six inches of what I assumed was her latest project, possibly another afghan. This one was smaller and made of pastel yellow and green yarn. Monique needed one more item to complete the look: a wall plaque that read, "Stop Me Before I Craft Again." She could even needlepoint it herself.

Monique was now lying on the couch in the fetal position, hugging a small blue teddy bear. The ribbon around the bear's neck looked fresh and unwrinkled, as if it had just been brought home from the toy store.

Cruz knelt in front of her, whispering something, but Monique pushed her away. Despite the psychodrama, Cruz's manner seemed maternal and loving. Only a few phrases from their conversation drifted my way. I got the impression that Cruz was peddling justifications that were turning out to be a hard sell. Eventually she grew frustrated by her failure.

She pointed an index finger at her sister. "You got yourself into this trouble. If you want me to help you out of it, you have to listen to me."

The word "trouble" seemed to follow Monique Ruiz everywhere she went, which made me wonder if she was as sweet and innocent as Rose thought she was.

Cruz was tugging on the teddy bear, trying to pull it away from Monique's face. "Talk to me, *mija*."

"Leave me alone!"

"Excuse me," I said, "but do you mind telling me what's going on here? Why did you come to my house? Is this some kind of shakedown?"

"You don't know anything," Cruz said.

"Then fill me in."

She lifted her chin into a pose that seemed determined, almost self-righteous. "Mr. Chatterton told my sister about you. He said you were a good person. He said if he ever needed help, he'd go to you first. I thought you might help Monique, too, but Mr. Chatterton was wrong about you."

Cruz knew that Chatterton wasn't Evan's real name, so I didn't bother correcting her. And I ignored the slam. Her criticism of me didn't even begin to equal my own.

"Just what did you think I was going to do for her?"

"It doesn't matter now. I can handle it myself."

"How? By selling lies about me to tabloid TV? How much did *Celebrity Heat* pay you anyway?"

Monique opened her mouth as if to respond, but Cruz shot her a look of warning.

Cruz stood. "We don't have anything else to say to you. Please leave."

"Fine, I'll leave, but if you think I'm going to stand by and let you trash my name to pay your sister's cell-phone bill, you're mistaken."

On my way out, I passed through the kitchen. Sitting on the counter was a funky blue backpack. I was willing to bet it was the same one I'd seen at Estela Sandoval's Oxnard beauty shop the day I went there looking for Monique. Hanging from a metal ring on the bag was a key chain. As I got closer, I noticed that it was made of beads, red and green ones. It looked like a red rose set against a green background, similar to the one I'd found in Evan's apartment. Except that the strings of beads on this one weren't broken. I'd assumed that Dara had made the key chain as a gift for her father. Now I realized how wrong I was about that.

"Where did you get this?" I said to Monique.

She hesitated. "It's just something I made."

"Did you make one for Evan Brice, too?"

Monique looked up at the ceiling as if checking for leaks in the dimpled tile. Her eyes remained focused up there for what seemed like a long time. When she squeezed them closed, two large tears spilled down her cheeks.

Once again Cruz knelt in front of her sister, folding her arms around Monique to comfort her. "Just leave us alone," she said to me.

Monique's tears seemed strangely inappropriate. Again I thought about the murder committed across the hallway, and wondered if she had been involved in some way. For a moment I let my imagination run wild. What if Monique had been stealing drugs or money from Evan's apartment? He found out. She killed him to stay out of jail. Except that it didn't fit. Monique was petite, almost frail-looking. Evan wasn't exactly a bodybuilder, but I didn't see how she could stab him to death without showing some physical signs of the struggle. Moreover, Moses Green seemed satisfied with her alibi. On the other hand, Green hadn't said anything about the alibi of Monique's boyfriend. Where had he been the night Evan was killed?

I didn't know for sure who had driven Monique Ruiz to Oxnard that night, or what time they'd left Venice. In fact, there was a lot I didn't know. A voice inside my head said, "Leave well enough alone," but as usual, I decided to ignore it.

-26-

i stood in the hallway outside Monique Ruiz's apartment, wondering what to do next. The way she'd reacted when I mentioned Evan's name, and the fact that she'd made that key chain for him, made me think there was more to their relationship than she was willing to tell me. It was possible she had a fantasy crush on him, or perhaps it was a full-blown affair. Either way, her boyfriend would not have been pleased.

Unfortunately, my suspicions were nothing more than prickles on the back of my neck. If I sashayed up to the LAPD homicide table with a cockamamie conspiracy theory about Monique Ruiz and her boyfriend, Green would laugh me out of the station. What I needed was information. I doubted that Monique or her sister would tell me anything now. However, if I could get the boyfriend's name, I could search a few databases—like the state prison's alumni rolls—to see if he popped up.

I decided to launch my latest investigation by interviewing Brenda, the self-appointed neighborhood parking vigilante. She seemed to keep close tabs on visitors to the neighborhood. She'd also had a few run-ins with Monique's boyfriend and might know his name. Unfortunately, Brenda didn't strike me as the kind of person who sat around a campfire singing "Kumbaya," so I didn't expect her to welcome me in the spirit of sisterly love. The situation required a little creativity.

I made my way across the street and checked the bank of mailboxes for her last name. It was Boyd. I headed up the stairs, past what was left of Brenda's bicycle, and knocked on her door. No one answered. I tried again. Nothing. I was about to leave when I heard a thump followed by the sound of glass breaking.

I leaned closer to the door. "Brenda? You okay? It's Tucker Sinclair. Remember? The one with the silver Boxster who can never find a parking place."

I heard movement. A few moments later the door opened, at least as far as the security chain would allow. I saw a flash of red—Brenda's favorite kimono—and a thin line of blue: Brenda's eyes, squinting at me with distrust.

Up close I could see that the sun had etched her face with wrinkles, which rippled across her forehead like drifting sand. She wore no makeup except for a garish shade of magenta lipstick that practically screamed, *free gift with purchase*.

"What do you want?" she said.

"Actually, I need your help." She didn't seem enthralled by that, so I hurried on. "I was parked out front the other night, and somebody dented my fender. I mean, the guy must have known he hit me. The damage is major. He should have left a note. Anyway, I was hoping you might have seen or heard something."

Brenda's expression remained frosty. Obviously she wasn't responding to my mojo, either. On the other hand, she hadn't slammed the door in my face, so I kept talking.

"If I make a claim with my insurance company, they'll

raise my rates, so I'd like to settle this off the books if I can. The problem is, I need the guy's name or a license plate number or something."

"Yeah," she said, "you got a problem, all right."

Words. This was good. I pressed on. "I know the car was black, because it left some paint on my fender."

On the word "black" Brenda cocked her head. "What day was it again?"

I calculated backward to the last time I'd seen the Latino's black Honda Civic parked outside. "Last Wednesday, I think."

She paused for a moment. "Hold on."

The door closed. Moments later, I heard the security chain slide on its track. Then the door opened wide. Immediately the oppressive odor of cigarette smoke, mingled with the even more oppressive aroma of patchouli oil, bombarded my olfactory system. When Brenda motioned me inside, I took my last gasp of fresh air and followed her into the living room.

In addition to her signature red kimono, Brenda was wearing a hand-wrought turquoise ring on the index finger of her right hand. It was a square, blue-green gemstone flanked by two smaller, bluer ovals, all set in a silver band. The larger stone was chipped. From what I could tell, she was wearing nothing else. Even her feet were bare.

My gaze moved across the neat and tidy living room. The couch was covered in a red fabric that had been repeated in the easy chair and on the lamp shades. The furniture had probably once been bright and cheery. Now it was merely old and serviceable.

Propped against the back of the couch was a waist-high pole with tubing coiled around it. Attached to one end was something that looked like a flat doughnut. At the other end was a set of headphones. It appeared to be one of those metal detectors people use to comb the beach for spare change and other treasures.

On an end table near the couch was a framed photograph of Brenda Boyd, standing on the beach next to a young Asian man wearing a U.S. Navy uniform. The photo looked recent. Unfortunately, it had been taken from too far away, as though the photographer had been more interested in capturing the flat gray ocean in the background than the tender look of pride on Brenda Boyd's face. The glass in the frame was cracked. I wondered if that had been what I'd heard breaking. If so, it helped explain her foul mood. The guy looked young enough to be her son, but I didn't want to insult her if it turned out to be a boyfriend.

I picked up the photo and smiled. "Nice picture."

She grabbed it roughly out of my hand and pressed it to her chest.

"Wait here."

She disappeared into what may have been a bedroom and returned a few minutes later, carrying a glass filled with ice and a clear liquid that smelled like gin. In the other hand was some kind of journal. On the front cover was a picture of a Japanese teahouse surrounded by cherry trees in bloom. She opened the book to a large rubber band that had been used to mark her place. She ran her finger down the page.

"Gotcha, you little prick," she said under her breath.

Brenda held up the journal and pointed to the entry. Three vertical lines ran the length of the page, separating it into four columns. The headings read, "Date," "Time," "License #," and "Comment." There were dozens of entries in small, cramped handwriting. I envisioned more pages and more books filling shelves and boxes and then rooms. Brenda needed to get a life.

"Mind if I take a closer look?" I said.

Reluctantly, she held the book close enough for me to see that a black Honda Civic had been parked on the north side of the street on Wednesday evening from five until seven-thirty. The license plate number was also neatly recorded. Under the comments column were the words "Took up two spaces AGAIN!!!!"

"Do you know the owner's name?"

"Asshole. Capital 'A.' " I wanted to ask if that was his first or last name, but I didn't think she'd appreciate my flippancy. "I wouldn't be surprised if he hit your car on purpose—the prick."

"Okay if I jot this down?" I said.

Brenda shrugged, but underneath the nonchalance she looked pleased. I copied the information onto a bank deposit slip I found crumpled in the bottom of my purse. When I was finished, she slipped the journal into a pocket of her kimono, took her drink, and walked over to a sliding glass door, which was corroded to a rusty patina by the salt air. She pulled it open and walked out onto the balcony. I followed.

Except for a few palm trees, Brenda's lanai offered an unobstructed view of the beach. Evan's apartment also faced the water, but the windows were on the small side and didn't take full advantage of the panorama. Maybe that was one reason why his rent was relatively low.

"I heard somebody across the street was murdered a few days ago," I said. "What was his name? Brice? Something like that."

"Who knows?" she said. "He called himself Tom around here. I heard it was because he didn't want to be bothered by us lowlifes. As if I give a shit that he was some Hollywood agent. Do I look like somebody who cares about being famous? Damn rich people think they're so special. Pisses me off."

She set her drink on the parapet and picked up a pack of Marlboro Lights parked on the seat of a bentwood rocking chair. If she planned to smoke, I hoped she'd do it out in the open air. The last thing I needed was black lung disease. As she tapped the soft pack against the side of her index finger, she scanned the street below, looking for parking scofflaws, I presumed. She pulled a cigarette from the pack and lit it with a match from a book she'd tucked inside the cellophane wrapper. Brenda seemed to spend a considerable amount of time smoking and spying on her neighbors, which made me wonder if she'd been on duty the night Evan Brice was killed.

"You know," I said, "it just occurred to me. I may be wrong about Wednesday. I was in the neighborhood on Sunday, too. I'm wondering if you could check to see if the Honda was here then, just to cover all the bases."

Brenda looked annoyed, but nevertheless pulled the journal from her pocket and flipped through the pages. Again, she held it in front of my face. I could see that Monique's boyfriend had been parked in front of Brenda's apartment between ten and ten-thirty the night Evan Brice was killed. Interesting, but the timing was wrong. According to Detective Green, Evan had been killed sometime between one and three a.m. That meant the boyfriend probably wasn't the killer. There was another one of my theories shot to hell.

"That's it?" I said.

Brenda studied her entries and then flipped to the next page. Her gaze lingered there for a moment. Once again she held the journal out for me to read. I scanned the page to see if the black Honda Civic appeared, and was rewarded with another hit. According to Brenda's records, the Honda had come back to the apartment at around one fifteen a.m., which put the boyfriend at the scene at around the time Evan was killed.

Brenda Boyd must be some kind of vampire. She never seemed to sleep at night. I was still considering what to make of it all when I spotted another listing near the bottom of the opposite page. At 2:15 a.m. a car had been double-parked for twenty minutes in front of the entrance to Evan's apartment building. It was a black Mercedes, license plate number 1GR8MOM—Claire Jerrard's car.

I was stunned. I tried but failed to think of any reason why Claire would have come to see Evan that night. As painful as it was, I also tried to think of any motive she may have had for killing him, but the idea was simply unthinkable. Somebody else must have been driving her car.

Cissy told me she'd argued with Evan on Sunday. Later that night she'd met a friend for dinner. She drank too much alcohol and asked the friend to drive her to Claire's place so she could sleep it off. It didn't take a rocket scientist to figure out that Cissy could have waited for her mother to fall asleep, taken the keys to the Mercedes, and driven to Venice. Obviously, the police had considered that, too.

I wasn't sure what Cissy had done after arriving at Evan's place, but I did know one thing: She lied about never being at the Venice apartment. And if she lied about that, she was probably lying about a whole lot more. It wasn't surprising that the police didn't buy her alibi; it was full of holes. I closed my eyes for a moment and let those old feelings of betrayal bubble to the surface.

"You ever talk to the police about this stuff?" I said to Brenda, nodding toward the journal entries.

She blew a lungful of smoke in my face. "You should know something about me. I don't talk to cops—ever." She patted the journal. "This information is going to somebody at 1600 Pennsylvania Avenue Northwest who has the power to do something."

Brenda Boyd's relationship with L.A.'s finest was obviously not of the warm and fuzzy nature. I wondered what events had soured the rapport—her vigilante justice or her bad attitude. On the other hand, who needs rapport with the local cops when you have juice with the president of the United States?

Brenda was sitting on information that could possibly send Cissy Brice to jail for the rest of her life or worse. I wondered how the police would react to her journal. Maybe they'd be thrilled, or maybe they wouldn't give much weight to a neighborhood busybody who may have slammed down a half-dozen gin and tonics before stepping out to take a smoke on her lanai that night. For all I knew, she had another journal hidden in the back room, where she'd also recorded Jimmy Hoffa, Amelia Earhart, and Elvis going into Evan's building that night.

I thanked Brenda for her information and headed back to my car. When I slid into the front seat, my first instinct was to call Cissy and confront her, but an uneasy tremor kept my fingers from hitting the right buttons on my cell phone. It took two failed attempts before I came to my senses.

If Cissy *had* killed Evan, I didn't want to tip her off that I had evidence against her. In my experience, people do crazy things when they're backed into a corner. And if there was one thing I wanted less than tar in my lungs, it was a sharp kitchen utensil.

-27-

pointing fingers is easy. Proving guilt is hard. I had no proof that Cissy drove her mother's Mercedes to Evan's apartment building the night he was killed. Brenda Boyd hadn't seen the driver, only the car double-parked in front of the lobby door. Even if Cissy had been at Evan's place, it didn't prove she killed him. To complicate matters, it appeared that Monique's boyfriend had likely been in the building around the same time.

Cissy's life was at stake. I couldn't go to the police with incriminating evidence without knowing more, like the boyfriend's name and whether he had any reason to want Evan dead. I had the Honda's license plate number, but I couldn't do much with that. It's all but impossible to pry information out of the California Department of Motor Vehicles ever since deranged fan Robert Bardo got the address of actress Rebecca Schaeffer from the DMV, then went to her apartment and shot her dead. The Screen Actors Guild lobbied to limit access to that information, and now, as far as I knew, only police departments or similar agencies could see those records. I was certain Moses Green wouldn't share information with me. Neither would Joe Deegan. As of two days ago, he wasn't even speaking to me. However, Charley Tate might be able to get the boyfriend's name through his PI contacts. Hopefully he'd help, because he owed me big-time for scaring the shit out of me on the 405 and ruining my perfectly good theory that Lola Scott's porn connections were responsible for Evan's death.

-28-

fter leaving Brenda Boyd's apartment, I drove to the
groomer's place to pick up Muldoon. In lieu of a
silly bow in his hair, she'd tied a spiffy red kerchief
around his neck. Not only did the pup smell great, he
looked good, too. As an unexpected bonus, she also sold
me a pair of doggie goggles from a small gift shop she
maintained. As compromises go, the goggles weren't perfect, but at least my new partner could hang his head out
the window without getting a bug in his eye. When we
got back to the car, I double-checked Charley Tate's address on his business card and headed for Culver City.

Tate Investigations was in a small two-story building
located on a pie slice of land between Washington Boulevard and Washington Place in Culver City. After parking
in the only available space the toy lot had to offer,
Muldoon and I were forced to make one complete circum-
navigation of the building before we located the entrance.
On the glass door was a name lettered in gold: "Manny
Reygozo, Esq." A piece of tablet paper was duct-taped
below that. It read, "Tate Investigations, 2nd floor." Either
Charley Tate was a new tenant or he didn't rate gold.

Once inside, Muldoon zeroed in on a patch of carpet

near the door, sniffing like crazy. I coaxed him upstairs as quickly as possible so he wouldn't go territorial on me. The door to Charley Tate's office was unlocked. I stepped inside and found a small but pleasant lobby. There was no receptionist, just a reception desk devoid of ornamentation except for a telephone and an old-fashioned bell shaped like a mini Bundt cake. Hanging on the walls were several framed posters of famous art, and a bulletin board covered with papers and cartoons thumbtacked to the cork. Many seemed to be lawyer jokes: "What do you call twenty lawyers skydiving from an airplane? Skeet."

At the far side of the room, next to a closed door, stood a dusty plant that looked as if it hadn't been repotted since Woodstock. I rang the Bundt-cake bell, and moments later the door flew open.

Charley Tate stood in the doorway. He had on brown huaraches, white Bermuda shorts, and a yellow Hawaiian shirt. His legs were muscular and hairy.

He frowned when he saw me. "How'd you get in here?"

I nodded toward the door. "It was unlocked."

"Damn you, Reygozo," he muttered as he stomped over and turned the dead bolt. "Just because he owns the building doesn't give him the right to come into my office anytime he wants. I hate lawyers."

Muldoon objected to the angry tone in Tate's voice and let out a rolling growl that picked up speed like the Coast Starlight leaving Union Station. Tate seemed to notice Muldoon for the first time. Not much of a detective if you asked me.

"For crissakes," he said, "what's with the mutt?"

"He's my new partner."

"Get him out of here. I'm allergic."

"Too bad. The mutt stays."

He paused. "Fine. I'm not going to trade spit with you. What are you doing here anyway? I gave you Lola Scott, and I don't give refunds on a freebie."

"I'm not here about Lola. I need your help with something else."

He crossed his arms and squinted at me. "I hope you came with more than a wish and a smile."

"I can pay, if that's what worries you."

He studied me for a moment longer. Finally he shrugged. "Come on in."

Muldoon and I followed him into a back office, which was in stark contrast to the neatness of the reception area. Along one wall was a row of three-drawer file cabinets as imposing as Buckingham Palace guards. An ornate oak desk was buried under mountains of paper. Apparently, Tate was enamored with yellow number-two pencils, because at least a dozen of them were lying on his desk, surrounded by eraser crumbs. The guy was obviously prone to making mistakes. His electric pencil sharpener looked like a sci-fi fire truck: red with all sorts of dials and flashing lights. A few slivers of wood had spilled out of the chip catcher and were floating in a cup of dead coffee. More file folders spilled onto the floor, blanketing the gray industrial carpet in a layer of manila. In the midst of all the chaos was a five-by-seven silver frame, which held a photograph of an attractive dark-haired woman who could have been his daughter but probably wasn't.

"Sit down."

Tate gestured toward his two guest chairs, which were covered in a wintry green and blue plaid. Both were piled high with file folders. Subtlety seemed like a waste of time, so I dumped the debris on the floor and gave the seat a quick dust-off before I sat.

He flashed a crooked grin. "Excuse the mess. I'm kind of in the middle of something."

What, I wondered. *A tornado drill?*

Out of the corner of my eye I saw Muldoon lifting his leg over what looked like an old blue sweatshirt wadded up on the floor. I didn't want to stress the pup out by drawing attention to his lack of etiquette, so I decided to wait until the smell demanded explanation. Luckily, Tate was oblivious. As he lowered himself into his desk chair, he seemed to grimace in pain. The look disappeared so quickly, I wasn't sure if I'd seen it at all.

"So," he said, "what do you need?"

"A name to go with a license plate number."

He held up his arms in surrender. "No can do."

"I thought you were a private investigator."

"I am, but you have to have juice to get that kind of information."

"You used to be a cop. Isn't that juice enough?"

"You got that right. Used to be."

"It's important I find out who owns a certain black Honda Civic."

"Why? Some lowlife key your Porsche?"

I leaned forward and looked him straight in the eye. "Cut the crap, Tate. You offer a service. I'm a paying customer. If you want me to take my business down the street, just say so."

He smiled awkwardly, realizing that he'd pushed the snappy-repartee game too far. "Okay, okay, let me see what you got."

I pulled out the deposit slip on which I'd written the Honda's license plate number. Tate studied it a moment and then retrieved a three-ring binder from his desk drawer. He licked his thumb to leverage the pages, studying each one as if it were a box of his favorite chocolates. He stopped at one page in particular, massaging his chin as he read to himself. A few moments later he looked up.

"Wait outside."

"What did you find?"

"Probably nothing. Mind if I keep this?" he said, holding up the deposit slip I'd given him. "My copy machine's down."

I looked around but saw no copy machine.

"Down where?"

He rolled his eyes and gestured toward the door. "Do you mind?"

I saw no reason to argue with him, so Muldoon and I returned to the tidy reception desk in the front lobby. Muldoon curled up at my feet while I amused myself by reading jokes from the bulletin board: "How can you tell if you're a Californian? If a really great parking spot moves you to tears." That was too close to reality to be funny; just ask Brenda Boyd.

Fifteen minutes later, I was beginning to feel antsy when Tate opened the door and motioned me back into his office. I saw Muldoon eyeing the sweatshirt again, so I held him on my lap.

Tate lowered himself into his chair. "Why are you so interested in this guy? Is he dating your sister or something?"

"I don't have a sister."

"Good, because the kid's a problem. He comes from a good family, but every time he's faced with a decision, he makes a bad one. He started out stealing checks from his mom's purse. A few bounced so good they were scouted by the Lakers. Since then he's been picked up for truancy, shoplifting, robo-tripping, you name it."

"Robo-tripping?"

"As in Robitussin cough medicine. Hard to believe these kids get wasted on something you buy over the counter at Rite Aid. See, the stuff has this nifty little ingredient in it called dextromethorphan. It makes you stop coughing, but if you drink too much of it, it makes you high. It also makes you mean."

"Mean enough to kill?"

"Sure. I've heard about several homicides associated with robo-tripping. I suggest you steer clear of the guy."

"Yeah, yeah, yeah, I'll be careful. Just give me his name."

Tate shrugged and skidded my deposit slip across the desk with a flip of his wrist. Next to the license plate number he'd written a name: Gilbert Ruiz.

I frowned. "Ruiz?"

"Yeah. Lives with his parents in West Covina."

Monique Ruiz's parents lived in West Covina, at least according to Rose Miller. Ruiz was a common name but not that common. There was only one explanation for the coincidence. The Latino with the black Honda Civic was not Monique's boyfriend; he was her brother. In my head I ran through everything I knew about the Ruiz siblings. Every fact I came up with was linked with the word "trouble."

Gilbert's problems were obvious; Tate had just outlined the particulars for me. As for Monique, she seemed like a good person—responsible and compassionate, at least where Rose was concerned. She went to college and held two jobs. She obviously had a cordial relationship with Evan. She'd made a key chain for him. Yet both her sister and her aunt had implied that Monique was in some kind of trouble. Maybe they were hiding the fact that she'd killed Evan herself, but somehow it seemed doubtful. I thought of other problems she might have: financial worries, health issues, or parental pressure to move back home.

The night Evan was murdered, it must have been Monique's brother, not her boyfriend, who drove her to Oxnard. Brenda had seen Gilbert's Honda parked in front of Evan's apartment at ten, probably when he picked up his sister. The car had been back again at one-fifteen, which gave him plenty of time to drive to Oxnard, drop off Monique, and return to kill Evan Brice. Only, what was his motive for wanting Evan dead?

Learning the identity of Monique's brother solved one puzzle but raised another, more intriguing one: Who was her boyfriend? Not even Rose had met him. That seemed odd, given how close the two women were. Why was Monique keeping him such a closely guarded secret? Was he part of the trouble she was in? Then I thought of her gray pallor, the teddy bear, the small pastel afghan, and came up with another kind of trouble altogether: baby trouble.

My throat felt dry and constricted as I considered the possibility that Monique Ruiz was pregnant. Then I thought about her reaction to Evan's death, Evan's phone call to Amy Lynch about the Catholic Church and abortion, the mousy "deer in the headlights" girl at Evan's party. Evan the poet . . . Evan the drug addict . . . Evan the womanizer. I also thought of the roses in Evan's apartment, in Evan's poem, and on the key chain Monique had made for him. Perhaps the flower had been some private symbol of her love for Evan. And his love for her?

I wondered who'd be most upset about Monique's pregnancy. Her family, no doubt. Evan was a married man. But Evan must have been upset as well. He was just out of rehab and trying to mend his shattered family life. The last thing he needed was a pregnant girlfriend. Maybe he told Monique to have an abortion, and she objected. I thought back to something Eugene had said: "When your baby's in jeopardy, you'll do anything to save her." He'd been talking about Mr. Geyer's mail order catalog and maybe even about his cat, Liza, but those words could be used to describe Monique's sentiments as well. What if she had asked her brother to intervene on her behalf? That could have transformed Gilbert Ruiz from volatile, robo-tripping troublemaker into macho avenger of his sister's honor.

On the other hand, I couldn't overlook another person who'd be deeply affected by Monique's unexpected pregnancy: Cissy Brice, a woman who viewed money as a protective cloak and who had turned the family's finances over to a money manager to protect her assets. What would she do if she were faced with losing thousands or even millions of dollars in a paternity suit? Worse yet, what if Evan planned to leave her and marry Monique Ruiz?

I felt overwhelmed by what I did and didn't know, and wondered how much Charley Tate would charge to help me sort everything out. More than I could afford right now. I was sure of that. I'd just have to tackle the issues myself.

Muldoon was getting restless sitting on my lap. I put him on the floor, handed Tate my card, and told him to send me a bill for his time. When he rose to see me out, again I saw pain etch a deep furrow between his eyes. The guy wasn't any spring chicken, so his discomfort could have been caused by a variety of ailments: bad back, arthritis, or something worse. That worried me. Tate wasn't an easy person to categorize. He was cranky yet appealing. I didn't like the thought that he might be compromised in any way.

As we made our way back through the lobby, I again marveled at the disparity in neatness between the two rooms. Tate apparently noticed my scrutiny.

"My receptionist quit," he said with a forced chuckle. "She and I had a difference of opinion about my filing system. I'm looking for a replacement, so let me know if you run across anybody who's looking for a shitty job with even shittier pay."

For a moment I wondered if Eugene might be interested. Then I thought, nah. They'd drive each other crazy. In the end, I told Tate I'd keep my ears open for somebody who was looking for the kind of unique opportunity he offered. If he needed help right away, I suggested he call Amy Lynch at Premier Temps. I wasn't sure if she was still there, but she'd be great at writing messages.

-29-

After I left Charley Tate's office, I tried to think of where I could find evidence to prove that Monique was pregnant with Evan's baby. Confronting her seemed futile.

I was waiting at a red light at Venice Boulevard when I remembered the medical bill that had been mixed in with the stack of junk mail Jakey had stolen from Evan's apartment. The statement had been sent to Thomas Chatterton at the Venice address instead of to the Brices' business manager. I thought I knew why. Evan didn't want to let his business manager or his wife find out about Monique Ruiz's pregnancy.

It was too early for Lola Scott to have forwarded the stolen mail, even if she'd been true to her word and done as I'd requested. It had only been a few days since the last bill arrived, so I doubted there was an overdue notice waiting in Evan's mailbox. However, since I was only ten minutes away from the apartment, I decided to stop by and check with Rose. Maybe Monique had mentioned something to her about seeing a doctor. If so, she might remember a name.

I turned onto Seagate Pathway and scanned the surrounding streets to make sure Gilbert Ruiz's car wasn't parked anywhere nearby. It wasn't, but nonetheless, I left the Boxster out of sight in the lot down the street. With Muldoon in tow, I made my way to the lobby. I opened Evan's mailbox and found a few pieces of junk mail, but nothing from the clinic and nothing from Lola Scott. I was disappointed but not surprised.

Rose was on the telephone with her daughter when I arrived at her door. I didn't want to interrupt their conversation, so I told her I would come back in a few minutes. To kill some time, I walked down the hall to Evan's unit. I still had to dispose of the bed and decided to use his phone to call the women's shelter. I'd make them an offer they couldn't refuse. If they took the bed, they could have the telephone as a bonus.

When I opened the door to his apartment, a strange, stale odor embraced me like an old man's unwanted hug. I stepped inside and flipped on the lights, nearly tripping over what turned out to be a padded envelope lying by the door. My name was scrawled on the outside. When I opened it, I found the stolen mail, a key, and a note from Lola Scott telling me she'd taken the bed.

The key was no surprise. Obviously, that's how Jakey had gotten into the apartment in the first place. It annoyed me that she'd used it without telling me, but there was nothing I could do about it now. At least the place was empty. My job was finished.

I sorted through the mail until I spotted the clinic envelope. Inside was a statement for an office visit for Monique Chatterton. On the bottom was a friendly handwritten note, asking her to call at her earliest convenience to schedule prenatal care visits.

Perhaps Evan was just being a nice guy by paying Monique's doctor bills. From all accounts, he'd done that sort of thing before. Except that Monique had used the name Chatterton. Why would she do that if Evan weren't the baby's father?

Cissy must have known or at least suspected that something was going on between Evan and Monique. After all, she was the long-suffering wife who'd put up with Evan's serial cheating throughout their entire marriage. By now she must know the signs. I had to speak with her again. This time she was going to tell me the truth. If I caught her in another lie, she was going down. I'd see to that myself.

⁕ ⁕ ⁕

THE CLOSER I GOT to Benedict Canyon, the more nervous I became. I couldn't believe that a friend whom I'd once considered a sister was capable of murder. Still, the evidence against Cissy Brice was piling up just as the list of other suspects was dwindling. I'd already eliminated my most promising lead: Lola Scott. I'd have to do a lot more research if I was ever going to pump life into the idea of a conspiracy between Amy Lynch and Evan's personal assistant, Jerome Fielding. Connecting Jerome to Evan's murder was probably a nonstarter. Moses Green hadn't even mentioned the guy's name. Jerome was probably just trying to get into Amy's good graces by helping her jump-start her screenwriting career.

Several media vans, including one from *Celebrity Heat*, were again congregated along the narrow street outside the Brices' house. Evan had been dead for a week already, so the number had diminished. I guess the faithful were just marking time until the next big freeway chase.

I didn't see Darcy Daniels. She was probably inside the van getting her lips reglossed. I considered asking Muldoon to hunt her down like a rat in a hole, but I didn't want to generate any new tape for her evening show, nor did I want to end up in the back of Deegan's detective car.

There was a guard minding the gate—different guy, same uniform, same procedure as before. Muldoon was wearing his goggles, so I let him hang his head out the window while I waited for the guard to call the house for permission to let us in. Unfortunately, this time there was a glitch. The powers-that-be inside the house said no. Frustrated, I asked to speak with Cissy. She wasn't there, nor was Jerome. I had to know when she was coming back, so after pleading, coaxing, and cajoling, the guard reluctantly called the house again.

Julia, who turned out to be Dara's nanny, answered with an English-accented hello. When I explained who I was, she told me the police had come early that morning to search the house. Cissy had been distraught and had decided to leave town for a few days. I wondered if she was in her green Jag, with a blond wig and a sack of hundred-dollar bills, heading for Tijuana. *Celebrity Heat* would love that.

"At least she got Dara away from all the craziness," I said. "How come she didn't take you, too?"

The woman hesitated. "She didn't take either of us. Dara's here with me."

I'm not a mother, but it seemed odd that Cissy would leave her child at a time like this. Dara had to be freaked out, too, losing her father, hounded by the media, and now dealing with the trauma of a police search.

It was a letdown to find out that Cissy wasn't around. On the other hand, maybe I should try once more to pry information out of Jerome Fielding. I didn't expect his emotional floodgates suddenly to open, but even a trickle might help solve the case.

"When will Jerome be back?" I said.

"Shortly, I suspect. He's just out running errands."

"Mind if I wait?"

She hesitated briefly. "I suppose that would be all right."

I looked around to see if Darcy Daniels had emerged from her news van, but she was nowhere in sight. I handed the phone back to the guard, who listened to Julia's instructions. Moments later he opened the gate, and I eased up the driveway. I didn't plan to be gone long, so I told Muldoon to stay in the car. He looked unhappy about my decision and wouldn't even let me take off his goggles. To make amends, I left the windows down so he could get some fresh air, and suggested he take a nap.

I expected Julia to be a plump woman in her sixties with sensible shoes and a Mary Poppins hat. As it turned out, she was petite and in her early twenties. She ushered me into the house with the nonchalance of somebody who still thought people were basically good at heart. Obviously, she was new in town.

The house looked intact. Either the police were extremely tidy, or somebody had straightened up after the search. Nanny Poppins told me to make myself at home and disappeared down a long hallway. A moment later I heard a door close. I was alone.

I waited restlessly on the couch for a few minutes before wandering out onto the patio. A cool breeze rattled the leaves of the potted plants around the perimeter of the pool. I glanced over at the cabana and noticed a padlock on the door, which was hanging open. Before, I'd assumed that the building housed pool equipment, but on closer inspection I didn't hear anything that sounded like the humming of machinery. Perhaps it was a playhouse for Dara.

I set my purse on one of the round patio tables and walked over to see if she was inside. The shutters were closed, blocking my view. If Dara was in the cabana, I didn't want to frighten her. I called her name but got no response. I pushed on the door. It slowly creaked open.

Inside, two walls were lined with built-in shelves filled with hardback books. To my right was a love seat and étagère, the shelves of which were crammed with antique toys. In the center of the room was an inlaid wood table, which held a neat stack of papers and a laptop computer.

Nothing looked out of place. Either the police hadn't searched in here or it had been cleaned up, too. On top of the desk was a file labeled "Dara," which contained a child's drawing of a woman with red hair and round blimpy arms and legs—Cissy, no doubt—and several report cards from an exclusive private school in Bel Air. Obviously, this wasn't a child's playhouse. Since Evan used the Venice apartment as his getaway office, I assumed that this work space belonged to Cissy.

Out of curiosity, I lifted the lid of the laptop and lightly brushed my finger over a red toggle switch embedded in the keys. Moments later, a word-processing program appeared on the screen. I positioned the pointer on the menu bar and highlighted "File." At the bottom of the pop-up menu was a list of nine recently created documents. To my surprise, I saw one labeled "Monique." I clicked on it.

A letter appeared on the screen. It was addressed to a Beverly Hills financial management company, instructing them to disregard Mr. Brice's prior instructions and cease paying any and all bills related to Monique Ruiz, aka

Monique Chatterton. It claimed that more detailed instructions from the Brices' attorney would follow. Cissy Brice's name was typed at the bottom of the letter.

This letter proved that Cissy knew about Monique's pregnancy. I wondered what else she knew. She told me she'd argued with Evan the day he died, and hinted that the fight was over her fear that he'd contract AIDS because of his drug habit and multiple sex partners. I'm sure that was a concern of hers, but there had obviously been another: Monique Ruiz.

Evan had obviously taken responsibility for Monique's medical bills and may have offered to pay child support. If he had died before he could make good on that promise, it would help explain why Marta Cruz showed up at my door, asking if Evan was an honorable man. Maybe she'd already approached Cissy on her sister's behalf and gotten the cold shoulder. Perhaps she knew that Cissy and I had once been friends, and hoped I'd persuade her to help Monique.

According to James Brodie, the night before Evan died, he was worried about information that was going to sink somebody's boat. I just didn't know whether the boat was Monique's or Cissy's. Perhaps he planned to tell Monique he couldn't marry her as she'd hoped, because he wasn't single Thomas Chatterton; he was married Evan Brice. Or maybe he'd informed Cissy that he was leaving her for a new wife and baby. Maybe he'd decided to dump both of them and start a new life somewhere else.

I wondered if the police had searched the cabana, and if so, why they hadn't taken the computer. A moment later, I opened "Finder" and discovered that the Monique file had been created only minutes earlier. I was still thinking about the ramifications of my discovery when I heard a voice coming from somewhere behind me.

"Tucker?"

I turned to see Cissy Brice standing in the doorway, wearing designer jeans and a pair of strappy high-heeled sandals. Her hair looked lank. Her blond roots had grown out a quarter inch or so, providing a stark contrast to the red dye job.

"Jeez, you scared me," I said. "I thought you left town."

"I did, but I came back to get Dara and take care of a couple of things. What are you doing in here?"

My excuse sounded phony, but I offered it anyway. "I wanted to let you know everything is out of Evan's apartment. I'm ready to turn over the keys."

"I thought you were working with Mom on that."

"I am, but—"

"Never mind. Come in the house. I'll make a pitcher of margaritas." Her gaze traveled to my hand, which was still resting on her laptop computer. Her eyes narrowed. "What were you looking at?"

It was time for the truth. At some point I'd have to confess what I'd learned, either now or in front of a jury if it came to that.

"When did you find out Evan was the father of Monique Ruiz's baby?"

The color drained from her face. "What are you talking about?"

"Cut the crap, Cissy. I read your letter."

She let out a breath of air and let her chin collapse onto her chest. When she lifted her head again, she seemed resigned.

"Okay, I knew. So what?"

"When did you find out?"

"Friday. Our business manager got a bill for the Ruiz girl's lab work. When she saw the phony name, she called me right away. She thought Evan was doing drugs again. Playing sugar daddy was always the way it started."

"When you saw Monique's name on the statement, you realized it was something worse than drugs. It was a threat to your future."

"It just blew me away. I thought things were finally good between us again, but all the while he was screwing some nineteen-year-old house sitter. We argued off and on all weekend, but on Sunday we had a huge fight. It was a good thing Dara was on a sleepover. I said some pretty terrible things. Evan left the house. I went to dinner and had one too many martinis. When my friend drove me home, Evan wasn't there. I figured he was with Monique. I didn't want to stay at the house alone, so I asked her to take me to Mom's. I think I passed out for a while."

"But later you woke up and couldn't stop thinking about what a shit Evan was."

"What are you getting at, Tuckie?"

"You lied to me, Cissy. That's what I'm getting at. You said you'd never been to the Venice apartment, but somebody saw your mom's car parked in front of the building around the time Evan was killed. I think you drove it there."

As she processed the information, her confused expression slowly changed to one of horror. "You think I killed Evan?" Her tone was so low and raspy, it barely sounded human. "I swear to you, it wasn't me."

"You were there that night."

"Okay, I was there, but he was already dead."

"Why didn't you call the police?"

"It was a mistake. I know that now. I just wasn't thinking straight. I'll call Detective Green. Tell him every-thing, whatever you say. Just please believe me, I didn't do it. I swear."

For a moment I didn't know what to believe. She seemed so earnest, so fragile. Maybe she was telling the truth. The problem was, I knew Cissy well enough not to trust her.

"Look," I said, "I'll take your word for it. I'll even go with you to the cops, but no more lies."

"Sure, Tuckie. I understand. The truth. I owe you that much. You've been so good to me these past few days. I can't tell you how much I appreciate it. Just wait here. I want to look in on Dara first. Then we can go. We'll talk in the car. I'll tell you everything."

That suited me just fine. I wasn't about to follow her inside the house, where she may have access to a weapon. I also had no plans to chase her down if she decided to run. I'd leave that to the cops.

"I think it's better if we take separate cars," I said. "I'll meet you in the driveway."

She nodded and hurried out, closing the door behind her. I looked around for my purse before remembering that I'd left it outside on the patio table. I was about to leave when I heard a rough scraping sound coming from somewhere outside. I pushed on the door. It wouldn't open. I pushed harder. Nothing.

"Cissy, are you still out there? The door is stuck."

Silence. I threw the full force of my weight against the door. It didn't budge. That's when I realized it wasn't stuck. It was locked. I wondered how loud I'd have to scream to be heard by Nanny Poppins. Pretty loud, I guessed, but it was worth a try. I started pounding and shouting. No one came.

All the windows were nailed shut. There was no telephone in the room. My cell phone was in my purse outside. I checked the laptop, hoping for an Internet connection so I could e-mail for help, but evidently Cissy hadn't yet entered the age of wireless.

I suddenly realized why Moses Green thought Cissy was guilty: She *was* guilty. I felt like such a fool. Worse yet, I was trapped inside a cabana, with a killer outside holding the key. That's when I felt the first twinge of panic.

-30-

i put my ear against the locked door of Cissy Brice's cabana, listening for sounds, like the sounds of somebody coming to rescue me. I didn't hear anything like that, but a moment later I did hear her voice. It sounded frazzled.

"Are you all right?" she said.

"No, I'm *not* frigging all right. Unlock this damn door, okay?"

"Please don't be mad at me, Tuckie."

"This isn't helping your cause. Let me out of here. We'll go to the police."

"I'm not ready yet."

"Then when?"

"I'm not sure."

"Look, give yourself up. I'll help you find a lawyer."

"Lawyer? You're talking like you think I'm guilty. I told you, I didn't kill Evan."

"Then why did you lie to the police when the truth would have worked just as well?"

"It's a long story."

It felt stupid trying to talk through a piece of wood. Both of us had to shout to be heard. I pushed on the door again to see if she'd had second thoughts and unlocked it. No such luck.

"Don't bullshit me, Cissy. I want to know what you were doing at Evan's apartment the night he was killed."

The silence went on so long, I began to wonder if she'd walked away and left me trapped inside the cabana.

Finally, she said, "Okay, I'll tell you the truth, but you're not going to like it." There was another long pause before she went on. "I knew Monique was pregnant. I confronted Evan about it on Friday. He said he'd just learned about the baby, too. He felt ashamed of himself and sad for the girl. He said he hadn't decided what to do about it yet. Well, *I* told him what he was going to do about it—nothing. He said it wasn't that simple. That made me really mad. Like I said, we fought all weekend. On Sunday he walked out on me."

"I got the impression from Evan that he was committed to you and Dara."

"I thought so, too. That's why I couldn't stop thinking about how horrible it would be for Dara if she lost her daddy. After I got to Mom's, I finally realized that instead of making him want to stay with us, I was pushing him away. When Mom fell asleep, I took her Mercedes and drove to Venice to beg Evan to come home. By the time I got there, he was already dead."

"I still don't understand why you didn't call the police."

"I was going to, I swear. Then I noticed he wasn't wearing his wedding ring. That's when I knew he was leaving me for good. I was devastated. I couldn't face telling the police and my daughter that Evan had chosen the mother of his illegitimate child over me. All I wanted to do was to get out of that place."

"Did you ever stop to consider maybe he just forgot to put the ring on that morning?"

"No, you don't understand. Evan stopped wearing it years ago when things got bad between us. Last week he put it on again and promised this time he'd leave it on. He was wearing it when he left the house that day."

"Where is it now?"

She paused. "The ring? I don't know."

"It hasn't turned up in his things?"

Her tone was hesitant. "No, but I didn't worry about that. It wasn't valuable like it had diamonds in it or anything."

"The police told me nothing was taken from the apartment. What if the ring was stolen? Maybe it was a burglary gone bad after all."

"I don't think so. He was still wearing his Rolex. If the killer didn't take an expensive watch, why would he take some cheap old ring?"

I didn't want to tell her, but the police might construe the theft as a sign: After Cissy had killed her husband, she took the ring to symbolize that the relationship was over—for good. I wondered if it was one of the objects named in the search warrant.

"The value of the ring doesn't matter," I said. "What's important is that it might be a clue. You have to tell the police what it looks like, if it's inscribed, anything that distinguishes it from other conventional wedding bands."

"Oh, come on, Tuckie. Evan was never conventional. You know that. First of all, he didn't even want to wear a wedding ring. I bugged him about it so much, he finally agreed, but he never liked anything I picked out."

"But he got one eventually."

"Sure, eventually. A few months before our wedding, we were on our way to Scottsdale to visit my grandparents. We stopped in some Podunk town in Arizona to have lunch. There was a pawnshop across the street from the diner. The ring was in the window. The owner told us he bought it from some old Indian who made it himself. He called it a dead pawn, because the guy never came back to claim it. Evan loved that. He made up a story about the Indian being a shaman or a cowboy poet, something cool like that. He thought the ring was some kind of omen for our marriage. I was mad at him, because he paid eighty bucks cash for the thing. I thought that was stupid, because one of the stones was broken."

My mouth felt dry as my thoughts jumped from omen to Arizona to Indian—maybe Navajo—to broken stone and finally to the ring I'd seen on Brenda Boyd's finger. Somehow I already knew the answer to my next question, but I asked it anyway.

"What did the ring look like?"

Not surprisingly, she told me it was a hand-wrought turquoise ring with one square, blue-green gemstone flanked by two smaller, bluer ovals, all set in a silver band. The center stone was chipped. Evan may have been right about one thing. Perhaps the ring had been an omen—a bad one. Maybe I'd been wrong about everything.

"Cissy, open this door. We have to call the police."

"I told you, I didn't kill Evan." Her tone was loud and strident.

"Fine, but you have to tell them about the ring."

"No. They'll take Dara away from me. I'm innocent. Why can't you believe me?"

"Stop screaming. I do believe you. Just open the door."

A few moments later I heard barking. It sounded like Muldoon. He must have gotten bored waiting in the car.

From the other side of the door I heard Cissy yell, "Get away!"

"Don't panic. It's just my dog."

"He's barking at me."

"I can hear that. Stop bellowing. He doesn't like loud noises."

"What's wrong with his eyes? They look weird."

"He's wearing goggles so he doesn't— Oh, never mind. Just let me out of here."

"I don't like dogs."

"Then open the door. I'll calm him down."

"I don't know . . ."

"Damn it, Cissy! I'm trying to help you."

"Okay, okay."

A moment later the padlock rattled. The next thing I saw was Muldoon, nudging the door open. He stopped briefly to lift his leg near an antique tractor on the bottom shelf of the étagère. Then he buried his nose in a patch of carpet, trying to identify the source of an old smell. I had to admit that the goggles made him look like a fluffy white larva from some killer-insect movie.

Cissy stood at the threshold, looking pale. We stared at each other for a long time, each waiting for the other to speak. Finally, she said, "I didn't know you had a dog."

"I don't—yet."

"I'm sorry I locked the door, Tuckie, but it's been a really bad day."

Mine hadn't been that great, either.

I spent the next few minutes trying to persuade her to speak with the police. That turned out to be a hard sell. In the end she agreed to let me call my lawyer, Sheldon Greenblatt. Shelly doesn't handle criminal defense work, but he transferred me to one of his associates who did.

After listening to the facts, the woman agreed to accompany Cissy on an interview with Detective Moses Green. Meanwhile, the attorney told her not to discuss the situation with anyone. I guess that included me.

When Muldoon and I got back to the car, I adjusted his goggles and headed for a showdown with Brenda Boyd.

• • •

FORTY-FIVE MINUTES LATER I knocked on Brenda's door but got no response. The Volvo was parked in a sweet spot in front of her building, which meant she was probably still in the neighborhood. Maybe she was out kicking ass and taking names. I was trying to think of where else to look when I remembered the metal detector I'd seen in her apartment. Maybe she was out searching for treasure.

Muldoon and I headed toward the beach, crossing a wide bike path and a patch of grass dotted with palm trees. The moment I stepped off the lawn, the sand began seeping into my shoes and abrading my heels. Muldoon was accustomed to running barefoot, so he went ahead, looking for something to sniff at.

I spotted Brenda strolling near the water about fifty feet away from me. She was wearing a pair of beige shorts and a pink tank top. Covering her ears was a headset, which was connected to the metal detector's battery pack. With wide zigzag motions, she swept the doughnut-shaped end of the detector over the sand. Occasionally, she'd stoop to inspect something she'd found, before dropping it into a plastic grocery bag that hung from one of the belt loops on her shorts.

My calf muscles strained as I maneuvered through the sand toward her, stopping a couple of feet away. The turquoise ring was no longer on her finger. I tapped her on the shoulder. She looked up, startled. She pulled the headset off and draped it around her neck like a horse collar.

"How's the fishing today?" I said.

Brenda shrugged. "Not bad. You nail Asshole yet for the damage to your car?"

"No, but I found out his name. Gilbert Ruiz. His sister lives across the street. Maybe you know her."

"What kind of car does she drive?"

"I don't know."

"Ask me again when you do." She started to put the headset back on her ears.

"Brenda, I didn't tell you this before. That guy across the street who was murdered, he was a friend of mine. He had a daughter. All she knows right now is that her father isn't coming home. Someday I'd like her to know that his killer got what he deserved."

I thought that would appeal to her sense of vigilante justice, but all she said was: "So Tom had a kid. Big deal. Lots of us have them. I don't see why I should worry about some rich kid getting justice when the rest of us get nothing but a bum deal."

Brenda definitely had an agenda. I wondered what events in her life had shaped her attitude.

"When I was at your place the other day," I said, "you were wearing a turquoise ring."

Her eyes narrowed. "It's mine. I got it fair and square."

"I'm sure that's true, but I need to know how you got it and where. I think it was my friend's wedding ring. The killer may have stolen it."

On the word "wedding," a light flickered briefly in Brenda's eyes and then faded. "I don't know anything."

"Please, I need your help. You'd be doing the right thing."

Brenda rolled her eyes and put the headset back on. There was nothing more I could do. If she didn't want to talk to me, I couldn't make her. I rounded up Muldoon and was about to head back toward the bike path when Brenda called out to me.

"I'm not talking to no cops. The lazy-ass pricks. You can't even get them to write a parking ticket anymore. They say it's the DOT's job, but that's a bunch of bull. I wrote a letter to the chief to complain. Now they're watching every move I make."

Brenda seemed a tad paranoid, so I didn't want to mess with her fragile psyche by lying to her.

"Look, the police will have to interview you, but I'll do everything I can to make sure you're not hassled."

Her eyes darted back and forth as though she were watching a tennis match or thinking deep thoughts. "I didn't steal it."

"I believe you, Brenda. Did somebody give you the ring?"

She shook her head.

"You found it, then. Where? In the sand, with your metal detector?"

"In there." She pointed toward a round garbage can, which was a stone's throw from her balcony. Apparently, in addition to all her other talents, Brenda was also a Dumpster diver.

"When?"

"Right after Asshole threw it there."

I felt a surge of adrenaline. "Are you talking about Gilbert Ruiz?"

"If you say so."

"Tell me what happened."

In drips and dribbles, guesses and nods, I was able to

pry the following information from her: Shortly after one-thirty a.m. the night Evan was murdered, Brenda was out on her lanai. She saw Gilbert Ruiz, aka Asshole, come out of the lobby of Evan's apartment building. He walked toward the garbage can and threw something inside that clinked against the metal sides. Then he headed toward the beach. A few minutes later he returned. His shirt was off, and his pants looked wet, as if he'd gone for a swim. That made her suspicious. A few minutes later, he got into his car, wet clothes and all, and drove away. After he was gone, she took a flashlight and searched through the trash can until she discovered the ring, covered with what appeared to be gunk from the garbage. She cleaned it up and decided it was a keeper.

It was unfortunate that Brenda Boyd had washed away Gilbert Ruiz's fingerprints, but bloodstains were more difficult to remove. Hopefully, there were still traces of Evan's DNA or that of his killer in the cracks of that broken turquoise gemstone.

Charley Tate told me that taking large amounts of dextromethorphan, found in over-the-counter cold remedies, could lead to murder. Gilbert Ruiz was hooked on the stuff. I wondered if Monique's hotheaded brother had been high on cough syrup when he killed Evan Brice.

Gilbert could have taken Monique's key that night to gain access to the apartment. Maybe he was ready to graduate from robo-tripping to real drugs and hoped that Evan would be his source. Perhaps he was just angry about his sister's pregnancy. Whatever the case, he went to Evan's place to confront him and lost control of the conversation. He killed Evan and took his wedding ring as some kind of trophy. When he got outside, he had second thoughts. The ring was evidence that could lead the police directly to his doorstep, so he discarded it in the trash can in front of Brenda Boyd's apartment. Too bad for Gilbert that she had seen him do it.

What I didn't know was if Monique had been an accessory to the murder. Detective Green told me he'd verified her alibi, presumably with her aunt, Estela Sandoval. But the aunt may have lied.

Perhaps I didn't know the whole story, but I had enough credible speculation to interest Detective Green. I was about to call the number for Pacific detectives when my cell phone rang.

-31-

i pressed Talk on my cell phone dial pad and heard the frantic voice of Rose Miller. "I'm so glad you answered. I thought you said you were coming right back, but maybe I got it wrong. My memory isn't that good anymore."

"Your memory is fine, Rose. I forgot. I'm sorry. Are you okay?"

"Yes, but I'm out of my heart pills. The pharmacy can't deliver until tomorrow, and Monique isn't home."

In my peripheral vision, I saw Brenda Boyd pick up her metal detector and hurry through the sand toward her apartment.

"I'm just outside your building," I told Rose. "I'll be right there."

She must have been waiting with her hand poised above the knob, because she immediately opened the door when I knocked. She was holding two neatly pressed twenty-dollar bills, probably from that white envelope of hers, and a piece of paper on which she'd written the pharmacy's address.

"Getting old is for the birds," she said. "You're a burden to everybody. Most of my relatives were dead by this age. Makes me feel like I've been overlooked. You don't have a cholesterol problem, do you?"

"Nope, not yet."

"Good. Hope your luck holds out. Mine didn't. Too many brown-and-serve sausages, I guess. Anyway, I'm sorry to bother you. My daughter says I inconvenience people. She wants me to move to a retirement home in Scottsdale, but I can't stand the heat."

"I'd miss you if you left."

"Thank you, Tucker. I'd miss you, too."

I didn't want to drag Muldoon to the pharmacy, so I asked Rose to entertain him until I got back. On the way to pick up the meds, I called the Pacific homicide unit to tell Moses Green what I'd learned about Gilbert Ruiz. He wasn't at his desk, so I left an urgent message for him to contact me. I'd just picked up the prescription and was heading back to my car when my cell phone rang. It was Green, calling me back.

"I know who killed Evan Brice," I blurted out.

He hesitated. "Yeah? Who?"

"A kid named Gilbert Ruiz."

I waited for him to say, "Wow! No kidding? Good work." But instead, all I heard was silence. Undeterred, I told him what I'd learned about Brenda, Monique, and Evan's turquoise wedding ring. That got his attention. Before we hung up, he promised to bring Ruiz in for questioning.

I drove back to Rose's, listening to a CD of Chinese tea ballads that belonged to Pookie, and feeling relieved that the search for Evan's killer was finally over. When I turned onto Seagate Pathway, I spotted a parking space smack-dab in front of Evan's building. Finally, my luck was changing. As I got out of the car, I saw Brenda Boyd standing out on her lanai, holding a highball glass and a cigarette. She must have needed a pick-me-up after our little talk on the beach. She held up her drink in a salute. I waved back.

A moment later, I glanced down the street and saw Gilbert Ruiz's black Honda Civic cruising toward me, stopping inches away from where I stood. My heart pounded as the passenger-side window slowly descended.

Gilbert was wearing that white silk shirt again, the one with the flames. My gaze swept from his hands on the wheel to the car's interior, half expecting to see telltale traces of blood under his fingernails, on the leather seats, or on the hard plastic molding of the dashboard. On the surface, the car looked clean, but I suspected that a crime scene investigator would find telltale traces of Evan's blood.

Ruiz leaned over. "You leaving?"

I shook my head. "Just got here. By the way, if you came to see your sister, I don't think she's home." Apparently he didn't notice how tense I was, because he flashed a smile that was free of malice.

"I know," he said. "I just called her cell. She told me she'd be here in a few minutes."

It was amazing to realize that at the other end of his violent mood swings was that beatific smile. A hundred thoughts flashed through my head. Among them: How had this kid's life gone so wrong? What had Evan done to incite his wrath? And how fast could I get to my cell phone and call the police?

My reverie was broken by the sound of Brenda Boyd, yelling from her balcony. She had apparently stopped inhaling gin long enough to see and recognize Ruiz's car. At first I couldn't make out what she was saying, because her words were slurred. Then her shouting grew louder. That's when the real nightmare began.

"There he is, Tucker. That's him. The one you said

killed your friend. You're going to burn for what you did, you prick."

Ruiz slowly turned his head toward the balcony where Brenda was standing. He stared at her for a moment while processing her words. Then he turned back toward me. Wraparound sunglasses masked his eyes but not his smile, which slowly curled into a grotesque parody of itself. It sent a chill down my spine. Moments later, he pressed down on the Honda's accelerator, made a U-turn, and sped away.

Gilbert Ruiz was on the run. In a couple of hours he could be out of town and possibly out of the country. I had to warn Moses Green. Brenda was still ranting as I pulled my cell phone from my purse and once again punched in his number. This time nobody answered. I pictured the telephone ringing in that empty trailer while Evan's killer drove off into the sunset. Frustrated, I tried to call the station's front desk. The line was busy. I considered calling 911, but Detective Green hadn't had time to tell anybody about the new evidence I'd uncovered. Ruiz would be in Guatemala by the time I explained the situation to the 911 operator and convinced her that I wasn't a total banana fish.

I was angry at Brenda for her gin-addled, paranoid mind and at the City of Los Angeles for its inability to provide the police with adequate telephone service. Mostly I was incensed that those two things combined might allow Gilbert Ruiz to escape justice. I couldn't let that happen. I slid into my car.

All I planned to do was find out which direction he'd taken, while I continued trying to reach Moses Green. I assumed that Ruiz would head for the freeway, so I drove to Venice Boulevard, where I knew there was an on-ramp. By the time I got there, the Honda was nowhere in sight. I pulled over to the side of the street to take stock of my options. There weren't many. The area was a warren of small surface streets. Ruiz could be on any of them. Again I tried the telephone number I had for Detective Green. Again nobody answered. I was at the verge of giving up on the idea that Ruiz would ever be caught, when I saw his Honda pull onto Venice Boulevard from a side street about a block ahead of me.

I followed, positioning myself so there were enough cars between us to serve as a buffer. The freeway was just ahead, so I was surprised when Ruiz turned left on Centinela, in the direction of West L.A.

By the time we approached the intersection of Centinela and Palms Boulevard, the veil of cars had dwindled to one—a Lexus sedan. Unfortunately, the Lexus turned off into the corner gas station, which left me directly behind the Honda at a red light.

I saw Gilbert Ruiz's sunglasses tilt up as he stared into his rearview mirror. They remained fixed there for a beat too long. That's when I knew I'd been made. He stepped on the accelerator and darted through the red light onto Palms, nearly sideswiping an oncoming SUV.

The light turned green. I turned the corner, too, and started up the hill after him. Moments later, he gunned his car over the crest of the steep hill ahead.

I dreaded what might be waiting for me on the other side of that rise. I felt as if I were on a roller coaster car as it crept up that first big summit: that torturously slow click, click, clicking sound when you know that at any moment you're in for a big fall. I groped for my cell phone but gave up. I needed both hands to drive.

When I reached the crest, a series of images flashed at warp speed before me: hazy blue sky . . . jagged Century City skyline . . . distant San Gabriel Mountains . . .

eclectic, orderly houses . . . neatly landscaped yards. There was nothing at all about the stunning view or the quiet Mar Vista neighborhood that could have prepared me for what came next.

Just ahead, the Honda barreled down the hill, swerving as it picked up speed. Halfway down, a man was using a garden hose to herd a large pile of leaves from his yard into the street. A moment later, Gilbert's wheels hit that patch of wet leaves.

For the next few seconds, I felt as if I were caught up in a slow, frame-by-frame horror film. Gilbert's car fishtailed to the left across the centerline. He turned left to correct the skid. Overcorrected. Then countercorrected to the right and spun completely around toward the left side of the street again. His vehicle jumped the curb. It slammed hard into a wooden utility pole. It rebounded and came to rest a few feet away. On impact, the pole cracked. It teetered. It listed at a thirty-degree angle.

Moments later I saw an explosive flash of light. I heard what sounded like sticks of TNT detonating inside a trash can as the power lines snapped some distance from the pole. After flailing in midair like a wrangler's whip, the lines dropped to the ground except for one, which came to rest atop the hood of Gilbert Ruiz's black Honda Civic.

I screeched to a stop. I cut the engine and swung open the car door. For a long, eerie moment there were no other sounds except for the lyrical Chinese tea music drifting from my car's stereo. It melded erhu, pipa, guzheng, and di. I also heard the fuzzing sound of thousands of volts of electricity from the severed utility lines.

The man with the hose stood like a statue in his yard, wide-eyed with shock. He was completely unaware that the menacing flow of water continued to gush out into the street and down the hill, closer and closer to Ruiz's car.

When the Honda's door slowly opened, I bolted out of my front seat. I wasn't an expert on electricity, but I knew you shouldn't use your hair dryer in the bathtub if you wanted to live another day.

"Stay in the car!" I shouted.

Gilbert turned his gaze toward me and frowned as if he was confused by my strident tone. Then recognition flickered in his eyes. I jogged down the sidewalk on the opposite side of the street from where his car had settled on the pavement. I stayed far away from the power lines and the moisture but close enough for the hose man to hear me shouting to him.

"Turn off that water. Go call nine-one-one!"

He blankly nodded. He dropped the hose and ran toward his house. I inched closer to Gilbert until I was directly across the street from him. He appeared dazed. The air bag had deployed, and he was covered with a ghostly gray powder.

"Gilbert, listen to me. Don't get out of your car, or you're going to die. The utility lines are down. There's water everywhere. We're calling somebody to cut off the power and get you out of there."

He shook his head a couple of times as if to clear away some mental fog. Then he pushed the air bag away. He twisted around in his seat, first to the left and then to the right. He carefully scrutinized the teetering utility pole and the downed power line resting on his car.

The man with the hose had apparently shut off the water but too late to prevent it from creeping, seeping, and saturating the pavement around and beneath Gilbert Ruiz's Honda.

Finally, Gilbert shifted his focus toward me. "I'm not crazy. I see the lines. I'm not going to touch them."

"You don't have to touch them directly to be electrocuted. If they're energized, anything—wood, water, even your body—can complete the circuit. If you step out of that car, you'll end up fried." I had no idea if what I was telling him was the truth. I just hoped it sounded convincing.

He seemed unsure of himself, weighing my dire admonitions against his instinct to run. "That line on my hood . . . If it was dangerous, I'd be dead already."

"Maybe, or maybe the car or the rubber tires are protecting you. Who knows? I think you're safe as long as you stay put. Why take a chance until we know for sure?"

For a moment he looked confused. "Did you tell that guy to call the cops just now?"

"No. He's calling nine-one-one. They'll send the power company and maybe the fire department."

His eyes narrowed. "You're lying."

"Fine. Don't believe me. But before you do anything, think of Monique. How will she feel if something happens to you? It's bad enough that her lover is dead."

"He was nothing."

"If he was nothing, why did you kill him?"

"I didn't kill anybody."

"No? Brenda Boyd saw you leave his apartment building that night. She saw you go down to the beach, where I assume you washed off Evan Brice's blood. She found the ring, Gilbert."

"She's crazy. Nobody will listen to her."

"Maybe not, but they'll listen to me, and here's what I'll tell them. Your sister met Evan when she moved into her apartment. She had a crush on him right away, or maybe he pursued her. Either way, I'm guessing one night he invited her over. They hit it off. Maybe they had drinks, did drugs, but for sure they had sex, because she got pregnant. Am I right so far?"

"My sister never did drugs." Even from my vantage point I could see the spit flying as he shouted. "Monique is smart. She was going to be a lawyer or a teacher. He ruined her life and dishonored my family."

"Monique thought Thomas Chatterton would be happy about the baby. But he wasn't. In fact, he wasn't even Thomas Chatterton. He was Evan Brice, and he was already married. I'm guessing he broke up with Monique Sunday night. She was upset and needed to talk to somebody who'd be sympathetic to her situation. So she asked you to take her to Oxnard to stay with your aunt Estela."

"That's right. My aunt will tell you I was there."

"Sure you were—for a while. But you came back. Somebody saw your car in the neighborhood a few hours later. Evan was dumping your sister. You couldn't let him get away with that, so you killed him. You also stole his wedding ring, but when you got outside you had second thoughts and threw it in the trash can. What you didn't know was that Brenda Boyd was standing on her lanai, watching you do it."

The cords in Gilbert's neck were taut with fury. "I didn't steal it. I didn't take anything from him. I went there to make him marry my sister."

"But he didn't want to, did he?"

"He said he already had a wife. He stuck that ring in my face to show me. He deserved what he got."

Sirens could now be faintly heard in the distance.

Gilbert's face registered fear. Then calm. His head collapsed against the headrest of his seat. "You called the cops." It was an accusation.

"No. I told you, the man with the hose called nine-one-one. It's probably the fire department."

"No. That's a cop siren."

"Look, what does it matter? Help is on the way. They need sirens to get here faster."

"You told me the power company was coming. You lied to me about those lines being dangerous so you could keep me here until the cops came."

Just then I heard a cracking and splintering of wood. My gaze shot up to the utility pole, which had begun to groan and list closer toward the ground. The pavement beneath the Honda was glistening with moisture. I thought of Evan Brice and Frank Jerrard. I felt tortured by guilt, knowing that I hadn't been able to see death looming ahead for either of them, not as I saw it now, threatening Gilbert Ruiz. Even with this newfound insight, I was still powerless to change anything.

"Look, Gilbert, this is no time to play chicken. Stay where you are until help gets here."

He paused, twisting his body right and left once again, checking out the utility pole and the power line lying flaccid on the Honda's hood. He cocked his head, listening to the sirens, louder now, closer. An instant later I watched wide-eyed with horror as he grabbed the top of the door and bolted from the car.

-32-

neither CPR nor ER had been enough to save Gilbert Ruiz. As soon as he stepped out of his Honda, he'd slumped to the ground. By the time the power company had arrived and de-energized the lines, and the fire department paramedics had transported him to the nearest trauma center, Gilbert Ruiz was DOA.

I finally reached Moses Green, who'd arrived within minutes of my call, or so it seemed. After that, I hadn't felt like doing much of anything, especially answering questions. I'd delivered Rose's heart pills, picked up Muldoon, and headed for home.

A few days later, I dropped off the keys to Evan's apartment at the management company's office in Century City. On my way home, I stopped by Claire Jerrard's house. As usual, she greeted me warmly and said how grateful she was to me for helping Cissy. After that, I welcomed any small talk that might postpone my having to tell her the real purpose of my visit. When I could no longer delay the inevitable, I pulled out the piece of yellow lined tablet paper from my pocket.

"Claire, there's something I should have told you a

long time ago." I took a deep breath and let it out. "Frank called me the day he died."

She looked puzzled. "Really? I guess I'd forgotten that."

"No, you didn't forget. I never told you. He asked me to write down some of your favorite recipes. I should have given them to you back then. I'm sorry. Anyway, I wanted you to know he was thinking of you till the end."

I handed her the piece of paper, on which I'd scrawled the recipes her husband had dictated so many years before. As she read, I watched her eyes become glossy with moisture. A moment later, she dabbed at her nose with a tissue and smiled.

"I forgot about that Salisbury steak. It was awful, wasn't it? Frank could never say no to a saltshaker."

I wasn't going to let her defuse the situation this time. "Claire, don't you understand? I may have been the last person he spoke with. If I'd been thinking clearly, I could have talked him out of it. I could have saved him. I failed. I can't tell you how sorry I am."

She looked at me for a long time without responding. "I'm not sure what you think you could have done, Tucker, but you couldn't have talked him out of it. No one could have done that. The truth is, Frank called a lot of people that day, including me. None of us had a clue what he was about to do. It made me really angry with him for a lot of years, but I finally realized that those calls were just his way of saying good-bye. Not a good way, but his way. I'm at peace with it now. I regret he didn't just take you aside and give you some pearl of wisdom that transformed your life forever, but he didn't. I think it's time for all of us to stop wishing things had turned out differently."

-33-

On a balmy evening in late April, about five weeks after Evan's death, I answered a knock at my door. Joe Deegan stood under the porch light, looking unusually handsome in a tux and one of those shirts with a butterfly collar—the perfect outfit for Eric's wedding.

I'd had second thoughts about the orange Caltrans dress. I'd taken it back to the Santa Monica mall and exchanged it for a sleek, black sheath that by some miracle of design made me look curvy instead of straight.

Deegan studied me for a moment and whistled softly. "You look beautiful."

Cissy had said those words, too, at her house, the first time I saw her after Evan was murdered. Somehow it felt more satisfying hearing it from him.

Deegan waited for me outside on the deck while I closed up the house. I didn't have to worry about leaving Muldoon alone, because he wasn't there. He was staying with Pookie and Bruce for the weekend. The moneymen controlling Bruce's trust had finally approved the purchase of an older two-story building in Santa Monica. The newlyweds were currently using the top floor as an apartment, while the ground floor was being remodeled to accommodate Bruce's yoga studio. The issue over custody of Muldoon hadn't been settled yet, but for now, sharing felt okay.

A few days after Gilbert Ruiz's death, I'd run into Deegan at the Pacific station while filing yet another police report. He'd been pretty decent about my ordeal. In fact, he hadn't lectured me once. I decided to give him a second chance. Vice versa, I guess.

Evan Brice's homicide investigation was now officially closed. Naturally, Cissy had been cleared of any suspicion, but that might have happened sooner if she'd told the truth from the beginning. A few days after she found out, I got a call from her. She thanked me for helping and told me that she and Dara were going to London to stay with friends for a couple of months, to get away from the media. I assumed that meant I wouldn't be hearing from her much anymore, which suited me just fine.

Darcy Daniels must have been crestfallen when she heard that Cissy was leaving town. *Celebrity Heat*'s ratings had skyrocketed because of the coverage of Evan's murder. In the process, Darcy had dredged up enough sludge to start her own Roto-Rooter franchise.

Monique Ruiz was naturally distraught to learn of her brother's death, but she was shattered by the news that he had killed Evan Brice. Shortly after Gilbert's funeral, she'd moved back home with her parents to await the birth of her baby. She'd lost her independence, but at least it was temporary, which was more than I could say for Rose Miller. With her unofficial caretaker gone, Rose had been forced to move from her apartment to an assisted-living facility near her daughter's home in Scottsdale. Her new place didn't exactly sound like a geezer ghetto, but it didn't sound like paradise, either. The transition continued to be a rocky one, so I'd been calling her every few days to cheer her up.

As far as I knew, Charley Tate was still PI to the stars, although I heard he dropped Lola Scott as a client when he found out she'd dumped Jakey and was now dating her lawyer. His pique didn't surprise me. Tate hated lawyers. I guess the thought of Lola sleeping with one was just too much for him to stomach. If you ask me, Lola made the right decision. Her new boyfriend is a big player in the entertainment biz. I hear he's working hard to pull the Richard Burnett project out of development hell.

I don't know if Charley Tate ever found a new receptionist. Maybe I'll call him one of these days to find out.

Deegan offered to drive us to the church, which was fine with me. On the way, he asked how work was going. I told him Eugene had returned from his trip to Palm Springs with a healthy cat and a muumuu prototype for the Hula Bitch line. The focus group had given it rave reviews. They especially liked the matching tote bag and hand-knit scarf accessories. Mr. Geyer was so delighted by the outcome, he had hired me to write a full-blown strategic plan for his business. Eugene was thrilled. Quite frankly, the whole episode had forced me to look at a lot of things in a whole new light, including muumuus.

I'd picked up a few other jobs as well. The Sinclair and Associates client list still couldn't compete with the one I'd built in my heyday at Aames & Associates. Not yet, at least. I guess building something solid takes both time and patience. Deegan thought I was onto something there.

All in all, things were running pretty smoothly for me. Even my aunt Sylvia and her lawyers seemed to be on hiatus from trying to steal my house. I knew the calm wouldn't last, so I decided to enjoy the respite while I could.

Eric and Becky's wedding was being held at the First Congregational Church, an impressive Gothic-style building in the Mid-Wilshire area of Los Angeles, not far from the office where I'd interviewed Amy Lynch. As we got closer, I began to feel tense. In a short time, I'd be seeing people who used to be friends of Eric's and mine, and who after the divorce had become friends of Eric's, and who were now friends of Eric's and Becky's.

My ex-in-laws would be there, along with a slew of Eric's more distant relatives. I wasn't sure how they'd feel about seeing me again, except for his aunt good-bye-and-good-riddance Lena. I was pretty sure how that reunion would go down.

As soon as Deegan parked the car, I felt the energy drain from my body. "Maybe this isn't such a good idea," I said. "Let's just go somewhere for dinner and call it a night."

Deegan caught my gaze and wouldn't let go. "You invited me to this thing to show your ex that you've moved on. You *have* moved on, haven't you?"

"I think so . . . but I could be wrong."

Deegan patted my knee. "Come on, take your medicine like a man."

"Is that what your father used to tell you?"

He smiled. "Nah, my mom." He got out of the car and walked around to my door. He opened it and gave me that come-hither gesture with his finger.

I took a deep breath. "Okay, you're right. I can do this." I swung my legs out of the car. Then I swung them back inside. "It just feels weird, that's all."

He rolled his eyes. "Look, give it a rest. You're not the only person in the world who's divorced."

I raised my eyebrows. "Yeah? Who else?"

"That's for me to know and you to find out."

"Don't patronize me."

Deegan took hold of my arm and gently pulled me out of the car. "There are a number of things I'd like to do to you, Stretch, but patronize isn't one of them."

"Okay, okay."

The resonant sound of pipe organ music was drifting through the door as we walked up the steps into the church. It left me yearning for enough alcohol to dull the pain. The chapel was decorated with truckloads of flowers. Big, fluffy white bows with streamers hung from the ends of each pew. This was a far cry from my wedding: city hall, dinner at Mario's, back to our apartment to study.

I knew I was being silly. I didn't still love Eric, not in the romantic sense of the word. I'd stopped loving him that way long ago, just as I'd stopped loving Evan Brice. At the same time, I knew my ostracism from the Bergstrom tribe would be final once I heard "dearly beloved" and saw the groom's cake cradled in net and tied up with ribbon, which would surely be imprinted with "Eric ❤ Becky."

An usher escorted Deegan and me down the aisle. Eric's parents were already seated in a front row. A few minutes later, a thin, well-dressed woman, whom I assumed was Becky's mother, entered on the arm of a young man. Her hair was teased, lacquered, and shaped into something that looked like one of the Jetsons' space helmets. She smiled stiffly as she sidled into the pew.

From a door near the front of the chapel, Eric emerged, followed by six groomsmen dressed in some type of formal attire that I couldn't quite name. He looked dazed.

Before I could read more into his expression, the organ went silent. Then came the sounds I dreaded most: "DUM-DUM-TA-DUM" and the deafening roar of yards of *peau de soie*.

"Shit," I whispered to Deegan. "I hate this part."

He grinned. Then he took my hand and massaged my palm with his thumb. I was really enjoying that until I glanced toward the aisle and caught a glimpse of a distinguished gray-haired man. It was Eric's new father-in-law, his first one ever. He looked uptight and pathologically neat, as though he wouldn't be caught dead with a loose buttonhole thread.

I closed my eyes for a moment, hoping he'd disappear. When I opened them again, he was still there. So was Becky. Her tiny little face was barely visible behind her billowing veil. A single ringlet of cinnamon hair had escaped from her headpiece, making her look like a ladybug that had taken a wrong turn into a cream puff.

Somehow I made it through the ceremony and the post-wedding receiving line. Becky thanked me for coming. Eric's parents hugged me and said how glad they were to see me again. Eric shook Deegan's hand and, in a tone that was both sincere and completely oblivious, said, "She's a great girl. Isn't she?"

Deegan flashed me a sly smile. "The best."

We stayed through dinner, dancing, and champagne—lots of champagne. In the morning, I knew my eyes would be stuck together like Ziploc bags. I chatted with several people I used to know, and practiced how to be coy while fielding questions about Deegan.

At some point during the evening, I realized I was having fun. Not just because of the champagne, although that certainly greased the skids, but because I was at a party with a man who was funny and charming, even if it was in an old-fashioned way.

Moments after Deegan and I had returned to our table, hot and sweaty from dancing, the waiters began serving the wedding cake. The idea of carrots in a dessert always gives me pause, but this stuff was delicious. I ate the whole piece and pushed back my plate.

"*Now* I've moved on."

Deegan grinned and leaned close. "Good. So are you ready to go?"

"Go where?"

He shrugged. "I don't know. Let's be creative."

"We could go for coffee, but that seems sort of silly. We can get that here."

"You're right. Maybe we should go for something we can't get here."

"Like what?"

A mock frown appeared on his face. "I'm a patient man, Stretch, but I have my limits."

I thought for a moment and then leaned close enough to whisper in his ear, "Did I mention that Muldoon is away for the weekend?"

About the Author

PATRICIA SMILEY is the author of the *Los Angeles Times* bestseller *False Profits*. To learn more about her, you may visit her Web site at www.patriciasmiley.com.